THE PLASTIC
TOMATO CUTTER

Michael Curtin

FOURTH ESTATE · *London*

This edition first published in Great Britain in 1996 by
Fourth Estate Limited
6 Salem Road
London W2 4BU

First published in Great Britain in 1991 by
Fourth Estate Limited.

Copyright © 1991 by Michael Curtin

The right of Michael Curtin to be identified as the author
of this work has been asserted by him in accordance with
the Copyright, Designs and Patents Act 1988.

A catalogue record for this book is
available from the British Library.

ISBN 1-85702-472-9

Designed by June Cumming
Printed in Great Britain by
Clays Ltd, St Ives plc

CHAPTER 1

The House of Montague

My office at Montague's looked out on the main street and I could observe the procession of roughs idling to the snooker hall overhead the shop. ('The Shop' was our inverted euphemism for the grandeur of Montague's then.) Now I must admit I had been up there myself as a youngster. That is what wild oats are for. But the Phil Thompsons, the Wally Kirwans, the Butsey Rushes, I shook my head at that lot. Hoping for a pension. And that guttersnipe Charlie Halvey. He shouted remarks in the window.

The boy Simpson did not seem to me as natural a street-arab as the rest. He approached as though about to pass us by and suddenly faded in the door. From my own time upstairs I recognized the respectable guilt. I surmised he was not allowed to haunt pool rooms. It was a cold, wet day, but Simpson did not have an overcoat or even a mackintosh. Prime boy Phil Thompson affected a gaberdine and erstwhile fawn scarf for all seasons and a moustache and cloth cap and perennial butt in the mouth. Butsey Rushe sold the newspapers at our corner. Enough said. And the third musketeer, Wally Kirwan, showed the pictures in the Lyric. Need it be said, Thompson never worked a day in his life. I knew those merchants from my own innings upstairs and none of them was ever my cup of tea.

On our manager, Mr Sloan's instructions, I myself taped the BOY WANTED envelope to the window and as I looked out on the street I saw Simpson staring at me. I was about to shoo him off for his impertinence but he turned from the envelope and walked in our main door. Our Mr Todd immediately had him by the collar and the slack of his trousers and was aiming

1

him in the direction of the pavement when Simpson protested. 'I only want to ask about the job, Mr Todd.' But Mr Todd – quite rightly – ejected him. Simpson stood outside adjusting his crumpled shirt inside his ragged Fair Isle. Mr Todd barked: 'Go on now, be off.' Scorning the rain, Simpson ran his tongue along the palm of his hand and with three strokes tried to tame his hair.

When Mr Todd turned his back Simpson put his face around the door. 'Mr Yendall,' he appealed to me directly, 'can I ask for the job please?' Furious, Mr Todd went for him but I cut in: 'All right, Mr Todd. Let me.' I gave Simpson an index finger direction towards my office. He stood before me as I sat down, one hand in the pocket of his short pants.

'Take your hands out of your pockets, boy.'

'Sorry, Mr Yendall.'

'Now then, where are your manners – you don't walk in off the street and *ask* for work.'

'I was afraid, Mr Yendall, that if I went home and wrote it down someone might have got it before I came back. And in most places you just go in and ask.'

'Montague's is not most places. Age?' I addressed an application form. He was fifteen, an only child, council house, father killed in the war. With training in our ways I was sure he would do.

'I'll inquire if Mr Sloan can see you. Wait here.'

Mr Sloan was impressed by his powers of advertising and Simpson's prompt application. I led the way back to my office. Simpson's hand was in the pocket. I pulled his elbow. Mr Sloan read Simpson's details.

'The position carries seven and sixpence, Simpson. Subject to the provision of the usual scholastic, parochial and commercial references, you may start Monday. You will report to Mr Yendall.' Mr Sloan raised his head towards the ceiling. 'And Simpson, no up there while on duty.' I was twelve years older than the boy and maybe eight years younger than Mr Sloan. We were far apart, the three of us.

'Yes, Mr Sloan. Thank you very much, Mr Sloan.'

2

Once Mr Sloan had left Simpson confided: 'Mr Yendall, I have to ask my mother first.'

'You should have told me that. Well, go and ask her then.' He must have run home and back. His mother had one condition: Night school. I was vexed to have to bother Mr Sloan again but he simply nodded: 'I should have insisted on it myself, Mr Yendall. He will do book-keeping.'

CHAPTER 2

The Society of Bellringers

There had always been a chaplain attached to the Society of Bellringers – a lame duck, a codger, an alcoholic, someone with a weakness best kept within the community. According to Donat, when he and Sam Brown and Charlie Halvey were newcomers, the incumbent was an ex-child molester. Occasionally – once in a blue fucking moon according to Charlie – we had a boss who was unremarkable. In the tower only Sam Brown failed to see the office as a sinecure. Clutching the hem of a cassock a new chaplain climbed the steps to the ringing chamber, cleaved a presence through the trap door and said: God bless the men. He was shown the photographs on the walls of all the ringers down through the years and sometimes went on up the ladder from the ringing chamber to see the actual bells. And then the chaplain withdrew, puzzled by the complexity of change ringing and was not seen again until the token appearance at the Christmas community dinner. No more was expected of him. Except by Sam.

On this hot and humid August Saturday evening we were coming out of a three month interregnum and expecting a new chaplain, Father Brock, a retired missioner. Hence my suit. The jacket hung from my finger over my shoulder as I strolled up the town. The peal was for the novena to Our Lady of Perpetual Succour, a crowded sodality of supplicants seeking a cure for cancer or the luck to pass exams – the simple largesse for which at some time or another we all thrust out the palm. I passed four houses of worship on the way and had left two more behind me, all within the city. Throw in half a dozen schools, two libraries, a few cinemas, a theatre, the

4

enmeshed shopping and commercial sector, the pubs; one was all the way swaddled in the municipal cloak. The beauty of so much grey stonework held its own with the Georgian medical district when Donat reigned. The town then blended quickly into the necessary evil of the suburbs, but only for an acceptable distance before you were mercifully released into the countryside.

When I raised my eyes the tower and steeple of the Redemptorist church dominated and I was part of its elevation and on my way to play that part. Me, an agnostic Londoner. Going up the steps to the tower I slipped my arms through the sleeves and adjusted the knot of the tie. I was early but Sam Brown was there before me. He was wearing his best suit. Sitting down, smoking, apparently relaxed, Sam didn't fool me. He was excited. He lived for the bells. I walked around with my hands in my pockets. I didn't smoke, not since the day Jimmy Johnston took twenty quid off me in the Fulham Cosmo and told me the weed murders your game. Jimmy Johnston once took a ton off Tony Meo. So I gave them up when I was fifteen.

'New chaplain tonight, Sam.'

Sam waved his cigarette: 'For all we'll see of him, Tim.'

But I caught the hope in his voice. He shook his wrist free of the white cuff to see the time. 'We'll be lucky to have six with this heat.' That was settling for the worst muster. By Sam's standards all eleven members should have been present to meet the new chaplain, all wearing their best. We heard quick steps on the stairs. I opened the trapdoor. I said; 'Charlie.' But Sam knew Charlie Halvey's steps as those outside the bells might know another man's knock. Charlie owned the Statue of Liberty bar. He was a small man, stocky, and though he had thick grey hair he always wore a hat, a check, peaked affair with a tassel on top, the type beloved of otherwise sane golfers. Tonight he wore purple sneakers with yellow laces, the bottom of a green tracksuit and a red T-shirt. As he came through the trapdoor, he winked. 'God bless the men.'

Sam exploded: 'I suppose you think you're a comic, do you,

Charlie? I suppose you think wearing rags worse than your usual rags is a blow for the tower, do you?'

Charlie dismantled his grin. 'Fuck me pink! Are you listening to him, Harding? You black English Protestant, do you hear him? I leave my fine pub in the hands of criminals, Jesus Christ Johnny Skaw is robbing me blindfold while I'm standing here and what do I get for thanks? I get shit for thanks. Sam Bollix Brown, I'm here, aren't I?'

'You could have put on something. Just for tonight. It wouldn't have killed you.'

'Like you? A suit? In this fucking heatwave? A tie strangling my neck and for what? Go on, where's the law says you're better dressed than I am, Sam Brown, get out the book, show me where it's written down.'

Sam would never be on Charlie's wavelength. And Charlie wouldn't bend. Sam looked at his watch again. 'Dr Donat's always here by now . . . five minutes . . .'

' . . . Dr Bollix . . . Dr Cunt . . . '

Outside of Sam, Donat and myself, all the other ringers were capable of arriving with seconds to spare. Charlie walked around, whistling, scratching his balls. Charlie sings in bank queues; he shouts at people across the street; roars up at painters on ladders. ' . . . there's old Sloan . . . Jasus, will you look at the cut of Phil Thompson . . . look at bollix Yendall coming up the street . . . Simpson, smile and give the face an excursion . . . ' Sam lit another cigarette. More footsteps. I turned to Sam: 'Paddy, George.' Sam took off his jacket. When they came through he asked immediately: 'Any sign of Dr Donat?' They both wore suits. No. No sign of Dr Donat. We all stripped – except Charlie – then Midge came. He didn't rush the stairs. He was the oldest since Jack Molyneaux retired. By the time Midge had his sleeves rolled up – a summer shirt inside a sleeveless jumper, Sam couldn't win them all – we were ready to ring. Only six. No Dr Donat. No chaplain. Mine was the number four bell over the trapdoor. I looked at Sam. He was sweating from more than the heatwave, the tower was cool. He nodded at me, said: 'Right.' I closed the trapdoor and we stood to our ropes.

Just as Sam was about to ease the treble out of its socket we heard a very slow step. I opened the trapdoor again. I said: 'Must be the chaplain, Sam.' Sam came to stand beside me watching the new chaplain negotiate his inaugural wheeze up the stairs. Sam greeted him. 'Father Brock, welcome to the Society.' Sam only had time to introduce himself and add his own title, Secretary. Brock sat down, out of breath. Sam launched us on the treble.

Standing on the trapdoor, ringing the number four in a six bell peal, I had the best seat in the house: I could watch Paddy, George and Sam in an arc to my right and when I was obliged by the changes to face left I had Charlie and Midge in my sights. And the new chaplain sitting. Brock had a bullet head with the vestiges of an old gym-hand's crew cut, accentuated by a round, fleshy face that he grabbed and pulled meditatively throughout the peal. But I could not tell if he was interested or just feigning attention. Sam's face was needlessly red since we were all good ringers and there was no danger of a clanger – for all his iconoclasm Charlie Halvey took his rope seriously. We finished the peal and Sam introduced Brock to 'the men'. Then Sam showed Brock the photographs. Sam was in most of them, from the early short back and sides to his present trendy if sparse fullness. Then Brock showed his jowled good humour: in response to Sam's invitation he looked mischievously up at the ladder leading to the belfry. He pleaded his age and said: 'Mr Brown, if you say the bells are up there I'll take your word for it.' Paddy, George and Midge laughed, the obedient appreciation of any old *mot* issued by those in authority. Charlie hated the black army. Sam was hurt. I didn't laugh. Then Sam started: 'It's a pity you missed our Dr Cagney, Father . . . ' Charlie slid out of his mouth: 'Dr Prick.' Brock nodded away at Sam until he was able to shoot in: 'Well, I must thank you all so much, most enjoyable, I'll say goodnight to you now . . . ' Even before Brock reached the foot of the stairs Sam was sitting with his fags out. 'He's not going to get in our way,' Sam said, loosening his tie.

I walked down town with Charlie. 'Harding, you black English Protestant, tell me how you stick it here. If I had your looks, your hair – Jesus to swap London for this kip – and that accent, I'd ride all round me. I'd shove it up from one end of the day to the other . . . '

'Charlie – '

' . . . when do I get my hole? I have to go to London for it. Know what a city is, Harding? All I want from a city? Fuck art galleries, and cathedrals and all that bollix I'll tell you what's a city. Give me an apple stand, a chipper and a brothel, that's a city and fuck the rest. To have the horn in this heat . . . '

'Charlie, I felt sorry for Sam tonight.'

'Fuck Sam. Did you see that big fat cunt back from the missions with the chubby cheeks and the belly. And they telling us all our lives don't have your usual full slice of bread and dripping during Lent, cut down on this, give up that, say your prayers to the statues in case you'd think of a pair of tits and your mickey'd stand up. Brock the bollix. And Sam's tongue hanging out to lick his fat arse. Oh, such a pity you didn't meet our Dr Cagney, Dr Donat. Dr Bollix . . . There's the Wank Mitchell, hey, Wank, how're they hangin' . . . '

'Thirty for a tenner, Charlie?'

'Fuck off. Forty. You black English Protestant robber.'

Outside the Drapers' Club Charlie grabbed my arm. 'It's sinful, isn't it, Harding, going in to a stuffy room to play snooker with the sun splitting the rocks. Fuck 'em. All the years they walked on us, you should be out jumpin' ditches in this fine weather, you should be on your knees, you should be in bed, you should be holy, you should be this, that and the other fucking thing. C'mon, we'll commit sin.'

The five tables were taken up. We watched old Simpson, Phil Thompson, Butsey Rushe and Wally Kirwan shuffle around in a four-hand. They seemed to take a month. When we were setting up the balls Charlie tied to psyche me. 'Get your tenner ready, Harding.'

I ate him. Charlie had to go to his Statue of Liberty. I went on to meet Donat in the Professional Club.

The Professional Club dated back to the turn of the century. Dr Donat Cagney was now its president, as his father, Dr John, had been before him. A founder member had given over the top floor of his Georgian town house for the Club's purpose. It was a place where the professional class met for a drink. Nothing more. But today the rest of the building was let in offices and the Club was a shabby couple of rooms catering for billiards and cards. It was a stipulation of the beneficent member's will that the top floor be retained by the Club through its trustees in perpetuity at a shilling a year. The professional class was an elastic term – doctors, solicitors, judges, Protestant clergymen, undertakers, dentists and later – by a nose – accountants, until Donat was finally goaded to sneer: 'Today, Tim, judging by our membership, auctioneering has become a profession. And building contractors. *Building contractors*, by Jove.'

It was early for the Club. I had a half of Guinness. De Courcy, a solicitor, and a guest were at the billiard table but of course they were playing snooker. I heard Donat once refuse De Courcy: 'Snooker? I'll have you know I'm a doctor, not a bookie.' In the far room I could see the television shadows flicker on the wall – a condition of its admittance had been that the set would not be visible or audible from the bar. I sat back in the cushioned armchair and waited for Dr Donat Cagney of Sexton Square.

He was carrying his bag which accounted for his absence from the tower. He wore a white flannel suit against the heat. Sockless sandals – attended at his Sexton Square residence every fortnight by a chiropodist. He was as handsome as he often said he was, the blond hair streaked with silver yet full of growth, curling over his shirt collar and around his ears. His affectation – a blond moustache – was nicotine stained. He bought his gin, sat in the chair opposite me, languid leg hanging over the arm.

'We lost Granny Eades, Tim.'

'I guessed we lost someone when you didn't make the bells. The new chaplain was there.'

'Lung cancer. She didn't smoke, remember that.' This as he took out his Players Medium. 'Her delirium aside, she would have resented a locum.'

'Good family?' I had heard him talk often enough with Jack Molyneaux about this Granny Eades.

'I interpret your inflection, Tim. I don't believe it becomes you. Yes, good family. We have a new chaplain?'

'Father Brock. Ex-missionary. He didn't go up to see the bells. Sam's disappointed again.'

'I wish you wouldn't warm to that fellow – '

'I wish you would.'

'A bony head.'

'I'm a bony head myself then.'

'Not with your blood.'

Jack Molyneaux came in. I hadn't known him in the bells. The stairs to the tower had caught up with him at seventy-five, yet at eighty he could make the top floor of the Professional Club. He was an undertaker. His sons and grandsons ran the business now – sorry, profession. It was one of only two undertaking firms in the city, over a hundred years in operation. It was not a business one broke into. People did change doctors nowadays – in their *Reader's Digest* wisdom according to Donat – but they were not so adventuresome over the last lap. Donat got him a drink.

'Granny Eades,' Molyneaux pronounced as he eased into his chair. He was reduced to a glass of stout.

'You've been there?'

'Just after you. The house is private. Sad, but I can understand, Donat. Not many of the old stock left. I prepared the insertion myself, one of the few I do now. Those "bony heads" as you call them, they swarm all over reception these days to compose their own. Imagine it, factory workers and the like, every one of them an instant obituarist with heads clipped out of dress dance snaps. I leave those to the grandsons. And how is young Tim, tonight? Not content to hunt the treble indifferently, I trust?'

'Of course not, Mr Molyneaux.'

'That's the lad. And how was Kilkee, Donat? Twice – no, three times – I was only down three times this year. Not able for the grandchildren, I'm afraid. Too lively. In my day you'd cower if your grandfather looked out over his glasses at you.'

'Kilkee is finished, Jack.'

'You don't say?'

'Caravans. What they are pleased to call mobile homes. How one wishes they were mobile and they might move – out of one's sight.'

Molyneaux shook the head. 'I said it years ago, Donat. Giving every Tom, Dick and Harry the vote. Every idler, nincompoop and chit of a lass. Without distinction. Such nonsense! But you're fortunate, Donat, your lodge is well away.'

'They pass by on their way to the Pollock Holes. I hear talk of a site behind me. I shall damn well sell out.'

'Donat!'

'What can one do? As you know I breakfast in the garden after my swim. Last weekend Molly had no sooner put the orange juice before me when there is a pair of heads looking in over the wall. Two bingo women, I've no doubt. I shouted at them: "Mind your business."'

'Quite right, Donat.'

'They guffawed. By the power invested in them by their medical cards, they guffawed.'

A few more came in. Soon we would have a circle around us, Donat the centre, cocktail conversation. I would be out of it.

'I'll leave you gentlemen,' I said, standing up. Donat raised the old eyebrows. I bent down and whispered: 'The pub fuck.' That hurt him. But then I hated being his son.

Two snobbish old farts like Donat and old Jack Molyneaux

would have driven me to the Statue of Liberty if I was never in search of the pub fuck. Charlie's was crowded. It always is. On the shelf behind Charlie's head as he serves you is scrawled on cardboard: THE MANAGEMENT RESERVES THE RIGHT TO SERVE EVERYBODY. That included all three sexes; the arty crowd; criminals; the slummers; the pseuds, the characters; the respectable, the poor, and above all anyone barred from another pub or from every other pub. Charlie told me that he was torn between calling the pub the 'Statue of Liberty' or 'The Three Cripples'. He wasn't so far out tonight in that only Bill Sykes and Bullseye were missing. Phil Thompson – the Steve Davis of his day according to Charlie – was nailed to the counter surrounded by the newsboy Butsey Rushe and Wally Kirwan. You could sit on a high stool at the long bar where Charlie was helped by his sister, Hannah, or you could stand by the fireplace or sit back against the wall or squeeze into a corner or just stand up in the middle of the crowded floor. My spot was in the corner by the fireplace where I could reach up to my drink safe on the ledge. The minute I went in Charlie caught my eye and served me a quick pint and muttered: 'Don't do it to me tonight, Harding, please. Don't let me see you.' He meant the pub fuck. Said it grigged him. I sat down to suss out the prospects.

It's hardly a challenge in the Statue of Liberty. You could throw one over your shoulder and take her home in the fireman's grip. But I prefer to cope with some sort of obstacle course, however token. I like a leg and there I was handicapped by the arty crowd who wore dungarees, or clown's trousers held up by braces, or minis that give it all away brutally. Monica was at the bar and she had it all, legs, tits, lipstick and a gobbler's mouth. I knew from Charlie that she was game ball: 'Harding, what is this world coming to? Monica Miller was here the other night. After hours. Nicely pissed. I said, Charlie, now's your chance. So I sidled up to her. "Any chance of the ride, Monica?" Nice and pleasant. What does she do? Ups off her stool. Shouts at me: "You male chauvinist pig." Can you imagine it, Harding? Male chauvinist pig. I said what's wrong with you. I only asked for the fucking ride. She makes a swipe at me with her handbag. Half the town rides her, Harding, but I'm a male chauvinist pig. Why? Because I'm not good-looking enough for her.'

Monica would do. But if it was going to be a hot Monica night, then I wanted to time my race for the pub fuck. It isn't done on one and a half pints. You need six or seven and the other party four or five gins, or whatever takes your fancy. Anything goes wrong, blame the drink. When both are married there are mutual interests to protect, no recriminations and no coming back for more. One married, one single, run a mile from it. Both unattached, use a johnny. Otherwise it's a free world and how can you go wrong? I went down on my pint and held up the finger to Charlie. He knows what I'm up to when I drink quickly. On my third pint the pub darkened and Monica glowed and I had to slip my hand in my pants pocket to flatten the stiff prick against the abdomen. Monica was with a crowd – no contest there – and it was time to start giving her the look.

And then *she* came in. Excused herself through the crowd to the counter beside Phil Thompson and his mates. She was taller than I am, a velvety jade cloche hat with a brooch perked on fair hair that reached straight down to her shoulders, shoulders carrying the pads of the clinging, heat-wave, thirties style patterned dress. Long and slim and unbusty, she flaunted her height in jade stiletto heels. She stretched her neck to get Hannah's attention. In the crowded pub one of the queers did have to be leaning on the fireplace giving the smile down to me. They give me the creeps and I don't care who knows it. As Charlie puts it: Gay my arse, those fuckers are bent. I was propelled to move towards my vision precipitatively. I carried my glass and managed to squeeze through just as Hannah was putting the small whiskey on the counter. 'Please let me,' I cut in with a smile and a beseech of the eyebrows. She smiled at me in turn, ever so sweetly, bent close, and hiss-whispered in my ear: 'Get lost, Buster.'

Her smile was gone and I was looking at steel. And then at

13

her back. Instead of showing what a great PF man I was, my glass was up to my mouth as a crutch and I found myself edging back through the crowd to my mercifully still vacant corner seat. I put the pint back up on the ledge and was grateful for the friendly presence of the hovering queer who had the hots for me. She did not turn round once in another twenty minutes, but I caught her voice above the racket a couple of times talking to Hannah. 'Oh it was so divine' and 'It was absolutely wonderful.' And her voice was divine and wonderful to me.

My next full pint was unsipped on the ledge and Monica forgotten when I noticed the queer bloke miming the offer of a fag. I was so rattled by her nibs that I took the cigarette, my first in thirteen years. I accepted a light, coughed, just like the very first time ever. And then the OOPS happened. My friend the fagman's arm slipped along the top of the fireplace and upset my pint, which came cascading down over my head on to my suit and shirt. And as he made a grab at the glass to try and save the day, he tipped over the pictureless frame that was all so typical of Charlie's appointments. So there I was with my head sticking out of the frame, dripping, the cigarette sogged, the suit and shirt destroyed and himself trying to wipe me down. The bar roared, everyone's head thrown back. Except hers. She alone alone looked at the comicality without laughing. The other asshole was calling a replacement pint. I assured him I was fine, no I would not let him pay to have the suit cleaned, porter didn't stain and so on. It blew over. She turned back to her whiskey. Reading the entrails I was not dealing with pub fuck material. But she was, after all, a woman, a fine one, and if I had to work for my oats then so be it. Charlie came out collecting glasses and feeling half the customers and he had the big grin on his face. 'Your lovely suit, Harding, that you put on in this heat for Sam and that fat prick missioner.' I pulled Charlie's arm until his head came down and I could whisper: Who is she?

'Forget it, Harding. That's Sloan's daughter.'

14

CHAPTER 3

The House of Montague

It is easier to develop an intimacy with a messenger boy than with those not quite so far beneath one, the type of familiarity I supposed once associated with a valet or a batman. One does not need to be on one's guard. I learned from Simpson that he handed up five bob out of his seven and six, and kept a half crown for himself out of which he put a shilling in the post office. I thought it just to pass this knowledge on to Mr Sloan and he nodded commendingly at this evidence of thrift. As I knew he would. Simpson played upstairs on his half-day and before going to night school and on Sundays, sometimes for a side bet of a threepenny bit against Phil Thompson, Butsey Rushe or Wally Kirwan. That lot were gods to young Simpson. Money was scarce, the loser paid, everybody was a safety player. Simpson got points from Thompson, Rushe and Kirwan and sometimes scraped home on the black. He improved. Because of his progress the lotus-eater, Thompson, was obliged to cut Simpson's handicap to fifteen at snooker and down to thirty from forty at billiards. This information I did not pass on to Mr Sloan.

Simpson went out in the morning and bought the milk and biscuits for our elevenses. He cycled the bike with the low front wheel and high basket on deliveries. From the bar hung our legend: 'Horace Montague, High Class Tailors'. He pushed the handcart to the station to meet the goods train. When our Mr Todd was out sick with his cough Simpson helped Mr Sloan to move the stock around, the Clubman shirts in their erect boxes crossing the floor to face, headless, east instead of west. He assisted Mr Sloan in dressing the dummies, if only in an acolyte capacity, responding to the

15

commands 'Shirt', 'Cravat', 'Cap'. Some of the dummies never wore anything except vest and underpants. Once when Simpson was tending Mr Sloan that creature, Charlie Halvey, passed by and I could hear the shout from my office: 'Hey, Simpson, how come none of the dummies has a prick?' I opened my door a crack. Mr Sloan was a stiff man. I saw him look at Simpson and I saw that Simpson was ashamed. Again I wondered what the world was coming to when a gentleman such as Dr John Cagney would allow his son, Donat, ring bells up in that town with the likes of Halvey.

I was developing in my own way, about to marry, set up home. I met my wife at the local debating society, a motion on the Suez crisis, we both spoke for Eden. And Mr Sloan, after five years of marriage, was about to become a father, joyous news to us all. In the light of all the excitement Simpson's one-tune despatches from the snooker hall declined from the piquant to the monotonous. As I remembered the hall it was an unhygienic place frequented by bums. And I was disturbed by the lack of youth in young Simpson, never heard him mention rugby or that occupation more suited to his station, soccer. I pressed him just the once: 'Simpson, what do you do after school?'

'I go home, Mr Yendall.'

'Straight to bed, eh?'

'I do a bit of book-keeping, Mr Yendall. I might listen to the wireless and have my tomato sandwich. Then I go to bed.'

Out of grotesque curiosity I probed the ingredients of his sandwich and, yes, it was a tomato sandwich every night.

'You don't weary of the staple, Simpson?'

'No, Mr Yendall, I love tomatoes.'

Whatever about Simpson's restricted social activity we had no fault with him at the shop. Making due allowances for his breeding he had a good manner. He was clean. He learned to communicate: I heard him one morning when Sir Thomas Ainsworth called to be outfitted for spring. Simpson carried the tweeds out to the station-wagon. 'Clement weather, Sir Thomas.' He was tossed a florin for his agreeability. On a different occasion, a delivery of shirts to Dr John Cagney of Sexton Square, Simpson so impressed the maid that she reported Simpson a likely lad to Dr John, who conveyed his satisfaction to Mr Sloan. Yes, Mr Todd's cough apart, we enjoyed a deal of contentment at the shop. And then, the tragedy.

Mrs Sloan had the best of care. Of that let there be no doubt. Mr Sloan was not one to draw in his horns in that or any other department of such importance. The accouchement took place in St Anthony's with Dr Pearse Farrell in attendance. We were all on happy tenterhooks that morning. Young Simpson was careful not to make a clatter with his bike. I declare Mr Todd had control of his cough. About midday the call came through from Dr Farrell and it was to me he wished to speak. I must confess that his consideration of Mr Sloan was a burden on me that I was scarcely able to bear. I had to hold my head in sorrow for minutes before I could gather myself to go out into the shop. I led Mr Sloan gently to his coat and hat. A call from St Anthony's, Dr Farrell required his presence there immediately, I lied. Mr Sloan did not demand more. He must have known. We did not speak going around the corner. Dr Farrell and the nurses were waiting. Dr Farrell put his arm around Mr Sloan's shoulder and brought him into the room. I stayed outside in the corridor.

Afterwards we saw the baby, a girl, who would be christened Cecelia after her mother. The healthy infant did little to alleviate Mr Sloan's distress, so bereft was he; that consolation was for his later years. From St Anthony's I took him to the old family home and put him in the care of his sister, who was to sacrifice her bloom in her devotion to the child. I hastened to Montague's, informed the staff and closed the shop. Mr Molyneaux, the undertaker, caught the evening paper in time and succeeded in having the remains in church that night. I was sad to observe in the notice that the house was private. Not the done thing but surely evidence of Mr Sloan's disconsolation. There was an excellent turnout at the church including Sir Thomas Ainsworth, who had the good grace to shake my hand and declare: 'I know how you must feel, Yendall.' It was a gesture that sustained me in the face of the outrageous appearance of those pool sharks, Thompson, Kirwan and Rushe, the newsboy and that blackguard Halvey, who saw fit, dressed in some sort of cowboy's jacket, to condole with Mr Sloan. I was also heartened that the well-scrubbed and neatly attired Simpson kept his distance from the buffoons.

Later that night Dr John Cagney rang me from the Professional Club. 'Yendall, my dear fellow, I have only just now this instant heard the distressful news from Pearse Farrell here. Now, Yendall, I want you to bear up, you understand, and keep an eye on Sloan.'

'Most certainly, Doctor.'

'And do you know, I was sitting back a moment ago mentally consulting my wardrobe, and I'm damned if I can think of anything suitable in black. Could I impose on you, Yendall, do you think? Send your boy round to the Square? My measurements remain unchanged, I'm happy to say.'

'Immediately, Doctor.'

'Good man. Talk to you at the funeral. '

I looked at the clock. There was time to intercept Simpson as he came back from night school. I brought him with me to the shop where I packaged a three-piece and boxed the Homburg. I loaded up his basket and sent him off and waited for him to return, garage the bike and lock up. When he came back he opened his hand: 'The maid gave me this, Mr Yendall.' It was a half-crown. Too much, I thought, but presumably that had been Dr Cagney's instruction.

'Good for you, Simpson. Here. You may as well add this to your hoard.'

'Thank you very much, Mr Yendall.' He had not let us down that day. I felt he had earned my sixpence.

'Goodnight, Simpson, enjoy your tomato sandwich.'

'Goodnight, Mr Yendall.'

There was a splendid turnout next day. Sir Thomas came again. Dr Cagney was elegance itself and complimented me on the cut. Mr Sloan bore up well, yet I knew there were wretched days ahead. Mercifully none of those bums appeared. There was a touch of the east wind. Mr Todd coughed so much that I was obliged to take him aside and suggest he tuck himself into bed with a hot drink.

CHAPTER 4

The Society of Bellringers

For the Saturday night novena, the twelve o'clock Sunday morning mass and the Sunday evening devotions we rang a peal; chimes sufficed for the Monday to Friday evening mass, and though Wednesday was my allocated night to ring the hymns, I was sufficiently committed to attend most nights and keep company with whoever was on duty. And then on to Charlie's for a few pints where I mooned thinking of Sloan's daughter. 'She doesn't part – for no one, Harding,' Charlie insisted. But then any woman who does not walk naked into the Statue of Liberty and hand him a whip is a prick-teaser according to Charlie. She worked in London for some publisher. That was all Charlie knew about her, he didn't know her first name, only that she wouldn't part. I heard her again: 'Oh, it was so divine,' 'It was absolutely wonderful.' Cocktail currency. It was only in the last few months that she had patronized the Statue of Liberty, coming home every few weekends now that old Sloan was getting on. The Statue of Liberty might have been a kip, but it was the only kip in town without a television and without *Sun* and *Mirror* and *Star* worshippers talking football.

My office at Fagender had a desk and two chairs, an ashtray, waste basket, copies of *Texts & Tests: Mathematics*, Parts 5 and 6, a scrap pad and a biro, a telephone and answering machine. I did not have a picture on the wall, a letterhead, compliment slip or business card. I had three clients that week, one new and two ongoing. My expenses were the rent and one line in the small ads of the local newspaper. The newcomer opposite me sat back, elbows out, fingers entwined across his chest. Ted Mulcahy, solicitor, forties, occasional member of the Professional Club. Apart from shaking his hand and indicating the chair I hadn't spoken.

'Acupuncture?'

I shook my head.

'Hypnotism?'

'No.'

'I have it. Mock fags that give you nausea.'

I pointed to the ashtray. 'Mr Mulcahy, please feel free to smoke.'

'American bullshit, motivation, that sort of thing.'

'How many do you smoke?'

'You think I count them? Twenty to thirty, I don't know.'

'Say two packs?'

'Okay. Two packs.'

'What brand?'

'Gold Flake . . . '

As a mathematician I did it in my head. 'The fee is one month's smoking. In your case a hundred and eighteen pounds. That's if you're telling the truth, that's if you're not a three or four pack man.'

'Boy, you've got some racket going . . . '

'If you smoked a cheaper brand you'd get it cheaper.'

'I like it.' Pulled them out, lit up. 'Charlie said you were a wizard.'

'Charlie said he was in your office. He was there for a half-hour. He said you smoked six. He said you said that you wished to Christ you could give the fucking things up . . . '

'All right, smart ass, sell yourself.'

'Mr Mulcahy, when did you smoke your first cigarette?'

'I was thirteen.'

'What were the exact circumstances, can you remember?'

'We had a half-day from school. Boy I was with went into Mary Conway's shop, bought five Gold Flake. We were going to the Lyric. *Untamed*, starring Tyrone Power and Susan Hayward. I smoked two. He smoked three.'

'You've got a good memory. Did you know before going to

the cinema that you were going to smoke, I mean outside this shop, did your friend say, Ted, I got two for you. Or did he just offer and you accepted?'

'He offered and I said I didn't smoke and he said how come and I said I didn't like them and he said how did I know if I didn't try. Something like that. What does it matter?'

'Whatever reason you had for smoking that day it's not the same reason you're smoking now. Why are you smoking now?'

'Come on. It's a habit.'

'Are you sure you want to kick the habit?'

'I must be. I'm here.'

'You've tried before?'

'Yeah . . . can't say I killed myself trying . . .'

'Okay. Why do you want to stop? To save money?'

'Good joke. The usual reasons. I'm spitting like a corner boy for the first hour of every day. People dying from long illnesses bravely borne, to wit, cancer . . .'

'Why do you think you can't give them up just like that?'

'I think I'm too busy. I have a fag lit and smoking before I know I'm doing it. It's high-pressure work, you know?'

'You chaps are gone from your offices early Friday afternoons. Long weekends to relieve the pressure. Your work takes its own time. Your clients suffer the pressure.'

'We chaps socialize. We're as busy socializing as when at work.'

'Okay. We're both busy. We're agreed we're dealing with a habit. Nothing more. I want you to try something for me. I don't want you to stop smoking but tomorrow when you have your first – when do you have the first cigarette?'

'Half-nine in the office.'

'At half-nine tomorrow just as you are about to light up I want you to do something else instead. I don't know what that is. Let's say your secretary is your mistress. At half-past nine you screw her . . .'

'Jesus . . . what am I doing here? I'm a busy man . . .'

'Or you stand up and look at your framed credentials on the wall or you read your bank statement if it's healthy . . . '

'What age are you anyway?'

'Twenty-eight.'

'I must be off my game. A twenty-eight year old English kid. Donat Cagney eats the damn things and he's a doctor. Why isn't he sitting here being told to count his blessings?'

'Donat wants to smoke. He doesn't want to stop.'

Mulcahy stood up. 'What do I owe you for your time so far?'

'Ring me Friday. I'll tell you then.'

Thursday Sam Brown was on duty. I relieved him for a couple of hymns so that he could have a cigarette. 'Our man gave a fantastic sermon last night, Tim.'

'Father Brock? You go to mass every night, Sam?'

'I'm not that much of a saint. I just heard he was guesting at all the masses this week, so I went to see what he was like. Mao Tse-tung, Hitler, Joe Stalin. I usually fall asleep during sermons but he had me gripped.'

'Praise indeed, Sam.'

On Friday I had to go and see one of the ongoing clients, Mrs Lillis, at her home. She had broken out again. 'Now, Mrs Lillis, so what? You don't drown by falling into the water. You climb back out, change your clothes, and enjoy dry land.' When I returned to my office in the late afternoon the answering machine instructed me to ring Mulcahy. His secretary said he was engaged. I explained I was returning his call. She put me on hold for two minutes. Then:

'Harding, I haven't smoked for three days . . . Harding?'

'Yes, Mr Mulcahy.'

'Oh, you're there. I haven't smoked for three days but now it's the weekend, how shall I put it, I don't have access to my secretary on weekends . . . '

'Do your best. And try to remember you don't drown by

falling into the water. You climb back out, change your clothes, and enjoy dry land.'

'What's that, Harding?'

'American bullshit. But it's true. Have a nice weekend.'

The holiday season was over. At the Saturday night peal we had all eleven ringers. Sam had been on the phone. He was never happy until seen to have done his bit. And he had called on Brock who, as it turned out, had not a notion of attending beyond his obligatory introductory presence. Donat, as conductor, called the changes and in the unusual event of a full house, picked the team. He had never included Charlie and he did not now. Sam was always angry at that, an anger he kept to himself. But he was also enraged as we were about to ring that Brock had not arrived. But just as we finished the peal we heard footsteps. Sam rushed to open the trapdoor as soon as I stepped aside. 'It's Father Brock.'

Panting, with his skirts gathered about him, Brock eased himself on to the long stool. Sam introduced those who had not been there the previous week leaving until last: 'Father, this is Dr Donat Cagney.'

'Please remain seated,' Donat ordered as he offered Brock his hand but Brock pulled himself up with Donat's help.

'Please to meet you, Doctor. Dr Cagney. Cagney, Cagney, Cagney . . . ' The trapdoor was opened; Charlie had his foot on the first step, pulling my coat sleeve, in a hurry for our game of snooker at the Draper's Club. ' . . . you could hardly be the young . . . no . . . impossible . . . or could you . . . ' Charlie yanked me after him but I caught: ' . . . Canton?' Down outside the door I said to Charlie: 'Wait a minute.'

'For what, for bollix?'

Sam, Brock and Donat were next in a threesome that did not quite include Sam. Outside the door Sam stood by, sweaty yet satisfied his star turn had been worth Brock's exertions to attend. Donat linked the chaplain a step or two out the yard.

'The nights are getting chilly, Doctor,' we heard. 'Would you care to join me in breaking open a bottle?'

24

I watched Sam Brown look after them. I loved Sam. And I hated my father, Dr Donat Cagney.

'Harding, will you come away from those bollixes 'till I beat the shit out of you.'

'Sam, come with us, we'll have a drink after in Charlie's.'

'In that kip, Tim?'

I would get him back in humour, sparking off Charlie.

On the way to the Draper's Club Sam and Charlie reminisced about the old days playing above Montague's. They recalled Phil Thompson, Butsey Rushe, Wally Kirwan, who were in the Draper's Club most nights. And they were on a table when we went in that night. We had less than ten minutes to wait. Charlie had no problem with time. He talks to himself or anyone who cares to listen. ' . . . would you care to break a bottle open, over their bollix heads I'd like to break the fucking bottle . . . look in now, bollix Yendall, a shower of dryballs, Simpson, although I have time for Simpson, and Sloan couldn't help himself, Jasus, he must just have been born that way but bollix across, Yendall, sly cunt that fella, hey, Harding, what are you giving me?'

'Thirty for a tenner.'

'You ate me last week. Forty.'

'Thirty-five.'

'Black, English, Protestant robber.'

I gave him thirty-five and took it handy for half the reds when he reached a lead of sixty-eight. I got serious but it was too late. Charlie had the confidence of the lead and the patience to indulge his murderous game of safety. Yet, I could draw on the balls and when he let me in I cleared them. But on the second black which I broke, Charlie – serious and sweating – pulled off a great long-table shot. 'Up your arse, Harding.'

I coughed up my tenner and, cool though I was, it hurt. I left him to play Sam – giving Sam thirty for fifty-pence – said I'd see them later in Charlie's – and went on to the Professional Club.

Jack Molyneaux had not yet arrived so I was stuck on my

own with Donat. 'You broke open your bottle, Donat, did you?'

'I detect sarcasm. It doesn't become you. He is from a good family, you know, Tim. Odd that in a Redemptorist. Our paths almost crossed, he was not long after me in Canton.'

'So what did you talk about them?'

'Hardly interest you. Malaria. Post-colonial birth pangs. Revolution . . . faith . . . '

'And the tower.'

Donat dropped the eyelids, smiled. 'No.'

I saw Jack Molyneaux come in. 'See you, Donat.'

'Where to now?'

'Well, if you'd like me to account for my movements, I've just had a game of snooker with Charlie, I'm going to meet Sam in Charlie's now . . . '

' . . . bony heads . . . '

' . . . the few pints first, then pick up the ride, collect the Kentucky Chicken, back to my place, bang her, chuck her out, up early in the morning for my run . . . goodnight, Mr Molyneaux . . . '

And to myself going down town: I'll get you, Donat, somehow, if it's the last thing I do . . .

Sam had room by the fireplace so I was able to stand beside him with my elbow on the mantelpiece and watch the door. He bought me a pint and a glass for himself. Sam is a once, maybe twice a week man.

'Well, Sam?'

'He beat me. I needed a snooker on the blue.' Sam looked drained. Fifty pence. All the old guys are the same, safety players, try as though their lives depended on the outcome. Charlie himself . . . the door opened and she didn't come in . . .

' . . . he was blessed, I potted the brown and went in off with the blue stuck on . . . '

For an hour there in the Statue of Liberty with Sam the door opened again and again and she did not come in. I kept my eyes on the door while I was listening to Sam and to Charlie roaring to anyone who would listen to him to observe his plucked pigeons, and God my knees buckled with every feminine sleeve that came round the door. And when Sam had his quota and went home I stayed on to have more than my fill, thinking of her all the time with a longing that induced a brewer's droop towards the pub fuck, and set off for my Kentucky Chicken, crazed, and to a salt and curried stained slump in the chair beside my bed in the flat. All that night I slept and woke and craved her, woke and hungered for a glimpse or even a hard look from her. And in the safety of my solitude I whispered her name; I said, I love you, Sloan's daughter, I adore you . . . .

On the Sunday morning I ran the liquor off up the three miles of river bank to the university, into the grounds for four miles lapping the track, back the river bank. I eat the Kentucky, talk about the ride, and run to buck Donat . . . 'grey haired men running through the streets, by Jove . . . ' All I had to do was ring her, all I had to do was to go over to London, all I had to do was call on Sloan himself if that was the form, announce my honourable intentions . . . But if I did ring her she might not come to the phone; if I did go to London she might refuse to see me; if I called on Sloan he might set the dog on me. Something held me back. I could rationalize: it was not the fear of thraldom, I longed to bend my knee; it was not dread that a longing satisfied might begin to pall, no, I yearned for satisfaction; it was not – Christ, I didn't know what it was but something held me back.

CHAPTER 5

The House of Montague

Wretched days ahead, I had anticipated at the funeral and the presentiment was not amiss. Gallantly, Mr Sloan came to work every day and though choking on emotion courteously attended to our solicitations on behalf of the child. 'She thrives, thank you, Mr Yendall,' Mr Sloan would answer, grateful for my concern yet tacitly pleading that I say no more. And I did not.

'Very well, thank you, Todd. How is your cough this morning.' 'Kind of you to ask, Simpson, And thank your mother, inform her the child is in capable hands.' But for all that Mr Sloan must have appreciated all our good wishes, he had a mountain of sorrow to climb alone. One morning, after three months, he came into my office.

'May I have a moment, Mr Yendall?'

'Of course, Mr Sloan. Please sit down. Sit here.'

'No, I'll stand, thank you. Mr Yendall, this is rather difficult for me to put to you. Mindful as I am of your consideration and that of Todd and the staff and even young Simpson. But the fact is, Mr Yendall, I find it wearing, that is to say, if you'll forgive me – I am finding it difficult as you can see Mr Yendall – Cecelia is flourishing I am happy to tell you, she is almost as well off in my sister's care as . . . the position is, Mr Yendall, I think it unnecessary that the staff inquire daily . . . I don't know if you would understand . . . '

'Mr Sloan, I understand perfectly. If you would like to leave it in my hands . . . '

'Yes. See to it in your own way.'

I had a quiet word with Todd and the rest of the staff and was severe yet diplomatic to Simpson, not quite pointing out the impertinence of his mother's curiosity. The woman should have known her place. Simpson could scarcely be faulted there.

Of course no such constraint was – or desired to be – imposed on Sir Thomas Ainsworth, who invariable referred to Cecelia in racing parlance. 'Filly coming along, eh Sloan?' Sir Thomas was celebrated for his good cheer and positively would not brook despondency. It was common knowledge that he was the life and soul of the British Legion and a cynosure of hilarity at the Curragh and Ascot house parties. But I must say he did have his work cut out with Mr Sloan whose revivification during a Sir Thomas visit did not, alas, endure.

Dr John Cagney preferred to express his professional interest through me. 'You feel, Yendall, do you, poor Sloan grieves overmuch?'

'I am afraid so, Dr Cagney. Not that it is my place to determine the degree of another's bereavement but I do wish his old spark would return. It is painful to watch.'

'You are quite right, Yendall. It may be that we shall have to do something for him. But not yet. Time, time is the fellow. We'll give it time, Yendall. I'll go and have a word with him now and you'll keep me informed?'

'Certainly, Dr Cagney.'

The thoughtful gentleman paused at my door-sill. Over his shoulder he spoke softly, sadly. 'It is doubtful if we shall hear "Absence" again.'

Mr Sloan's favourite and with which he was ever reliable to break your heart with the most soulful rendition. Indeed Sir Thomas would not have a party without insisting on Mr Sloan's attendance. Like all men of good cheer, Sir Thomas needed a respite from his own joviality and there was no better excuse for a good sniffle than Mr Sloan's 'Absence'. I only enjoyed the privilege myself at Christmas when the staff repaired to Arthur Skee's place around the corner, a splendid old pub, oak, mirrors, swords and muskets, stuffed heads and all sorts of comforting bric-à-brac. Spotless of course unlike so many establishments and Arthur Skee himself was of the old school, as able to fence with Sir Thomas in his cups as defer to Dr John Cagney *inter alia*. Mr Sloan was a regular every Saturday evening after we closed the shop but his time was too early for me. I enjoyed my sup, such as it was, in the Draper's Club.

Mr Sloan had always taken his wife to one of the European capitals on the summer holiday. He was a man for the art gallery and the cathedral, and of course the opera, which he patronized for a few days at his own expense in the autumn, a little excursion of his out of which he found time to call at the London branch and confer with Mr Dobson. The tragedy occurred in June necessitating the cancellation of a visit to Athens. We did not have a staff drink that Christmas. I must confess I did not enjoy the festive season myself thinking of Mr Sloan. The winter lingered, accentuating the general gloom. Despite our most judicious ministrations – jolly Sir Thomas, Dr Cagney's shrewd professional eye, my own subtleties – Mr Sloan did not rally. We could scarce enjoy the glorious contrast of spring. Outside our small little world the signs were ominous indeed. Noise emanated from my wireless that later I would be informed constituted an entertainment christened 'Rock and Roll'. And my informant was Simpson. The high priest of this bilge was an American young fellow called Presley who proved Barnum right by the original wheeze of avoiding his barber, dressing in sequins and trousers so tight that the contours of his genitalia were identifiable to the myopic, leaping about after the manner of those coloured tribes with rings in their noses one caught in the travelogues at the cinema, mangling a guitar to the point of discordance and grunting inarticulately into a microphone. And this was a refinement of that cross we were already bearing, pop music. It was difficult to avoid ill-temper.

The good news for a time – of which I was unconscious until he made a reappearance – was the absence of that scut Halvey. One grey morning I had to go out from my office to steady Mr Todd who was having a paroxysm. Behind my back the glass doors were pushed open and I heard myself addressed: 'Hey, Yendall, get a load of my blue suede shoes.'

I turned to be confronted by an apparition. He was indeed wearing blue suede shoes, and a black suit a size too small for him with a velvet collar and the trousers as narrow as those of a trapeze artist. I could see almost three inches of lilac sock and a lilac handkerchief in his breast pocket. His shirt was white but again, a lilac tie. He too presumably had not visited a barber in months. His hair was larded in Brylcream and swept back in the manner of the Presley delinquent. But I recognized the voice and the incessant leer. I went to run him but he as quickly back-pedalled out to the pavement from where he addressed me, unabashed by the numerous passersby. He said: 'Yendall, you're only a bollix.' I thought of all the money spent on education out of my taxes and not a policeman in sight when needed.

I was in touch with those aspects of the times outside my milieu perforce through the odd conversation with Simpson and that very day yielded one of the oddest. Simpson had been sent to our clothing factory to collect a suit that I had seen ready and wrapped the previous afternoon and he was not yet back, a half hour late with the milk and biscuits. I was in such a foul mood that I cuffed him.

'Mr Yendall, I'm sorry, 'twasn't my fault, I had to run after Charlie Halvey to get the bike back.'

I brought Simpson into my office. In truth I needed a chair.

'I was in plenty of time, Mr Yendall, I was coming down William Street when he called me and we were talking and he just sat up on the bike for a second, you know the way he does things, Mr Yendall, and suddenly he shot off, the turned into Catherine Street and up Thomas Street and around the block shouting out at everyone the way he does, until I was able to catch up with him and stand in front of him so's he'd have to knock me down.'

'But Simpson, it would never have happened if you hadn't stopped to talk to him in the first place.'

'Well, I hadn't seen him in a long time, Mr Yendall, I

31

couldn't ignore him, we were only bringing each other up to date.'

'And what is his most recent history, Simpson. Has he been in jail by any chance of good fortune?'

'Ah, Mr Yendall, he's not like that. He was over in England, in London.'

'Doing what?'

'Working in the factories and in the bars but he's come home to join a showband, Mr Yendall.'

'A what band, Simpson?'

'Guitars and drums, you know, Mr Yendall.'

'I didn't know he was musical, Simpson.'

'He'll only be playing the triangle, Mr Yendall, but he'll be the lead singer.'

'I suppose that does account for his dress.' It would follow. A disciple like Halvey would find a messiah in Presley.

'No, Mr Yendall, they'll be wearing cowboy suits in the band. That's what he told me anyway. He'll be called Tex. Tex Halvey. It's Paschal Larkin's band, they're calling it Hank Larkin and the Hoedowners.'

At this Simpson grinned but I froze him. 'All right, Simpson, make the tea. And Simpson . . . '

'Yes, Mr Yendall?'

'I can see it wasn't entirely your fault. I regret I lost my temper. I apologize, Simpson.'

'That's all right, Mr Yendall. Thank you, Mr Yendall.'

Halvey had not lied to Simpson. In the weekend local newspaper, in the *entertainment* section, there was a photograph of the cowboys. I recall musing at the time that there was no longer any need of a labour exchange.

Spring blew past and we were into a fine summer that contrasted more sharply with the mood of the shop. On the first anniversary of Mrs Sloan's death none of us could look at each other. It had been difficult to know what to do but I decided against a present and admonished the staff to abide by my example. We sent a simple birthday card with the inscription 'From All At Montague's'. Dr John Cagney called in that day, had a few words with Mr Sloan and came into my office.

'You see any improvement, Yendall?'

I shook my head. 'I have been unable to approach Mr Sloan on the subject of the roster. But I am in readiness to sacrifice somebody at a moment's notice should he feel he is up to a holiday.'

'When does he usually go, Yendall?'

'August, Doctor. August is his month but he has waited until September, depending on climate and so on.'

'Well then, we will give it to September, Yendall. After that I can no longer stand aside.'

'Yes, Doctor.'

I enjoyed my own holiday as best I could in Kilkee given my thoughts for Mr Sloan and the fact that everywhere one turned one met a Presley lookalike. And they were all about me on the streets when I returned. It struck me that alone of his generation Simpson remained true to the short back and sides. I put it to him. 'I notice, Simpson, you are singularly unaffected by this passing whim.'

'I don't think Mr Sloan would allow me to wear the DA, Mr Yendall.'

'The what, Simpson?'

Simpson blushed. He had the hand in the pocket, working away, despite my constant reproof. I dreaded to think that he played with his person.

'It's called the DA, Mr Yendall. It's . . . I don't like to say . . . it's a bit vulgar . . . '

'Simpson, you won't shock me. What is this Dee A?'

'The Duck's Arse, Mr Yendall.'

'I beg your pardon, Simpson?'

'It's like a duck's backside the way the hair comes together at the back.'

'Hm. I see. So this is what good men fought and died for, Simpson. Take your hands out of your pockets. Men like your

33

own father fought and died. For Teddy Boys. That will be all, Simpson.'

As he promised, Dr John Cagney saved the day. He called in on the first of October and took Mr Sloan out to lunch at the Royal George. I imagine they may have had a drink or two as Mr Sloan displayed something of the old animation on his return. He was off to London for a fortnight of theatre and opera, gallery and cathedral. Could I hold the fort?

It was as if we were on holiday ourselves for two weeks coping without Mr Sloan, rooting for him. I will not claim that after fourteen days in London Mr Sloan danced into the shop. That had not been his style *status quo ante*. But he was brisk again, enjoying his work. And from his visit to Mr Dobson at headquarters he brought back the command that we were to cut an inch off the circumference of our leg. Only Sir Thomas baulked. 'Dammit, man,' he bellowed at Mr Sloan, 'have you all gone mad?' Sir Thomas is long since gone. But, as I remember now, the rot set in. It was the beginning of the end.

CHAPTER 6

The Society of Bellringers

After the peal on Saturday night I led the way downstairs and waited at the tower door for Charlie. He came down with Sam. The three of us were about to set off for the Draper's Club when Donat called me. He made no effort to detach me.

'Tim, I'll stroll over and have a chat with Brock. Poor fellow can't have much company. I'd like you to join us, he comes from a good family, you know.'

'I'll follow you along.' This was treacherous to Sam. Charlie was well able to look after his own feelings. Oiling out of it, I said to Sam: 'If he came to the tower he'd have company, Sam. I'll see if I can't get him interested.' Sam nodded. Sam *is* innocent.

'Bollix. What about our game, you black English Protestant.'

'Sam can beat you tonight for a change. I'll see you later.'

I stayed at the tower door for five minutes chatting to a couple of the other ringers and then strode slowly across the yard to the presbytery. I was answered by a cleaning lady who skirted the slippery handiwork of her mop and pail and led me down a corridor to the door with Brock's nameplate.

'Dr Cagney said you can go straight in.'

I could hear Donat's voice. I obeyed the cleaning lady.

' . . . I have always dealt with things at source . . . Tim, sit there . . .'

It was a high-ceilinged room; a writing bureau, a large, polished mahogany table at either end of which Brock and Donat faced each other. I was directed to sit in the chair by the fire that was just beginning to bud. They had a bottle and a glass each. Donat pointed to his and a third glass, indicating I should help myself. Brock did not look at me, he stared straight down the table at Donat. I noticed Brock's bottle was half empty, Donat's – ours – almost full. I helped myself, said Cheers, got no acknowledgement.

' . . . as my father used to do and would today . . . ' They did not deign to précis what I had missed. 'Whereas the other ringers, for example, exemplified by Sam Brown, our secretary, they only woke up when the deed was done and some bearded lout was thumping his guitar at what we're told is a "folk mass". It was too late then for their ilk. Splinters of reform had already lodged in their souls, they were sapped of the outrage necessary for a major gesture – as chucking the church would be for a bony head. So they plod on.'

Without taking his eyes off Donat, Brock poured from his bottle. He drank half a glass, let the whiskey burn its way down. 'Keep talking, Cagney. I don't know what the fuck you're saying but keep at it.'

I was a credit to my blood. Having listened to Donat so often I was trained not to show astonishment. More so since I divined Brock knew my story.

' . . . they plod on. Africa and the East certainly contributed in my case. The execrable introduction of the vernacular, that was a factor. And by Jove, this lunatic notion of shaking hands with one's grimy neighbour as a sign of peace after the Lord's Prayer . . . one recoils. But it was ecumenism that pushed me out. I would have nothing to do with that. You don't dilute blood, you don't dilute religion. And then this Roncalli fellow . . . visiting prisons . . . so pathetic . . . such a peasant . . . '

Brock sipped, shook his head. 'You're a fucking snob, Cagney.'

'I had too much of myself invested in your organization. When it should have begun to fructify for me, the loins less restless, strictures easier to soak, you'd become over-ripe, too soft. That is unfair to me. I go my own way now.'

'And that's it?'

Donat opened his palms. 'The crown rests.'

'I wish I had some such excuse. Mine was sudden. I woke up one morning or turned a corner or crossed a street, I can't remember now, it doesn't matter a fuck – and it was gone. Just gone! Nothing led up to it. I had never turned native. I wasn't a man to read, never mind worry about encyclicals. My faith was founded on faith, not theology, your friend by the fire there could probably outfence me. Suddenly I didn't have it anymore. The thought of kneeling down and muttering through a grille to a man of my own make that I had been tempted to masturbate and indulged the thought was almost enough to make me laugh. Overnight,' Brock looked down at his glass, 'I saw consubstantiation as hocus pocus.'

Donat's cigarette fist propped his chin. Through the smoke he put in boldly to Brock: 'I think it's the fear of death.'

Brock laughed: 'Fuck you, Cagney. Of course it's the fear of death.'

They smiled at each other then Donat turned to me: 'Any light from our young English Protestant?'

I did my best. 'This young English Protestant is ignorant of the ways of older Irish men of the cloth. I didn't know priests swore.'

'I say fuck because I might wake up tomorrow and it might be back and then I might not be able to say fuck anymore.' He did not smile at me.

'Does it stop there with you?' Donat pried professionally. 'While you're in this state of diminished responsibility do you seek out the odd woman.'

'She'd want to be odd. I masturbate now, Cagney. I'm seventy-one years of age and I began abusing myself at seventy.'

'There are those who would consider that a boast at your age.'

'I enjoy it until it is over and I have to mop up.' Brock spoke coldly but I thought he could have cried. He was surely crying inside. What did he do on Saturday nights after Donat left? Did he sit with only himself and the bottle, did his eye fall on the picture of Our Lady of Perpetual Succour on the wall above the fireplace? Did he turn his head away? Did he rage? I didn't want to know. I felt grubby. They should not have had me in, not to listen to the preoccupations of the aged. I finished my drink and stood up to leave. I said: 'I hope you'll excuse me. I have an appointment.'

Brock ignored me. He refilled his glass. Donat's nod of dismissal was less emphatic than the Queen's.

When I got to the Draper's Club Sam and Charlie had just left. So I was informed by the 'legendary' Phil Thompson who was shuffling around in a trio with the newsboy, Butsey Rushe and Wally Kirwan. The club was quiet, a few of the young sharks – some of whom I took pains to chastise just to keep my eye in. Charlie was no challenge; a couple of antediluvians at the bar with the dead look, collars too large for shrunken necks, the last few thin strands plastered on the bald heads, probably drapers originally; and drinking by himself seated at the bay window – the pussers corner, Charlie called the bay window, where a member sits to fight with himself – Yendall, the gaffer. He was secretary of the Club as far back as anyone could remember. Like Sam in the tower no one else wanted the job. Charlie told me that back in the old showband days he was dressed in his cowboy suit – Tex was his name in the band – and loading the van when Yendall passed by. Charlie shouts: 'Hey, Yendall, we've got a gig tonight an' we need someone to demonstrate the Hucklebuck, want to earn a few bob?' Charlie simply has no respect for respect. I turned left when I went into the hall, away from the bay window but going out I had to see Yendall and he had to see me. Out of ordinary good manners as I neared the door I said: 'Goodnight.' Now I knew from the look on Yendall's face when I'm with Charlie that Charlie and anybody with Charlie gives him a pinch of distress. And from listening to Charlie incriminate himself I don't blame Yendall. He seemed surprised by my courtesy. He said: 'Oh, goodnight to you.'

My corner was gone in Charlie's but the mantelpiece held me up. Charlie was serving the usual six at a time; he was one wizard of a barman. I got my pint from Hannah. I wondered why Sam wasn't there. Then I started to try and not think of her, and try and not hope that she would come in. In ten minutes Charlie comes out. 'All quiet on the western front, think they'll never get enough of it, take 'em half an hour to drink it. That bollix Sam Brown took fifty pence off me.'

'He beat you?'

'I gave him thirty. Fluked the black and wouldn't go doubles or quits, his wife had fucking visitors. Domesticity, Harding, worse than heart disease. Country full of bollixes dead at forty and have to live till eighty goin' home to the wife. Fuck Sam and my grand fifty pence. He'll be in later when the visitors are gone and she lets him out. There's another crowd for you, fucking visitors, what's a visitor for Jaysus sake, why don't we tell visitors fuck off go home to your own fucking kip, but I may as well be talking to the wall.'

She was there. I turned to Charlie for a second and she was there, the door closing behind her, mounting the draughty stool opposite the door. Blue jeans and matching denim shirt, braces and mauve handkerchief, beret and high heels, the same rubbish Charlie or the art brigade affected and yet . . .

'Tell me about Dr Bollix and bollix Brock, did they break open the fucking bottle, what are you – aha, you can look but don't touch, she's here again, where's her sign, customers are requested not to handle the merchandise . . . '

A whiskey and water before her, legs crossed, one arm folded, a cigarette held poised, looking down the long bar. At me. Gripping my eyes and smiling. At me. Or had I gone round the twist? Looking at me, smiling at me and now flicking her head back in invitation. I put my finger to my chest and widened my eyes. She nodded.

'Excuse me, Charlie.' I made my way through, my pint in the air for protection. She smiled a welcome all the way until I was beside her.

'I think you're divine,' she sang and I swallowed – not my drink – and blushed, 'when you sat there with the frame around your neck after the drink was spilled on you, I thought

39

that's my man, you had an absolutely wonderful expression and it was so funny . . . '

'But you didn't laugh . . . '

'I didn't laugh but who are you?'

'Tim Harding.'

'Cecelia Sloan. I haven't much time, my father has a bad flu. I work in London. I only came this weekend because he sounded so bad on the phone even though my aunt is there but I just had to tell you, I've thought of you every day for the past two weeks . . . '

'I've thought of you every day.'

'No you haven't, buster, you were looking for an easy lay and when it didn't work you forgot about me. This isn't patter, I'm sincere and telling you simply because I can't help myself.'

What sort of gimmick was this? I put my glass on the counter.

'Listen to me for a change. I said I thought of you every day and I did. If you don't believe it then goodbye. And you're right, I was looking for a ride. This is Charlie's for God's sake. But now, now it's different. Please believe that.'

She looked at Charlie's clock – which had stopped, then at her watch. 'I have to go. Walk me home.' She looked down the counter for attention and drew Charlie.

'May I have a whiskey to go, please.' To me she said: 'For my father.' Charlie wrapped up the small bottle – in a piece of newspaper rescued from the waste bin – took her money and gave her the change without a comment. So unlike Charlie. I had known all sorts of women since I started at sixteen with one of the bingo hall girls in Fulham Broadway yet when I tried to lift my glass for a last drop my hand shook. She put the whiskey in her shoulder bag, landed from the stool and walked to the door. Where she stopped and waited. Until I copped on and opened the door for her. 'And who is Tim Harding, Tim Harding?' She pulled my sleeve to make me walk on the outside of the footpath.

'Tim Harding is a twenty-eight year old Fulham man,

graduate of Trinity, Dublin, and presently chief executive of the one-man business, Fagend – that's my office across there, overhead the auctioneers.'

'Fagend?'

'I help people to stop smoking.'

'Oh Gawd!'

'Hold on, I'm really a maths teacher. But I got into this racket by accident and it beats work.'

'If you're a maths teacher you should be teaching maths, Tim Harding.'

'I know. I will. Teaching jobs are scarce here. I suppose I should go back to London, they can't get enough teachers there, all the good ones are dead, dying or cashiered for pederasty.'

'Cross here. That's where my father worked all his life. It used to be a Montague's. Now look at it.'

'I know. All I have to do is walk down town with Charlie. "There's Mr Sloan . . . look at Yendall coming alone . . . would you look at the face of Simpson . . ." Charlie expresses it more colourfully.'

'I can imagine.' I stopped to look at the building where her father had worked all his life. To do the same thing all your life. Charlie climbed into my head with his myriad vocations. ' . . . since I was ten collecting slops from the lanes at a ha'penny a bucket . . . '

' . . . Tim Harding, you may hold my hand . . .' And so our love affair began. The throat dry I turned away from Old Sloan's prison to the smiling Cecelia with her hand down by her side. I held her hand tightly and went to lean towards her to kiss her.

'No. That comes much later. Keep walking.'

We walked across the bridge. I could wait for later. I could count my blessings. I was holding her hand. It was an autumn night. I was in love. I was in heaven.

Apart from Donat's Sexton Square across the bridge was the most fashionable part of the city. This was so simply because it once was and old blood still lived there. We

41

squeezed hands in silence until we reached the large wrought-iron gates, hundred yards' gravel driveway, garden with four oak trees and leaf covered lawn, the three storey red brick desirable residence of Sloan, Esquire. She let my hand go and folded her arms. 'This is it, Tim Harding.'

'You must be rich,' I pointed out.

'We haven't a bob. My father lived prudently. His own word. Goodnight.'

'Heeey . . . hold on there. Don't I at least get my goodnight kiss?'

'That comes much later. As it is I've knocked off six months to hold your hand. What was good enough for my father and mother will be good enough for us.'

'What do you mean?'

'My father walked out with my mother for six months. When he brought her home at night he raised his hat and thanked her for the evening. Then they held hands for three months. Then he proposed. She was wearing an engagement ring when they kissed. And a wedding ring when they made love. I think it was so wonderful, absolutely divine, don't you?'

'You're kidding?'

'Am I?'

'You're not kidding. But when will I see you again? When are you going back?'

'In the morning.'

'I'll go with you to the airport.'

'No you won't. My father will.'

'I'll ring you. Charlie said you're with a publisher, what publisher?'

'You won't ring me. I'm with William Drake.'

'Here's my card, you ring me.'

'Ha! You don't know William Drake, I'm afraid. I couldn't make a cross-channel call to James Joyce.'

'I know, I'll fly over to London, take you out to dinner . . .'

'No. Goodnight. I love you.'

She high-heeled it in the gravel.

42

I didn't go back to the Statue of Liberty for half an hour. After crossing over the bridge I went down the steps and walked along the quay thinking like a Fagender, counting my blessings. No more could I indulge the grievance of my beautiful mother taken from me when I was seventeen and the discovery that Dr Bollix was my father. I had Cecelia Sloan.

I reached Charlie's in time for one drink. Charlie is strict. Nobody is served after hours unless it is someone he thinks will give him the ride or Sam or myself. Sam was there. I congratulated him. Serving the drink, Charlie leered at me.

'Harding, you black English Protestant, I told you, Sloan's daughter? You'd have a better chance with Mother Mary fuckin' Aikenhead.'

'You cleaned his clock, Sam.' Sam started to tell me about the game but I don't think I caught a word. I was listening to the music. Cecelia, Cecelia, Cecelia. Charlie cleared the bar, stood Sam and me a drink, and came out to sit by the fire, drinking Ballygowan water by the neck.

'What about the bollixes, what do they talk about?'

'Loss of faith. Father Brock woke up one day and it was gone. Donat objects to ecumenism. Is there some part of the mass when people shake hands with each other, Sam?'

'The priest says: Let us all offer each other the sign of peace.'

'Donat won't go along with that so I gather he stays away from mass which I must say is news to me.'

'It's news to me. I just assumed he went to the Jesuits. He never did go to the Redemptorists as long as I know him. I'm sad to hear that, Tim. And Father Brock too?'

'It's funny. He "Fucks" away like Charlie there. If his faith comes back he won't be able to swear so he sins now while the going is good.'

'Sin, my bollix. I'll tell you a sin story. Listen to this, Harding. And you too, Sam, 'twill do you good. When I was Tex with Paschal Larkin in Hank Larkin and the Hoedowners. It's about half past two on a Sunday morning, we've been playing about five hours straight – we didn't have a relief

43

band, we were a fucking relief band. We pack away all the equipment and we're sitting in the back of the unheated van somewhere in the arsehole of Kerry waiting to start the three hour drive home. Bitterly cold. We knew how cold it got in the van so we're all sitting there wrapped in a blanket and muttering to each other like dispossessed fucking Indians. And the cause of our misery: Paschal has scored. Paschal did the Elvis bit, he used to have a French letter full of sand strapped to his leg so 'twould bulge out of his jeans even though his prick wasn't the size of my thumb. But he had this foolproof way of clicking. He'd scour the hall during the break until he'd find the ugliest, filthiest, scrapeist woman in the hall. This night he's gone to fucking town altogether. Grossly fat, this woman has encased herself in the tightest black dress you could imagine, great bands of flesh encircle her like fucking car tyres. Her hair is a bee-hive job that hasn't been dismantled in years and her face is one big splodge of sweaty make up. Now the rule of the band was that anyone who clicked took the shortest time to get the job done – usually in the nearest field – so we could all get home. But it's so cold that even Paschal's knob would shrivel, so he shoves her into the long seat in the front of the van and dives on her. Sound of clothes being yanked off and then: "You can't, you can't, it's me period." Grunts of disapproval from Paschal and then whispered instructions. Followed by a rhythmic rocking in the front seat. Then: "Me hand is tired, you're never goin' a come." Further whispered instructions from Paschal. "No, I don't like doin' that." Paschal with the poetry again. "Promise you won't come in me mouth." Paschal grunted his agreement. Then great slurping sounds and little squeals of pleasure from Paschal. Progress is being made. Her nibs trying to wrench out from under but Paschal just gets there. Explodes into the poor bitch. The rest throw off their blankets and cheer. And meanwhile, young Charlie, without manual stimulation of any kind has shot his lot in his pants. And here's the question, Harding, you black English Protestant, and Sam,

44

you statue licker, was what I did a sin? And if it was, how in the name of fuck could I confess it?'

Sam was nauseated. Charlie walking up and down, grinning, clutching his bottle of Ballygowan. It was the type of story I usually loved, typical Charlie iconoclasm but tonight Cecelia obtruded. Holding her hand.

'To think that you call people to church, you're a disgrace to the tower. No wonder Dr Donat doesn't pick you when we have eleven, I don't know how the tower isn't struck by lightning.'

'You don't? I'll tell you why. Because there's a lightning conductor up on it, you dumb prick. As for Dr Bollix conductor I knew his doctor bollix of a father before him.' Charlie's grin was gone. There was anger, bitterness in his face. 'Old Dr Cagney – Dr fucking John – with the usual bullshit reputation for being kind to the poor. You'd have had to get yourself a fucking underground shelter to escape from the poor in those days. Everyone was the poor then except for the likes of the Cagneys and a few more like bollix Yendall in the office in Montague's, and that shower of drapers looking down their noses at carpenters for Jayses sake. Drink up that there, ye pair of bollixes, I had to give it up myself, couldn't handle it. When you find yourself in a hotel room for a month and having the booze and the dock whores sent up to you and only putting on a vest to be formal answering the door, 'tis time to give up. I know their history, you see. Farmers. Farming stock. But for an Irish Victorian farmer 'twas as necessary to have a doctor in the family as a fucking silver-laden mahogany sideboard in the parlour. His people set him up in Sexton Square after he got his doctorate. John M. Cagney, Doctor of Medicine, on his shingle crying out from its daily polished brass surface. No abbreviations. 'Doctors by Courtesy' he used to call mere Bachelors of Medicine. A fucking snob from day one. Not too dumb, married money, one of the Dinneens, the timber crowd, a dowry of twenty thousand. In those days. Cute cunt. The present bollix was born with two silver spoons in his mouth. I remember as a kid watching them go to mass. The

45

Jesuits was only round the corner but such a stately fucking progress you never saw the like of it. How I know some of this is from this yoke I was bangin' who knew the Cagney's maid. Every Sunday the maid had to gong the dinner gong at twenty to eleven on the dot so that all hands were on deck, and ten minutes later out they'd come; we used to hang around to gawk at them. Cap and bonnet and parasol. Old Cagney in full morning dress, striped trousers, coat, tall silk, grey spats and gloves, rolled umbrella. And young bollix in a dark blue Norfolk jacket and boater with blue and white band, and we all gathered round to watch them with the snot running down our noses. They turn the corner. Half way down the street Old Cagney stops, looks up at the clock in Montague's clothing factory and takes out his gold hunter watch. What was the old bollix doing? Looking down at Montague's old clock with his snug opulent full hunter. Snaps the cover shut on the watch and on round the corner to the Jesuits with the rector waiting at the door. Cagney raises his hat with a full sweep, old bollix rector whips off his biretta and nails it to his chest and shakes hands all round with the washed. Into the porch there the collection plate is on the green baize table with another doctor bollix behind it or that prick Yendall. Old Cagney puts his half-crown on the plate with as much sleight of hand that a blind midget with a bag over his head sitting on top of the Matterhorn could see how much the cunt was offering. This was the nob porch, the other two doors were for the likes of me with our hot coppers and I collecting slops at a ha'penny a bucket when I was ten. Anyway, up the church with the procession of pricks to the heavy red rope railing off the north transept from the rest of us. The Jesuits. In the name of Jesus. Don't fall out with the establishment, that's their mission, to seek, find and nurture leadership. My bollix. And all for the A.M.D.G. Look at Harding smiling, fair play to you, a black English Protestant. Sam, you ignorant bollix, you know fuck all. I'd be the same if I had stayed at school, but I had enough brains to escape those mad Christian Brothers, bots that only wanted their hand on your leg, school guards following me all over town to bring me back by the ear. But after mass, wait till you hear this, out comes old Cagney and his troupe. Butsey Rushe used to move his stand up there on Sundays. Butsey dashes up with the folded *Sunday Independent* – that'll tell you their fucking politics too, boy – Law and Order, England Our Nearest Neighbour, God Bless the Pope But Don't Forget the Queen and the Gracious Queen Mum, ginsoddenould-fuckingbitch, Croppy Lie Down. "Your paper, Doctor," Butsey all polite. He couldn't normally put two fucking words together unless one of them was a fuck and the other off. Old Cagney says nothing. Paper paid for by the month. Takes out a shilling from some pocket I'd say specially stitched in by the Montague bollix just to hold the shilling, puts the bob in Butsey's grimy paw as if administering episcopal fucking chrism. Can't be seen actually carrying the paper, lowers the head and whispers, "When you come round, ring the bell, there's a good fellow, Molly will have something for you." His fucking gardener's cast off corduroys. You know, when I think back, Jasus doesn't know what the poor of this city had to put up with. But I'll say this much for old Cagney, that was then and this is now. You could just about take the likes of him, you had to, you had no choice and they were the times . . . But when I see that cunt Dr Donat going around with his father's walk and head in the air I go mad. Collecting slops from the old lanes at a ha'penny a bucket since I was ten and that bollix wouldn't salute me in the street.'

Charlie brought the grin back but could not hide the hurt in his face.

I could ring the airport, check the time of the morning flights, go out there and hide, watch her departure. Charlie and Sam were arguing. Whether or not Dr Donat Cagney was a snob, a bollix . . . or at least watch her coming out the gate of her house. Cecelia, Cecelia, I love you, Cecelia . . .

CHAPTER 7

The House of Montague

Mr Todd's cough lasted another two years. I will ever cherish Mr Sloan's Trojan tolerance. When Mr Dobson was due from London on his rounds, Mr Todd was despatched on a spurious errand, or to attend to a gentleman at the gentleman's own residence. Frequently Mr Sloan brought Mr Todd into my office – holding him by the shoulders – where we sat the poor fellow in my chair and did out humble best with the ministration of a glass of water. Of course Dr John Cagney was cognizant of our dilemma. As was Sir Thomas who opined characteristically: 'Flogging a dead horse, Yendall, knacker's yard if you ask me.' Dr Cagney was more circumspect. 'I was talking to Pearse Farrell in the club the other night, Yendall, Sloan's name came up. As you can imagine, Dr Farrell will always have a concern for Sloan and young Cecelia. Todd is not a patient of either of us, and one is reluctant to put in one's oar. Frankly, Yendall, we don't see the good in this, not for Todd, Sloan or your own self, Montague's. I don't know if you follow me.'

Mr Todd was admitted to the sanatorium, a dreadful place. While we awaited a definite prognosis Simpson was called upon more often to help Mr Sloan. I cursed my impotence for it was Mr Sloan's jurisdiction. But having a messenger boy unnecessarily about the place, customers in the shop, it was maddening. What next, Halvey in to join us at elevenses? We reaped in due time and it afforded me little satisfaction. Three months on while I was pained to observe Simpson actually wrapping a shirt under Mr Sloan's guidance – no matter that the customer was some tradesman with aspirations – the monkey Halvey made one of his phantom appearances and we were treated to: 'Hey, Simpson, watch out in there, that place is riddled with TB.'

Mr Todd did not improve. Between us – Mr Sloan and me – we fielded the insistent missives from Mr Dobson in London. But finally we were no match for a professional shake of the head from Dr Cagney. We could not look the other way for much longer. I drafted the advertisement for an Assistant Shop Assistant. I showed it to Mr Sloan in my office: we always worked in consultation. Desperately, Mr Sloan tried: 'I take it they're quite sure, Mr Yendall, they're quite certain about Todd?' I could not blame Mr Sloan for trying to avoid reality. Reality had taken his wife. I told him I was afraid so. He put the advertisement back on my desk. He called Simpson. I took an envelope from a stationery pigeon-hole and wrote the address. Mr Sloan sent Simpson to the newspaper office and returned to busy himself in the shop, weighed down once more. Outside my window Simpson was about to mount the bicycle. I saw him hesitate with his left foot poised on the pedal. He looked at the envelope. He rested the bicycle and came back into the shop. My door was always ajar so that I could keep an eye on things. I caught him approaching Mr Sloan – 'Mr Sloan, I was wondering' – as he followed Mr Sloan about the floor. A minute or so later they were both in my office, Simpson pushed in ahead by Mr Sloan. 'Simpson here has expressed a willingness to fill the position . . . Mr Yendall?' Mr Sloan spoke brutally. Of course it was a pre-posterous suggestion. But what were Mr Sloan and Simpson doing in my office? Mr Sloan repeated: 'Mr Yendall?' It was difficult to look at Simpson and see Mr Todd. Simpson's chin was low, eyes alert, and the hand working away in the pocket. Had he come to me directly I would have run him. He was getting too big for his messenger boy's bike and no mistake. But he was standing there with Mr Sloan. I had no idea how to deal with the situation. I probed: 'A probationary appoint-ment, Mr Sloan?' Mr Sloan snapped at me. 'All appointments are probationary, Mr Yendall.' I was snubbed. I was damn angry. At that I would do no more. Mr Sloan was the manager. Our codominium was prorogued. Let him do his own business. I was cold: 'As always, Mr Sloan, I will be content to abide by your good sense.' Mr Sloan frowned. He looked down at Simpson's shoes and then all the way up to the top of Simpson's head. He walked around Simpson's back and round my back to observe all dimensions of the grotesque. Mr Sloan was a thorough man but immediate in decision. He was not blind. I was shocked to hear the cry of surrender. 'What age are you, Simpson?' We were all being dragged through the muck. 'Your salary will be thirty-five shillings less deductions to pay for the morning suit and striped trousers. Mr Yendall will inform you of staff regulations.' That was not my brief. He was already washing his hands. At the door Mr Sloan recovered some ground. He closed his fist and pointed a finger at the ceiling. 'Out, Simpson. At any time of any day or night.' We were alone. I concentrated on my fingers tapping the desk, a habit of mine to control anger. I closed my eyes and thought of Mr Sloan bereft. Of the child, Cecelia. Tried not to think of Sir Thomas or Dr Cagney. At last I looked up at Simpson. That hand working away. I hissed: 'Take – that – hand – out – of – that – pocket!'

'Sorry, Mr Yendall.'

'Sit down, Simpson. Sit.' I instructed Simpson in the code of the house and concluded: 'To the rest of the staff you will of course be Mr Simpson. You understand?'

'Yes, Mr Yendall. Thank you, Mr Yendall'.

To the rest of the staff.

Only when I sat alone in gloom did it come to me Simpson's intelligence of the vacancy must needs have been gleaned from the letter on my desk when I stood to take the envelope from the pigeon-hole. I cursed myself.

Mr Todd passed on that very night. His was a modest funeral. Consumption was not a very popular way of dying. I attended the church next evening. Those ghouls, Halvey, Phil Thompson, Wally Kirwan and the newsboy, Butsey Rushe, rallied to the obsequies. I pondered what twisted sense of the macabre drew them to the removal of their betters. The newsboy wept into his snot rag. I felt so sorry for Mrs Todd and her children, humiliation piled on grief. I did not notice Dr Cagney at the mortuary but I saw him condole with Mrs Todd in church. Out of respect we closed the shop for two hours next day. Mr Sloan represented Montague's. I stayed in my office. Later that afternoon Simpson brought me the news from the graveyard. But it was that morning alone in my office that I received the telephone call from our factory: some madman had organized a stoppage as part of a campaign to 'unionize' Montague's.

J. Kelly. I consulted my records. He was the son of Patrick Kelly who was in our employment for over thirty years, a conscientious fellow, our senior cutter, on whose intercession alone we had taken on the son six months earlier. A storm in a teacup, I anticipated, some such nonsense. I put on my hat and coat and hastened to the factory to encounter Russell, our foreman uncharacteristically impotent.

'Well, Russell?'

'They want to form a union, Mr Yendall.'

'So? Why are they still on the premises?'

'It's principally Kelly, Mr Yendall. The other two don't know their – they're just easily lead. But Kelly is quite persuasive and his father is with us as long as myself. Outside of the job Patrick Kelly is a personal friend of mine.'

'I understand, Russell. But what is this orator's grievance?'

'Oh, the usual. Better conditions, better pay, shorter hours.'

'Did you talk to the father?'

'I did. The man is heartbroken, he's tried everything, but he's not a match for the son, Mr Yendall.'

'Let's see them, Russell.'

Russell led the way to the factory floor where we were confronted by this pup Kelly with a crucified look on his face flanked by two obtuse candle-holders identifiable to me down the years by their clock numbers. Stage left I noticed Patrick Kelly in a state of embarrassment. The poor fellow had my sympathy. In the background the rest of the workforce stood in a chorus of trepidation. I stepped out in front of Russell.

'Now then, what is this nonsense, Kelly?'

'Mr Kelly for a start, Mr Yendall.'

'I beg your pardon?'

'We won't be fobbed off with platitudes or sops, we're speaking in our capacity as representatives of the NDSP and demand equitable – '

'The what, Kelly?'

'The National Democratic Socialist Party . . . Yendall.'

There was a stir about the floor. Patrick Kelly entreated: 'Please, Jimmy.' If the agitator thought he could provoke me that easily then his drop through the scaffold would come all the quicker.

'I haven't heard of the august body, Kelly.'

'We are a breakaway from the Labour Party . . . Yendall.'

'I see. In what direction? The Labour Party perhaps not radical enough for you, is that it?'

'Exactly.'

'And you are National, Kelly?'

'We will be . . . Yendall. At the moment we three are an ad hoc committee formed to establish the party in this city, and our very first demand is that there will be no more "Mister" for you, while it is blunt "Kelly" for the rest of us.'

'In at the birth are we?' I had had enough. I looked over to the father. 'You have been with us thirty years, Kelly, is that right?'

'Yes, Mr Yendall.'

'Then you have some experience of the House of Montague. Are we fair employers would you say?'

'Very fair, Mr Yendall.'

' . . . for Christ's sake, Dad – '

'Do I exaggerate when I suggest that our positions are much sought after, wages higher than any "union" norm, conditions of employment, pension scheme, holidays the envy of every comparable establishment, do I exaggerate?'

'No, Mr Yendall.'

' . . . stop calling him Mister!'

'You listen to me, Kelly. Did Mr Russell here hand you the Code of the Shop when we employed you?'

' . . . your Code, not my Code . . . '

'Did he sign for it, Mr Russell?'

'Yes, Mr Yendall.'

'Right.' I walked over to Kelly senior and tried the quiet word. I said: 'You see the position, you can't want him sweeping the streets . . . '

'Mr Yendall, believe me I've tried. Mrs Kelly was in tears last night. No sleep for either of us, Mr Yendall. He won't listen. He was a year in London in a factory. God knows who he mixed with.'

'You're his father. For your service this is what I will do for you. Take him aside for five minutes. I will not mention it to Mr Sloan. Talk some sense into that boy and we will pretend it never happened.'

It was a sad business and no mistake. Kelly approached his son, but all he managed was 'Jimmy' before he was cut off with: 'Please, Dad, not here, don't speak here. I'm not a child, you can't see what I see, it's not your fault, my dignity means –'

'Mr Russell, give the man his cards – and anyone else who wants his. Back to work, please.'

I put on my hat and left. Going down town I could not have felt more sorry for Lear. Kelly, on his own, walked up and down outside the factory for three days carrying a 'Strike On Here' placard. We decided not to confer the dignity of an injunction. He gave up and went back to England.

Simpson's intelligence of the funeral was uneventful except that the four musketeers walked behind the hearse all the way to the funeral. And: 'Sir Thomas sent a wreath, Mr Yendall.'

'How did you spot that then, Simpson?'

'I didn't, 'twas Charlie – Charlie Halvey pointed it out.'

I caught Simpson blushing. 'Yes, Simpson?'

'Charlie just pointed it out, Mr Yendall.' He was blushing all the more, and the hand in action in the pocket.

'In what words exactly, Simpson, did Halvey make his observations?'

I was sorry for Simpson's discomfiture, Halvey's vocabulary was not Simpson's responsibility. But I was determined. 'The truth now, Simpson. You won't shock me.'

'You know the way he talks, Mr Yendall. It's just his way, he doesn't mean, he just said: "I see that langer Ainsworth sent flowers, fair play to him." He said "fair play to him" Mr Yendall.'

'That's all right, Simpson, I was simply curious. Back to your work.'

'Thank you, Mr Yendall.'

With the full phalanx of NDSP parading up and down outside the factory for the next three days I did not have leisure to entertain myself with Simpson's progress. Lady Ainsworth called in to see me.

'Good morning, Lady Ainsworth, lovely to see you again.'

'How are you, Yendall? Tommy's in a sulk, gone up to the Legion to drink whiskey, swamp fever in Boyd-Rochford's stable, all Tommy's colts caught it. He sent me in about poor Todd. Had the fellow capital, Yendall?'

'Not that I know of, Lady Ainsworth. I doubt very much that he could have had. He left seven children.'

'Oh dear. Of course. Tommy's always coming back from town with: Great cover, Todd, wife's foaled again. He can be quite irreverent, Yendall, you know.'

'Lady Ainsworth, we have long rejoiced in Sir Thomas's wit.'

'Indeed. Well, Yendall, I'll come to the point. I have a little cheque here that may be of help to Mrs Todd, that is, if you feel it appropriate, that no offence might be taken. Otherwise bung it in against Tommy's account.'

The cheque was for one hundred pounds.

'Lady Ainsworth, on behalf of Montague's and Mrs Todd may I – '

'Now, Yendall, stop that nonsense. Good day to you.'

'Thank you, Lady Ainsworth.'

I had tea and biscuits with Mrs Todd that evening. No offence was taken.

Let me confess that Simpson did not let us down. He was obsequious to Mr Sloan and to all our valued customers. And to the occasional riff-raff emboldened to cross the threshold by a windfall from the bookmakers Simpson was properly prim. The other assistants tended to be shirty at his appointment but Simpson knew his place and in time their resentment melted. He was three weeks behind the counter when Sir Thomas next called and the visit was without incident. 'Stable lad's a jockey now, Yendall,' Sir Thomas teased me and then showed his magnanimity, 'as it should be, Yendall, as it should be. Keep 'em down, then let 'em up, I say.' Of course Sir Thomas was always attended under the personal supervision of Mr Sloan. After a few months – at judicious intervals – Mr Sloan was in the habit of suggesting to me as an afterthought: 'Simpson seems to be settling in, Mr Yendall.' He had risked the accolade in the first place. He was gratified. I was happy for him and in a somewhat grudging way I was pleased on Simpson's behalf.

Now that he earned a man's salary, Simpson bought the paper out of his own pocket, and as I was taking my own one morning I overheard Butsey Rushe say to him: 'We didn't see you in a long time.' Simpson apologized : 'I'm not allowed now.' I thought I caught despair in his tone. That morning I made it my business to have a word with him.

'Miss the game, Simpson, do you?'

He lied. 'Oh, not that much, Mr Yendall.'

'You realize there are two good tables in the Draper's Club?'

'Mr Yendall, I wouldn't presume . . . '

'Rot, Simpson.' I cut short his Uriah Heep protestations. And I was impatient with his old-fashioned vocabulary in such a young man's mouth. I thought it artificial. Then again he was not picking up words in a natural way, among his peers.

'Because of your age, Simpson, not necessarily your occupation, you're eligible. Scarcely two-thirds of our membership consists of drapers now. Anybody reasonably respectable with the annual membership fee will find a proposer and seconder.'

I put him up myself and had him seconded and left him to enjoy his game. My own visits to the club were sporadic at that time and usually in a nineteenth-hole capacity. Mr Sloan never put a foot in the place. There should not, in the old order scheme of things, have been much more to say of Simpson – or any of us for that matter.

CHAPTER 8

The Society of Bellringers

Mulcahy called to my office during the week. He walked up to my desk and planted Exhibit A in front of me: a box of matches and a packet of Gold Flake.

'You can put those in your waste basket, Kiddo. I lied to you. Four packs, not two.' He put a cheque on top of the cigarette packet.

'That cover it?'

It was for two hundred and sixteen pounds. I said: 'Thank you.'

'Well, I'm a busy man. Some racket. I think you deserve it.'

I nodded.

'See you.'

'Thank you, Mr. Mulcahy.'

I went back to my *Texts & Tests*. In pursuit of the equation of the normal to a parabola I arrived at the equation of the directrix. To clear my head I switched to complex numbers. The Argand Diagram. Modulus of a complex Number. Polar Form. Loci and Transformations in the Complex Plane . . . plane . . . plane, up in the sky . . . Cecelia . . . Cecelia, Cecelia . . . my eyes strayed. I put Mulcahy's cheque in my pocket. I stared at the Gold Flake. I stood up, went over and turned the key in the door. Went back and looked at the Gold Flake. Seven in the packet. I took one out, put it between my lips, struck a match. Aaaah. Heaven. Cecelia, Cecelia . . .

After the bells on Sunday night Donat went over to Brock. I took a tenner off Charlie who got his fifty pence back from Sam. I skipped the Professional Club and stayed all night in the Statue of Liberty gnawing my finger. I had smoked all of Mulcahy's cigarettes, behind closed doors, and taken a bus five miles out of town to buy a few packets.

Donat startled us as we were tying up our ropes after the Sunday morning peal. 'By the way, I have been asked to make an announcement.'

He received immediate attention whereas Sam had to pluck us by the sleeves to listen to his notices. Even Charlie opened his eyes.

'Father Brock is being given a second-in-command, he's not in the best of health as you know.' We did not know. 'We'll see a new man here more often, a Father Clancy. Father Willie Clancy.'

Donat's 'Willie' told me the new man would be a 'bony head'. As Secretary the announcement – any announcement – should have come through Sam but he let Donat's story go unchecked until we were out in the yard. I was quickly behind Sam having smelt the same rat.

'Well, Dr Donat, is he a Republican?' Sam smiled.

'You have a wonderful imagination.'

'What's the story then?'

'Story?'

'Father Brock not being active enough to perform the duties of chaplain. There are no duties.'

Later, Donat told me that he had warned Brock so, and that Brock had told him to do it his own way. Brock had no interest in the tower and 'did not give a fuck about those bells'.

'I'm only carrying out instructions.' Donat reached for the unction. 'It wasn't my idea to keep it from *you*. This Clancy fellow is not on the run but he does have a problem. He's had a nervous breakdown. More than one. He was scarred from a one-man war against pornography and cinema courting up the country some years back. He had his own flashlight. Brushed past usherettes and routed all round him. Bookshop managers scarlet in his wake after his hurling bare breasted paperbacks at them, you understand?'

'He must have been kept busy. Why us? Why here?'

'Apparently it's our turn. That was some years ago and he's had relapses and now they feel he's well enough to start rehabilitation again. We are to show tolerance and understanding, we're comparatively enclosed. Brock wants me to encourage the delusion that Clancy is filling a void created by Brock's debility. He thinks – and I agree with him – that it's best not to spell it out to the others.'

'I won't tell them. I'm even sorry you told *me*.'

'Good. It's better in your hands. I can tell you this Willie Clancy doesn't sound like my type.' That went all round Sam.

Brock – looking healthy and well-fed – in titular exercise of his function, introduced Clancy that Sunday night. He treated Donat as the introduction of honour and immediately tried to appoint Sam as Donat's locum: 'I think we can leave you now in Mr Brown's capable hands. Coming, Dr Cagney?'

'I'll follow on.' For once Donat's blindness to sensitivity was outclassed. He had to stay. Our collective decorum demanded so.

Willie Clancy had everything in a man's appearance that I find disgusting, even though I know I should not judge a man by his appearance. But I do. Clancy was in his thin fifties, scrawny, a protuberant Adam's apple. His baldness seemed curiously premature, as though he had not bothered to fight its onset. And he had a grin that made me feel I might catch something from him. Charlie's fixed grin was the tip of a mischievous spirit; Clancy's, the rictus of obsession. Never had I been so repelled by the first sight of anyone. And I could see Sam wasn't exactly elated. It was bad enough that he had never been sent a chaplain who took interest; now they scraped the bottoms of barrels for chaplains who did not take an interest. Sam continued the introductions. Clancy inspected the photographs, Donat and the rest of us lingering out of politeness.

'I can see straight away who has given sterling service,' Father Willie grinned at Sam, and Sam blushed and tried to cover himself with: 'The bells are up above.'

'May I?'

Sam's carapace of indifference cracked. He looked at me. I nodded. Sam led the way up the ladder followed by Clancy, and I followed in case Clancy froze. Donat and the men escaped. As we had just finished the peals and the bells had not yet dropped for the midweek chimes, Clancy saw them with their mouths open when we reached the viewing platform.

'Fascinating,' Clancy said and Sam gave him a potted explanation of the mechanics. Bluntly: A ringer pulls the rope attached to his bell. The bell drops and the bell's clapper strikes the side of the bell. The bell continues its movement until it comes to rest in its original position. What facilitates its rest is a wooden stay that prevents the bell's continuous motion. Each ringer pulls his rope at a fixed interval after the ringer nearest to him and this constitutes a peal. The number one ringer – on Treble – is followed by the number two, and the number two by the number three and so on. When the conductor calls a change; for example, Three, One, meaning number three should follow number one, then it is axiomatic that number two should follow number three and four should follow two. As from 12345678 to 13245678. The principle is as simple as that. But in fact a ringer does not allow his bell to return to its original position but only so close that the bell is equilibrial. If the rope is pulled too lightly the bell fails to reach equilibrium, drops too soon and contributes to a cacophony. If the rope is pulled too strongly the bell passes equilibrium, breaks the wooden stay, continues full circle and causes as much dissonance as when pulled too lightly. The art is pulling the rope with the correct strength and holding the rope above one's head at a stretch that keeps the bell balanced until it is the ringer's turn to pull the rope again. Although Sam did not explain it as simply as I do, our new second-in-command was attentive. His eyes did not glaze. He did not yawn.

'Fascinating.'

In our sandwich we descended from the ringing chamber. Sam and I put on our coats. I bent down to open the trapdoor.

'I suppose, Sam, an old man like me could never learn new tricks.'

'Pardon, Father?' Sam was afraid to believe his ears.

Father Willie Clancy blushed. 'It's probably too complicated?'

Not traditional chaplain material. Sam was already taking his coat off again. 'You'd like to learn, Father?' Sam begged as from my disappearing eyes he caught my wink.

I skipped along to the Professional Club. Donat was lounged over his drink with Jack Molyneaux for company. Donat began immediately: 'A dreadful business.'

I said: 'What is?'

'Don't act the bony head. I've tackled Brock. I told him bluntly that I was not amused by his equivocation, he should have made known to me the type of individual I was expected to announce. By Jove I wasn't expecting much, but dammit. I told Brock that hale or ill Clancy was not our type. I was hot, I can tell you. Jack, I wish you would see this specimen for yourself. Food – no – banquet for a phrenologist.'

'You don't say. And you ticked off Brock, did you? Quite right too. Quite right, Donat.'

'Yes. But in the finish Brock helped me see it his way. We are unlikely to see Father Willie at all, Brock maintains, apart from the community dinner, and by then the fellow will surely have been transferred to an appropriate orchard or chicken run. Of course I didn't let him have the last word, I pleaded an engagement, left him to drink his bottle alone.'

Jack Molyneaux nodded. I came in: 'I don't think Sam Brown would agree with you there.'

'You don't say.'

'I do. Father Clancy expressed a willingness to learn and Sam is going to train him. To ring.'

Donat searched me to see if I jested. He could read me. So could old Molyneaux.

'You two are in for a time of it, it seems.'

Donat took a long draw that made me gasp for the hot Gold Flake in my pocket. 'We'll cope, Tim?'

'It looks like we'll have to.' I was close to him then. If a Father Willie Clancy could do it to me then I had to accept so many bony heads haunting Donat, with his trip-switch allergy. Old Jack, Donat and myself were warm together at last.

I can see my mother sitting in the Bunch of Grapes looking up at Dr Andrew Tait, the Harley Street gynaecologist with the flat in Hans Crescent. I know the Bunch of Grapes. I sat myself at the same table in the same corner. I can see my mother when she was leaving school at fifteen, setting out from Ospringe on the bus into Faversham seated beside her father, a man who wore a green coat behind the paint counter in Peacock's hardware. I can see Alice Harding, dutiful, tremulous, on her first morning in Madame Dillons across the road from Peacock's. Grandpa Harding, when not sending cylinders on the funicular to the office aloft for change, must have strained his eyes for an anxious glimpse of his daughter's initiation into the rubrics of *haute couture* à la Faversham. How quickly sped the years from that first magically slow day in Madame Dillons to inevitable impatience with small town life; to London and work as a seasonal casual in lingerie at Harrods where they were encouraged to refer to the emporium as 'the shop'. What posh. She was shy. During the five weeks before Christmas the only friends she made were two girls in the same department. Christmas fell on Monday. After work Saturday evening she and her pals went to the Bunch of Grapes for a drink. She stayed on when her two friends left at eight o'clock. I can climb into her mind. Her wages not much above subsistence. Sitting there thinking of the train from Victoria to Faversham next day and the bus to Ospringe, without clothing any more glamorous than she had setting out for London, without a metropolitan catch; on the table piled beside her gin and tonic a gift-wrapped panties and bra that she had nicked and managed to smuggle through security as a present for her mother, and a Harrods shirt that at staff discount price put her on beans for a week.

'Excuse me, would you object if I sat down for a moment, perhaps share in a seasonal toast?'

She looked up at Dr Andrew Tait. He was old/young in that his eyes crinkled with experience, while his trim thirty-seven-year-old body was clothed in three-piece Highland tweed and fob watch and he was doubtful of his reception. There was no possible correct response in the repertoire of somebody as young as Alice Harding. Flustered, she mumbles consent and arms the parcels to her side of the table.

'Thank you. Christmas shopping, eh?'

A man of Dr Andrew Tait's urbanity learns in a few minutes all there is to know of Alice Harding: Ospringe, Faversham, lingerie department in Harrods, two parcels. Then: Let me get you a drink. Andrew is undecided on whom to inflict himself for the holiday. 'I'm a man of the world and I'm lost.' His first Christmas as a divorcee. Hundreds of friends, parents in Edinburgh and cannot bear the thought of their sympathy. 'They'll say Poor Andrew and organize parties to match me up again.' He needed to talk to himself in the Bunch of Grapes without being arrested. It was considerate of Alice Harding to facilitate him there. And what lovely presents did she have in the parcels if he could be so bold. Alice Harding speaks. This is a friendly man, a gentleman. It is such a relief to tell someone who would promise not to nark, she had never taken anything before in her life, but she had nicked the bra and panties for her mother. Well, he slapped his leg and laughed and said bully for you and not to worry my dear, secret safe with Andrew Tait I can assure you. But take care, sharp that crowd in security, all ex-detectives, my advice don't try it again. Ever tempted, here, take my card, ever slightest bit tempted or in any spot of bother just ring that number and say Bunch of Grapes to receptionist. All right? Now let me get you another.

No, no, please, woozy already. Nonsense. Only comes once a year. Yes, damn lonely. At a complete loss, never realized it could be like this, never in the blasted position before. Boyfriend? No? Bloody fools. Not to worry, soon have them queuing up, take my word . . . You all right, young lady . . .

63

have to go to the . . . . . . steady. that's it, you can manage . . .
eh? Parcels? . . . safe with Andrew, oops, steady, steady, that's
it . . . take your time . . .

Ah, here we are, better now? Feel queasy. I understand. Tell
you what, young lady, what you need is a cup of strong tea,
my place is just around the corner . . .

Out of a lady's novelette, Dr Andrew Tait carried her
parcels while she linked him to stay on her feet. He sat beside
her as she sipped the strong tea and he felt her forehead and
said nothing to worry about there and held her hands and said
you are such a sweet creature and he kissed her. Sorry about
that, afraid I couldn't quite resist it. You needn't be sorry. Eh?
Well. So he stands up and pulls his hand through his hair
down to his neck while he wrestles with temptation, but a
decent man has only so much strength. He sits down beside
her again, again holds her hands, kisses her again and at last a
slip and slide kiss and they fumble and make love. Andrew
dexterously slipping on the johnny before easing in. More tea,
talk and yawns and love in bed.

Next morning he gave her twenty pounds, insisted that she
ring him at the surgery in the new year, and sent her in a taxi to
get the train home. Twenty pounds was almost five weeks'
wages.

She did not ring him. He walked into Harrods, to the
lingerie department, asked her size, paid, handed her the
wrapped parcel and the receipt all in front of her two pals and
then moved with her to the end of the counter. She went to
him that night wearing the parcel. Again he insisted on twenty
pounds. Altogether she was with him five times and always
tried not to take the money. Then he was moving back to
Edinburgh, ending her dream of becoming Mrs Tait. But if she
was interested, there was a colleague of his, not quite as
young, but a gentleman, rest your mind there, very willing to
be liberal with a lady of discretion.

She was in the business by referral. Colleagues recommended colleagues. There was a Dr Cagney from a town in
southern Ireland – a gentleman – who had a fine mind but few

to share it with, a model of rectitude, the Victorian thing, who needed a day out on her own terms. She entertained Dr Cagney twice a year for four years. Almost all her clients were doctors, a small, profitable market. She managed not to think of herself as a whore. A friend to the medical profession. She stayed on at Harrods, now on permanent staff. All that was missing from her life was what she had before she met Dr Andrew Tait: romance. And when romance is lost, you don't miss it, you shrug it off like innocence, yet unlike innocence romance can come again, as it did for me with Cecelia.

On a summer evening Alice Harding went home to her flat on the Gloucester Road to find a young man waiting at her door with a letter of introduction. I have it now.

My Dear Alice,

Please observe bearer to be my son, Donat, who is on an educational visit to the city. I would esteem it a great favour if you would look out for the boy, perhaps direct him to the same amenable and entertaining accommodation you were so courteous in providing for my own self and of which I have such fond memories. God bless,

Yours, etc.,

Cagney

She had never seen such a handsome individual, client or otherwise. Donat was no hick overawed by a big city and he was there to retain his poise and have the romance knocked out of him. But he was young and it was a slow operation. Alice Harding was his girlfriend for a fortnight. He took her to the theatre farces, museums, art galleries, the seaside. They held hands. They laughed. They looked into each other's eyes. They embraced and he vowed to return during Christmas leave from Trinity.

When she knew she was pregnant she wrote to Dr John Cagney for advice. She did so ingenuously. Cagney was on the next boat. He would not hear of abortion. That was not his style. Bastards had an honourable place in the world. She would be looked after. She was to forget she ever met Donat or Dr Andrew Tait or anybody she had accommodated. In time she would resign from Harrods. The confinement would take place in a nursing home of character and discretion. A colleague, Pearse Farrell, would come over from Ireland for the delivery. She would be in the best of hands. Subject to a successful issue she was to look for a house of her own desire in the eighteen hundred to two thousand category. He would buy the house on her behalf. She would be put in funds to the amount of fourteen pounds per week increasing pro rata as the general level of wages increased. On the child's reaching school attendance age a position would become available to her as part-time receptionist to a colleague. She was to cease immediately to entertain as heretofore; other than that her affairs were her own. He trusted she would not hesitate to contact him in any difficulties. God bless you, Alice.

When I was young enough Daddy was dead in Heaven, but when I reached the age of curiosity – what did he do, where was his photograph – Daddy was someone with whom she had had an affair and who had vanished from her life. I accepted that. It wasn't unusual. It gave me a certain status. I hadn't missed him anyway.

I came home one night to our house in Colehill Lane after a game at the Fulham Cosmo and sat by the fire trying to absorb the Franco/Prussian war. My mother sat opposite me under a table lamp putting a zip in my jeans. She said: 'Tim.' I said: 'Hmm?'

Nobody listens to his mother. You hear her when she's gone. She had to come again to elbow Bismark. 'Tim, how would you like if Granny came to stay with us for a while?'

'Mum, Granny hates London.'

'She's lonely in Ospringe. Or would you think of staying with her, you could commute.'

I let Bismark and his telegram slide off my lap on to the floor.

66

'Ospringe! Mum, you know I can't stand the place. What are you on about?'

I had not looked at my mother or listened to her before then. She was my mother, a doctor's receptionist, always there when I needed her to make my bed and cook my meals and buy my clothes, scold me for staying late at the Cosmo; interrogate me when she suspected I was screwing around. But now I saw her and heard her as she dropped the half-zipped jeans and lifted her clenched fists to her cheeks and cried: 'Oh God.' I dropped to my knees and held her shoulders. 'What's wrong, Mum?'

'I'm going to die, Tim. Oh God, I'm going to die.'

I put my arms around her and held her close as she had done for me so often and I had always taken as my due. When we parted I saw the sparkle of her tears inside her sewing glasses and I saw her frailty. That was my mother.

And my father? And his father?

'My father, Tim, was Dr John Cagney of Sexton Square. Daily communicant. Worshipped at the Church of the Sacred Heart. He was a Catholic in the French sense – he had a woman in London.'

The best way to meet Donat is to let him speak for himself. He stood with palm resting on the globe and knuckles gently sunk into the side of his cardigan while I was seated in the study listening as he must once have listened to his old fart of a pater.

'I was thirteen. The Reds were recruiting bellringers through appeals for probationers in all the local churches. My father had the novel idea of donating me. My mother said: "John!" But he hushed her. He said: "Donat may well see how the other half lives." To this day I have no idea where the dear old boy got such a daft inspiration. Sam Brown, that peasant Halvey, they were part of a crop of three. This house was in the route of procedure from a warren of lanes where Brown lived and the Redemptorist Church, so what would do the fellow but to take to calling for me on his way. Brown, Halvey. By Jove, I can tell you, Tim, there have been no indiscriminate appeals for campanologists since.'

Donat moved from the globe and sat opposite me, dipping into his cardigan for a packet of cigarettes.

'An undernourished gnat of a fellow, Brown. Threadbare coat let down at the sleeves to fight another winter and his dry mousy hair cut to the bone to stave off the next barber's shilling. My mother used to snip my own luxuriant blond crop. She would often declare that she wished she had it herself.'

He exhaled a long draw of his cigarette through the conspiratorial slit of a smile. There were riches to follow, I interpreted. But I would not show a flicker of interest.

'A Christian Brothers' boy, Brown. Molly, our maid – I was never ready when Brown called – Molly at first directed the bony head to the waiting room on the ground floor. But my mother corrected Molly: Please show Donat's friend to the sitting room. My friend! He sat with hands clutching the arms of the fireside chair, waiting for me to decide on crombie, duffel or jacket. So proud to know me, you must understand.'

Seasoned as I was to his crap I wanted to vomit.

'What on earth did we talk about? I do recall him once saying that he loved Saturdays, he always had a fry on Saturday. What *could* one say to that? Bellringing, we talked bellringing. Study. His Christian Brothers sounded a pack of bucolic savages and do you know he was grateful for what he referred to as the "education" they walloped into his bony head. And snooker. He played then over Montague's with such luminaries as Halvey and assorted newsboys. On my Jesuit side we must have impinged on my white cold breath as a scrum half on a muddy pitch before a shower. Brown had never seen a shower. In summer he threw himself into the doubtful waters of a creek – where I'm sure he had to bide his time lest he land on another bony head. When I of course would have been setting out from the lodge in Kilkee.'

Again I did not smile.

'He used to suck air in between his teeth, Brown, if we passed a girl in her first nylons and high heels. There was a virginal shyness over the land of the Christian Brothers' boy then, Redemptorist bellowing against passionate kissing. All gone the other way now. Now, the stiletto heel is the leper's bell of a wobbling apprentice whore.'

'But you love whores, Donat.'

'Before I went to university my father sent me to London to his woman – your mother. When I came back from London – educated – he would not discuss my future, that is, when I would have qualified. He said: Just qualify, just qualify and don't get a woman in trouble, use these. A packet of johnnies. I didn't know your mother was pregnant. But where was I? Brown. He landed one of those clerical positions with Aer Lingus and could . live at home. That's your Christian Brothers' education for you, to be able to live at home and have mammy iron your shirts. Boneheadedness at its quintessential. At home, where they can have frying pans in action seven days a week now. But wait: what adventure! Travel concessions attached to the job, holidays in places called, I believe, Torremolinos? Gran Canaria? And he met his wife in Dingle. Dingle, by Jove. One has to smile. Because one is smug and one knows one is smug and one knows that makes a difference.' I must have let slip the camouflage of my nausea. He added: 'You're sitting there still tainted with egalitarianism, Tim.'

'You said it, Donat. You're a smug man.'

'After university my father gave me a cigar in this study. He said: "This practice will be here for you in time but for the moment go away." He spun the globe. He prodded the West. "Not America. Go East, Donat. Do Africa." I asked him why. He said, "Because you're not finished and because I say so." A wonderful man, Tim.'

'You'll pardon me if I don't share that opinion.'

'No, I will not pardon you.'

'He knew she was pregnant. He fobbed her off with an allowance. He didn't tell you.'

'He was wise. Who knows what I might have done at that age? I might have hot-footed it over to London to assume what I might have romantically thought of as my responsibilities.'

'You don't regret you weren't told?'

'No. A gentleman does not compound his errors. I was twenty-nine when I returned to bury my father and inherit the practice. I married Simone, I became known as young Dr Cagney . . .'

'What is she like? Not a shop girl?'

'Of course not. She is elegant, not that you will ever meet her, at least not in your capacity as my son, though we do not have issue and you will be provided for.'

'I wouldn't take tuppence from you.'

'Quite. Sam Brown stopped me in the street. I must say I had forgotten the wretch. He introduced himself and after some thought I said: Of course. They cannot be properly insulted, you know. He asked me back to the tower. I enjoyed the idea of the practice in Sexton Square as I might never have done had I not been sent away by my father. It was an extension of that contentment that led me again up the stairs to the tower. In for a penny, in for a pound. The fellow clung to me. He told the other ringers: If Dr Donat can make it the rest of you can. Now, Tim, I need you there with me. You will have the community dinner to look forward to. The choir, confraternity secretaries and trustees, the priests, brothers, ourselves in the tower, we entertain ourselves once a year. I do Burlington Bertie. I use cane and bowler and modulated tone. How say you?'

I would give him this: he was as tough as any old blue comic who ever died a death in a Sunday morning Labour club. He must have known I wanted to puke on top of him yet he sat there in control. I told myself, fence flippantly, play it his way.

'Donat, I pity you. You're diseased. But an English Protestant ringing bells in an Irish Catholic tower does have its piquancy. I hear the call, I shall answer.'

'Trinity wasn't wasted on you.'

'I will continue to loathe you, Donat. You understand that.'

'Nonsense, Tim.'

'Put yourself in my position. In one night I hear the terrible news that my mother has leukaemia and that my father is alive and has condescended to visit me – at seventeen – next day. You come over, put up at a hotel, invite us to dinner, announce that I am to become a doctor and that I will inherit your practice and live like you and your father before you. I go home alone after that dinner. Did you make love that night?'

'Of course.'

'She told me. I was sick. I was damned for a start if I would become a doctor. An axe murderer, yes. A doctor, no. But I did go to Trinity and survived there on booze and fornication because I had one ambition. To destroy you. I went to America because you hated America. What you stand for I stand against. I am back here now because I can't pluck you out of my mind. She died without bitterness. You came back and arranged for her end in the hospice where you slept during the last few days. I watched you holding her hand and looking into her eyes as she died. That fool of a father you had, he destroyed your life as well as my mother's. She loved you. It if wasn't for that fool – '

'That old fool was no fool. Yes, at a tender age I might have been happy to marry your mother and it would have been disastrous. She would not have made a doctor's wife – go on, flinch – and I would not have made a shopgirl's husband. You do flinch. That is your age. You do not understand the world. But you will.'

'You are an evil man. I will hurt you. That, I promise.'

'Just so. But do it in style, please.

CHAPTER 9

The House of Montague

We are insular people and obedient to the words of the poet:

Be not the first by whom the new are tried,
Nor yet the last to lay the old aside.

We comply with Pope's latter exhortation through our path-finding ambassadors – Halvey *inter alia* – whose indefatigable exertions on our behalf lay at our feet the contagion of their travels. How innocently we blew the trumpet and brought out the band to welcome our returned scouts bearing the twigs of the great plague: the Sixties. Who could have foreseen how soon and quickly Macmillan would fall, pulled down by peripheral sluts and a gutter press? And the vacuum filled by that Humpty Dumpty, Wilson, no sooner in the saddle than taking the good ship *Tiger* to push the decent Smith of Rhodesia over the brink into the unilateral declaration of independence. But there is Kennedy, one told oneself, ever amenable to Macmillan's avuncular tutelage and perhaps sage enough to bear any burden however great, cut down! Leaving the shop late on Friday evening, my collar turned up and hat set against the breeze, I stopped for Malton in the Roche sisters' tobacconist around the corner, to find them both weeping with handkerchiefs to their noses. That is where I heard the news, to be confirmed on my emerging by a shout from across the street: 'Hey, Yendall, some mad bollix knocked off Kennedy.' I sat at home alone that night by the wireless; my wife went next door. I had been resolutely deaf to her entreaties and would not have a television in the house. Where she failed, the assassination succeeded: how would we keep up with events? The monster was installed before the funeral and now my mind was to be broadened – unlike our ambassadors' – by armchair travel.

After a couple of years Simpson was appointed shop assistant proper. He was in command of his job. I almost forgot how he had come to us. By the time he was promoted to buyer I no longer saw drama in his progress. I had my own life. When Simpson was in his late twenties, I was forty something and Mr Sloan fifty-odd. Our field was closer bunched, as Sir Thomas might have put it. I suppose we had grown on one another. The past receded. We were told by the government that the rising tide was lifting all the boats. Money lenders set up shop and called themselves finance companies. Fledgling hire purchase merchants proliferated and soon became nabobs. The poor could lay their hands on money: distinctions were blurred. The Provident Cheque was there to tog anybody out. The evolution in popular music continued apace; that is to say what standards may have ever been upheld in that branch of entertainment were now abandoned completely. I had become inured to a Charlie Halvey calling himself 'Tex' for the edification of his public, but now from my armchair I could witness a refinement of such incognito: four young fellows from Liverpool, with names I have no reason to suspect they had to be ashamed, armed apiece with the modern tom-tom, the guitar, chose to trade under the collective title of an order of insects. That they could not spell 'Beetle' correctly was no object of wonder to me: on the television I had already noticed that 'cat' was now 'kat' as in 'kat food' and 'night' had become 'nite' as in 'nite club'. As with the messiah, Presley, the four evangelists introduced a diverting line in tonsorial splendour that earned for them the affectionate sobriquet: mopheads. The world took them to its bosom, made them millionaires, decorated them at Buckingham Palace. And all the while a vestige of Mr Sloan's grief deprived the regulars in Arthur Skee's of 'Absence'.

I was intrigued one morning to look out my window and observe Halvey talking to Butsey Rushe – or should I say roaring his head off at all and sundry. But it was his raiment that arrested me. A strange outfit, I thought, even for a subaltern of Hank Larkin and the Hoedowners. I invited Simpson in to marvel with me.

'Have those fellows taken to Gilbert and Sullivan, Simpson?'

Simpson smiled at me as though I had uttered a witticism.

'That's the latest fashion, Mr Yendall.'

'You jest, Simpson. If I am not mistaken, Halvey's tunic is reminiscent of that worn by Confederate generals in the American civil war; his trousers would not be found in the wardrobe of the most colourful matelot ever to take to piracy. They are purple, Simpson. And he is shod in thonged sandals only affected in this city by the poor Franciscans around the corner. This is the latest fashion, Simpson?'

'Perhaps an exaggeration, Mr Yendall. He told me everyone is going around like that in London.'

'You've spoken to him? You believe him? Everyone in London? Our Mr Dobson, Simpson?'

I was irritated that Simpson had not shaken Halvey off. My tone wiped the smile from Simpson's face.

'Charlie says the young people have the purchasing power, he says they're going to take over, he says long enough older people have made a . . . his theory, Mr Yendall, is that young people won't want to wear suits as much as – '

'Simpson, spare me his theories. I prefer our Mr Dobson's facts. We should have something better to do than looking out the window at freaks. I see they are at work on Miss O'Sullivan's. I trust what new venture emerges will be in keeping with the street. A milliner of taste, Miss O'Sullivan. God rest her.'

I trusted in vain.

Our Mr Dobson came over from London – clad in sober three-piece – and had myself and Mr Sloan out to lunch at the Royal George. I learned a fact of life. The House of Montague was forced to lower the drawbridge. We introduced the Montague Budget Plan. It was with some difficulty that Mr Sloan and I salvaged the requisite of a guarantor. And though we did not say so to Mr Dobson, we would be damned if any Tom, Dick and Harry thought they could breach our portals.

Our divide narrowing with age and the propinquity of the job and the Draper's Club I began to find Simpson dull. As witness this scintillating anecdote of the type of non-sequitur that entertained him. I was sitting in the bay window of the club one evening when he joined me. I had been musing on how young the players now seemed to me. Apropos damn all, Simpson fished out of his pocket what I took to be some sort of gewgaw or folderol and grinned inanely at me. 'What do you think, Mr Yendall?'

I was impatient. 'What is it, Simpson?'

'Just what I asked my mother, Mr Yendall. She bought it in that Just A Pound place across the road where Miss O'Sullivan was. It is a plastic tomato cutter. She got a pair of sunglasses, a face tester and our friend here, all for a pound.'

Out of civility I examined the object. The plastic handle was a mere four inches in length and half an inch in height and was attached to a circular serrated plastic blade about the size of a half-crown. I said: 'Well, Simpson, I notice it doesn't have to be assembled.' My wit was wasted. He looked positively gloomy now.

'I've always managed slashing away with a breadknife, Mr Yendall. There are millions starving and yet somebody – a graduate of the Massachusetts Institute of Technology for all we know – somebody has applied himself to undermining the multitudinous aptitudes of the breadknife.'

I remember thinking it a pity that a man who had developed a vocabulary from scratch should waste it talking rot.

When he had taken his plastic tomato cutter out of his pocket, what I thought a piece of burr came out with it and fell on the seat beside him. But now, as I idly fingered it, I saw it was a narrow strip of red cloth with the letters K.O.Y.L.I. in gold stitching.

'Oh thank you, Mr Yendall. My father's.'

It was the shoulder flash of the King's Own Yorkshire Light Infantry. Of course I knew when we took him on that

Simpson's father had died in the war. But so had many. What was a statistic then took some shape now.

'He was attached to Horrocks' 30th Corps, Mr Yendall, fought under the Sign of the Boar at Alamein.' For once he spoke with assurance and not with the one-eye-on-my-reaction servility in which his cadence had been accoutred since he had first been emboldened to throw his leg over our bike. 'He survived Italy. And he bought it when they broke out of the Caen Peninsula at the battle for the Lower Rhine.' He put the shoulder flash back in his pocket. 'I like to carry it about, Mr Yendall.'

I nodded.

He went on. 'I had it the day you put the BOY WANTED notice in the window. And I had it when I asked to be allowed to replace Mr Todd. You see, it reminds me that he did his bit, my father. And that I should do mine, Mr Yendall.'

After the lame plastic tomato cutter saga I now felt chastened. I thought I understood something of how a mind such as his had striven to cope. I would grant him his sense of duty. Indeed I would not tolerate him without it. But a sense of duty without a sense of humour is a burden. Just then I thought him old, much older than I was. I was disturbed that he could not wear *gravitas* comfortably. It was as if he carried a large head on a thin body. I was in sympathy with him for the moment.

'You and your mother, Simpson, how have you managed without your father?'

'There was a pension, Mr Yendall, and my mother was adept at turning shirt collars for the neighbours as a supplement. But his loss turned her into a strict woman. She wanted to bring me up right. The snooker hall drew me against her interdict so that I used to lie to her. I'd lose the money for the pictures playing Phil Thompson and I'd come home with the doings at the Lyric supplied by Wally Kirwan — even unto the second feature and the trailer, because she was a great film-goer herself, Mr Yendall.'

We could all smile at that, I suppose. But I checked my appreciation: I wish to God he'd forget about those spivs.

CHAPTER 10

The Society of Bellringers

During the week, after the chimes summoned the congregation to the evening masses, Sam muffled a bell and began to induct Father Clancy in the art of peal ringing. I could not have imagined anyone with less aptitude than Clancy but that only fired Sam to spend more time with him. Clancy broke five stays in the first week. I said to Sam: 'You've a job on your hands there.'

'I don't mind. He's the first chaplain we ever had who took any interest at all. It'll come to him, Tim.'

Clancy was in the tower every night regardless of whether Sam was there to instruct him, and I found myself giving him a turn, as did some of the other ringers. At the peals on Saturday night and on Sunday morning and evening he sat on a stool watching us ring, his eyes moving from treble to tenor, giving every one of us a share of his vigil. And after a peal he remained to share his conversation among us. He was an itch I could not scratch. He brought religion into his speech. I could not say 'Chilly tonight' without getting in return: 'Yes, Tim, thanks be to God and his Blessed Mother'. Cute hawk, Donat, ignored Clancy by seeming to make more of him than the rest of us did. At the trapdoor – on his way down – Donat would say: 'Coming along in training, Sam tells me he is quite pleased with your progress.' And as Clancy prepared to be his sociable self and inflict his inanities, Donat took the steps three at a time, calling back: 'Look forward to having you in a peal.'

I thought it was just a chemical thing that I could not stand the sight of Clancy but in fact his presence constrained most of the other ringers. So much so that Sam and I were surprised one Wednesday night to find eight in attendance – five of them in caucus. Charlie was there because he sniffed entertainment. Sam was delighted with the turnout. Everyone took a turn to play a hymn and when we finished Sam said: 'We could have had a peal.'

George led for 'the men'. 'How long is he going to keep it up, Sam?'

'Who?'

'Father Clancy.'

'Keep what up?'

'Jesus, he's here every night.'

'So?'

'We always got on fine without a priest breathing down our necks.'

George looked around him for support. Sam followed his eyes. Paddy was the next brave. 'Sam, we have to keep watching ourselves in case we let a "fuck" slip out.'

'I'm sorry for your trouble, Paddy. You're a teacher. You manage at school all day without swearing. At least I hope you do. Now what is all this, is this why you're here? I know, it's Charlie, you got them up to this.'

'You big bollix, I've more to do but they're right. Why isn't he in Africa curing lepers, what's he doing here?'

'All right. Who else. I'm listening to whatever you have to say.'

Whoever spoke next would have to take Sam on. He was never a man for much of a joke where the tower was concerned. I was surprised myself to hear Finbar, the quietest man in the society, outside of Sam more doctrinaire than any of us in his adhesion to orthodoxy. 'Sam, last week he asked me to put my cigarette out. I'll admit he did it nicely. He wagged his finger and stood over me with his big smile until I nobbed it. He did it nicely, Sam. But he did it.'

Paddy and George nodded their support. I could see Charlie was having a ball. Sam lost control. 'Smoking is forbidden in the tower. It's a fire hazard. The notice is behind your head!'

Finbar came back angrily. 'Christ, Sam, you smoke yourself

in the tower. You're smoking now, there's a lighted cigarette in your hand.'

Sam should have laughed. He should have said 'what the fuck' and disarmed all by adjourning to the nearest pub. But he didn't. He dropped the cigarette on the floor and put his foot on it. 'Not any more. All the man has done is come along and show us a good example. I've slipped up, I'll admit it. None of us should smoke in the tower, we're only here twenty minutes for a peal. We can smoke downstairs. From now on it's out. As for language, we are attached to a church.'

I went to the Professional Club that night and reported to Donat and Jack Molyneaux. 'What will you do if he asks you not to smoke in the tower?'

'If who asks?'

'Clancy. *Or* Sam.'

'Brown won't. He'll make an exception of me to the men. Clancy? You know, Tim, I rarely smoke in the tower, I don't linger. And it is a fire hazard.'

And so Clancy came to be accepted for what he was – a nuisance. But we did not again have a superfluity of ringers at the chimes. I took to giving them a miss myself. Sam didn't comment. He did not discuss Clancy. He was set on not having an atmosphere about the place. Clancy trained on. When he no longer broke stays, I did something characteristic of me: showed my better nature. On Sunday morning I had my jacket off, shirt-sleeves rolled up. I saw Clancy on the form, for so long a cheerleader. I held out my rope: 'Father? It's so long since I sat one out.'

'No, no, Tim . . .'

'Good idea, Tim. Come on, you can do it Father.' It was all very well Sam seconding the motion but I avoided Donat's eye. Donat was the conductor. He – and no one else – selected the team. I could not have offered my rope to Charlie. It was probably from having been excluded so often by Donat that Charlie was inspired to come in: 'Come on, Father, get togged off, Phil Thompson is minding my pub, God only knows what's being robbed.'

We waited until Clancy stripped. He was a collarless sight in his shirt, braces and nervousness, Adam's apple galloping. Sam said: 'Ready, Father?' Clancy grinned weakly and nodded. Sam led off on the treble. Clancy made an absolute shambles of the peal. On his first pull he failed to reach equilibrium and could not correct the fault. He was like a driver on a hill who could not balance clutch and accelerator. Donat had to stop the peal. Sam said: 'Forget about that, Father. False start, we'll try again.' This time Clancy began all right and continued with every muscle rigid. I was tense myself at Donat's first change – three, one – which necessitated Clancy on four switching to follow two. But he was over the hurdle and I sat back at ease and thought of Cecelia. After ten minutes Donat began to change down and Clancy missed a call. We had a clanger. Donat called out 'Four seven, four seven' but Clancy panicked. Instead of holding his bell and waiting to follow seven he pulled too hard and broke a stay. That was that. Donat called: 'Finish' and everyone eased the sally to a halt. Charlie grabbed Clancy's rope and dropped the bell. I looked down at my shoes. Sam was embarrassed too. He took it as a reflection on his training. I was humbled, having promoted Clancy when he was not ready. There was a silence in the tower. Clancy was red in the face, close to tears. I had done enough damage and could not think of anything to say to dissipate his discomfort. I hated Donat for not stepping in. Anything he said would have sufficed – coming from him. But George had what it took. He tied his rope, walked over to Clancy and put his hand out.

'Well done. That's as good a first effort as I've ever heard and I'm here a long time. You were unlucky with the stay, that's all, right, Paddy?'

'I made a bags of it myself the first time.'

To an extent it was true that everyone falters at the first attempt. I did. Charlie slapped Clancy on the back. We all chipped in. Sam was proud. Only Donat stood off. He lifted the trapdoor and left as though nothing unusual had happened. Chancy thanked us. 'You're all so kind, so tolerant, the spirit of Christ is with you all.' Jesus, it was cruel to have to listen to such religiosity. 'I'm so sorry for letting you down, especially Dr Cagney.' He looked hungrily down the stairs after Donat.

Leaving the tower with Charlie it was music to hear his familiar: 'Dr Cagney – Dr Bollix.'

It finally did come to Clancy as it had come to all of us. Although on his next effort he again started tensely he suddenly slipped into relaxation and came through the peal with only as much blemish as could be detected by a learned ear. He would never be top class but he would get by. We all congratulated him. Even Donat was obliged to shake his hand. Sam had rubbed off on Clancy. He wanted to lick Donat. On the next occasion that we had a full house – now twelve – Donat as usual omitted Charlie. But he also left out Clancy. This was to show that he selected on merit, which was nonsense. Charlie was the best ringer in the tower after Sam.

And so there it might have been left. Brock happy that a niche had been found for Clancy, Sam Brown with someone who appreciated his 'sterling service', 'the men' melted by Clancy's going among them beaming his love of one and all, scattering benediction, Donat with another bony head to despise. I was happy myself, until the fifth Saturday passed without Cecelia coming home . . . and the sixth . . . and the seventh . . .

I must admit that I was not able to swallow Clancy whole and was not inclined to attend every night while he was about leaking goodwill all over the place and Sam curbing his needs for a cigarette until he reached the tower door. And now that I was a surreptitious smoker myself and could not light up at will I found myself with my tongue hanging out in the tower. One Tuesday night I had a Fagender client from the country who had fallen into the water again and I was saving her from drowning. She was a widow who only decided to give up cigarettes after her husband's death. I do not have parchments in psychology but a dog with a mallet up his arse could reason that the anti-smoking crusade had caught her on the rebound. I dipped into my bag of tricks, reminded her how wonderful it is to wake up without the cough and the spit, how even I in a short time noticed the sparkle in her eye and the freshness of her skin since she stopped smoking. She was fifty-eight and wanted me or anybody to throw the leg over but I was gone from all that since I met Cecelia. I wanted to tell my client to stay on the cigarettes and go to a Sunday afternoon tea dance, go home and let me take out my own cigarettes. Our appointment was for eight o'clock and I had a job opening the door at half-past nine.

After she left I went for a walk by the docks and held my cigarette cupped in the hand in case I would meet anyone who knew my business. It was probably the most satisfying smoke I ever had, acting the schoolboy, and helped me to understand why Tory ministers yearn to be spanked by whores in gymslips. Turning back I looked up and noticed the light in the tower. I was conscientious enough to investigate. Sam and Clancy were there, sitting down, talking.

'Sorry. I saw a light and just wondered . . . '

They were both excited, I could see that. They looked at each other. Clancy did his beaming act: 'Shall we, Sam?'

Sam nodded. 'Tim can keep a secret, Father.'

I was to keep it to myself for the time being. On his very first visit to the tower Clancy had deduced from the dates on the photographs that some of the ringers were over thirty years in the society. Clancy had written to the Holy Father. And he had just received a favourable acknowledgement from Rome. He had deliberately not consulted Brock as he wanted to give him a pleasant surprise also. He sought papal medals to commemorate the long service of Sam, Donat, Charlie, Midge and Finbar. The preliminary reply from a functionary encouraged Clancy to believe his request would be granted, but I was to understand that 'it was early days yet'. Best that 'we three' keep mum until the receipt of more substantial confirmation. It would not do to raise hopes that might ultimately be dashed.

Although an agnostic I was as much of a sucker for the charm of John Paul XXIII as the next man – I had grown out of the notion that feminists, queers, abortionists or married clergy had a leg to stand on. So I was chuffed for Sam. I said: 'Congratulations to you, Father. That sounds like good work. Congratulations, Sam.' Sam was so obviously elated that I squeezed his arm. And I almost warmed to Clancy.

I had given up cigarettes at fifteen when Jimmy Johnston in the Fulham Cosmo advised me that they were bad for my game. Now a secret smoker, I played Knobby Stevens, the full-time professional in the Draper's Club – that is, he lived on the dole. I caught him in three games for twenty quid a game, making a break of ninety-two in the third. Gold Flake were good for me.

Cecelia was pleased that I was smoking again. And by now we had kissed.

CHAPTER 11

The House of Montague

'Your notice?' Mr Sloan exclaimed, flabbergasted, having heard the expression come from that side of the divide for the first time in his life.

Simpson had consulted me first. I did my utmost to no avail. I was doubly stunned because I thought I saw him growing content in the niche we had allowed him. For months he had been quite the regular in the Draper's Club and in our April Annual Handicap – open to all comers – he had reached the quarter-finals out of an entry of sixty-four, beaten only through nervousness on the pink in the third frame. I did every damned thing I could to dissuade him. I called upon all my experience, my years over him, but no. He left me with no choice but to bring in Mr Sloan. I had to give Mr Sloan my chair, he was so shaken. He looked up at Simpson, standing. I had no need to X-ray Simpson's pocket. He was fingering away at the shoulder flash.

'You're mad, Simpson, do you realize that? Mad.'

I did not feel sorry for Simpson standing there submissive in the face of chastisement, even though I was professionally aware that Mr Sloan was not quite composed.

'Going – out – on – your – own, is it? We took you in off the streets . . . ' But Mr Sloan recovered, guillotined his emotion, and slipped into the inquisitor – as I had done. He adopted the paternal.

'All right, Simpson. To what extent have you rushed your fences?'

'I've spoken to the suppliers, Mr Sloan.'

'And?'

'They're happy with me, Mr Sloan.'

'Hmm. We were happy with you ourselves, Simpson. We did not know the sentiment was not reciprocated.'

'Oh no, Mr Sloan, I have been more than – '

'Finance, Simpson. Too many people have thought our business easy to invade. I've seen them open and shut.'

'The bank is with me, Mr Sloan.'

'I see. Not letting the grass grow under our feet, are we, Simpson? And where, if you don't mind me asking you, where did you intend to open?'

'Mr Mayhew is retiring, Mr Sloan. Mayhew's Medical Hall is available on a ninety-nine year lease.'

Mr Sloan glanced at me. I showed I was with him by coming in: 'Mayhew's Medical Hall is not suitable as a drapery, Simpson.'

'I know a lot of work has to be done, Mr Yendall – '

'It's not a good street, Simpson.' Mr Sloan was emphatic. Simpson had no answer. How could he? A pawnbroker's offal and spare rib merchants, hucksters of balloons and holy pictures, an Italian chip shop, low pubs, betting shops, the promenade of the poor on their way to the dispensary for free cod liver oil, the wonder was that they had not bankrupt Mr Mayhew, a decent man but undoubtedly eccentric to prosper in such a community. It was not a street I would have strolled through after dark. I suppose it was the last straw for Mr Sloan, the location. He capitulated.

'Simpson, if you won't listen to reason, you're of age, go your own way. Mr Yendall will vouch I did my best. Can I prevail upon you to reconsider, you have your mother to look after, you know.'

'Thank you, Mr Sloan. I've talked it over with my mother. She understands. I'd like to promise you, Mr Sloan, that I certainly will not move until you find a suitable replacement. I can assure you of that. I would not leave you in the lurch.'

'Simpson, it's best you go today. You can't very well stay on here drumming up your own trade. Mr Yendall, see to it. Goodbye, Simpson.' He shook Simpson's hand.

That was not how I liked to see things done. And I knew Mr

Sloan long enough to be aware of his true form. I told Simpson to take two days' leave and come in on the Friday. Then I knew Mr Sloan would have the run of himself again and we would have the whip-around organized to give Simpson a watch. It happened that Sir Thomas called in on Thursday morning and caught me in the act.

'Simpson's bolted, Yendall? Rum times . . . rum times.' But he was not as jovial as of yore. I thought his countenance florid and suspected he was no longer up to the younger man's intake of malt.

'Here.' Sir Thomas hauled out his roll but I was quick to protest.

'No, no, Sir Thomas, please – '

'Eh? A dashed fiver, Yendall. Can't take the bloody thing with me you know, one time have to come without the horse.'

I levied the rest of the staff at five bob a skull and put in a pound myself. Mr Sloan did not fool me at his buckram best during the two days, for I could see he was relieved when I invited him to my office.

'Mr Sloan, about Simpson. I hope you'll forgive me but I've taken the liberty – '

'Of course you have, Mr Yendall, I knew you would. I knew I could count on you. Now what am I down for?'

'Five shillings for our people here. Russell's taken up a collection at the factory – Simpson was popular with the men there. I have decided to contribute a pound myself if you agree with me that it meets the case. And though I tried to protest, Sir Thomas insisted on a fiver; he will not be denied his way, Mr Sloan.'

Mr Sloan smiled and how I welcomed his humorous agreement. He took out his wallet. He put a ten pound note in front of me.

This time I did know how to protest. 'I'm not having that, Mr Sloan. Simply out of all order. No.'

'Mr Yendall, I have been on the telephone to Mr Dobson. I have his imprimatur. Montague's has a reputation. I shall be reimbursed in good time, I can assure you.'

What could I say? That he was a liar? He had not been on the telephone to Mr Dobson. We did not ring London lightly and any trunk call had to receive my sanction. As for his being reimbursed the greater likelihood was that we would all be sacked for such a lunatic munificence however personal, establishing a ludicrous precedent. But Mr Sloan stood there while I sat down and brazenly he outstared me.

'Thank you, Mr Sloan. About a few words at the presentation, would you like me – '

'I'll attend to that myself, Mr Yendall, thank you all the same.'

He made a gracious speech. Simpson responded in humble fashion, too much so for my taste. We all shook hands with him and wished him well. But I can't pretend that we were happy, Mr Sloan and I. No, we resented Simpson's behaviour, no point in denying that. He was getting too far above himself as we saw things.

Be it said Simpson could not now satisfy his snooker indulgence and so I did not see him in the Draper's Club. He worked the long hours put in by anybody on his own who hopes to stay in business more than a month. He was open early, he closed late. He bought well – we trained him – and sold for as much as he could and that was cheap by our standards. But then so was his product compared to ours. Money was also cheap by now, to the point of reference to *disposable* income. I avoided his patch. I might never have seen him if he hadn't continued to patronize Butsey Rushe for the paper. After a few weeks I went out one morning and hailed him. He told me that at the end of the day he had just the energy to make his tomato sandwich and totter off to bed.

'I must congratulate you, Mr Yendall. I never realized how taxing and tiresome and time-consuming book-keeping is.'

I did not see why I shouldn't give him some advice. 'Just don't let it mount up, Simpson. Deal with it. That is the secret, deal with it.'

I reported to Mr Sloan but he cut me short with his feigned lack of interest.

Simpson bought a car, a station wagon, to do the work he once accomplished with a bike and a handcart, and at the end of his first year he moved to a house on the New University Road, a fashionable area to some, where what boorishness and vandalism abounded among the students was smiled upon as high spirits. It was the birth of Third Level, Open Markets, colour television, euphemism and prosperity. A person was carried along, in a hurry.

Mr Sloan and I found Simpson's cavalier departure hard to stomach. But in his replacement we received a double blow. Not that Mr Sloan would admit to seeing it that way. We wrote to Mr Dobson to advise him of Simpson's entrepreneurial rush of blood to the head. Mr Dobson wrote back exhorting us to struggle on as best we could for the time being. We did so – I should say Mr Sloan and his assistants did – for a month until we received a further communication from Mr Dobson: Montague's were sending over a young man in his twenties to do a two-year trainee manager's course. We were to induct him in all aspects of our trade, the shop, the accounts, the factory. Enclosed was a curriculum vitae. Mr August Gabrielides, of Cypriot/Pakistani extraction, though born in London. I am by no means racist. But as one who visited London infrequently, I was conscious of the changing colour of the capital and was always happy to return among our own. I put it to Mr Sloan: 'We have managed to staff Montague's for a number of years now with some success, though I say it myself.'

Mr Sloan prodded the curriculum vitae. 'Mr Gabrielides is quite an educated man.' The London Polytechnic!

'Simpson had no education at all when he came here.'

I had him there but he snapped at me: 'That was the exception, Mr Yendall, hardly the rule of our recruitment policy.'

I let it go. He was more upset than I was. I was sorry for him. He was alone. The very stuff of officer material.

I will say this for Mr Gabrielides. He proved to be a good man. I am happy to say so. But he was one of the many harbingers of changing times to which we paid little heed, such as Simpson's own success. Mr Gabrielides was deference itself behind the counter, and he had as good a voice as any Englishman, which of course he was according to the letter of the law. His hair was straight and cut short – unlike the Charlie Halvey-led apostles all over the streets now. His moustache was as neat as Mr Sloan's. Yet, having seen Mr Gabrielides for the first time, Sir Thomas put his head around my door. 'Calais's fallen, Yendall, what?' But he chuckled heartily. Yet when we sent Mr Gabrielides to the factory in his capacity as a student of time and motion his appearance almost provoked a strike. Mr Russell reported that the men did not want a 'black bastard' breathing down their necks. Since the men were all members of the Holy Family Confraternity attached to the Redemptorists' 'church' I was impish enough to invite a retired missionary from that community to address the men. We heard no more nonsense after that.

I have seen many changes in the past thirty fleeting years, some, I must concede, for the better. But since man first crawled out of the cave and ventured forth, I wonder have we ever taken a more disastrous turn for the worse than our abolition of pounds, shilling and pence? I cannot now recall the provenance of such a brainstorm, but I do remember laughing it out of court. How much in error I was, we know to our cost today. It will make things easier, we were told. Easier! Why should anything ever be made easier? All you have to do is divide by ten. We knew that there were twelve pennies to the shilling, twenty-four to the florin, thirty to the half-crown, one hundred and twenty to the half-note and two hundred and forty to the pound, not to mention half-pennies and farthings and our own hallmark at Montague's, the guinea. Did we have a problem? No. We had no problem. We could compute. But we were going into Europe and had to adjust our faculties – downwards – to oblige those Frenchmen to whom we were down on our knees begging to facilitate us.

I was sitting in my office fuming at this whole nonsense of 'going into Europe', having taken receipt of conversion table charts sent over by Mr Dobson. My beloved half-crown was about to be allowed simply to fall into desuetude just like our long-lost farthing, to be replaced by the inelegance of twelve and a half new pence, a motley collection of copper. Dammit, there was no need for us to 'go' anywhere, and certainly not brandishing the begging bowl. They had often enough been glad enough to see us coming. Worse, in our Gaderene haste we were going ahead of England – on foot of a plebiscite! Imagine putting such a question to the mob – I heard shouts outside my window and rose to investigate. I looked down at Butsey Rushe's stand. Rushe and Phil Thompson and that fellow Kelly, who had tried to trouble us at the factory in his capacity as head bottle-washer of the National Democratic Socialist Party, were standing on the pavement looking across the street at a Frenchman up on a step-ladder outside that Just A Pound place where Simpson's mother had bought her plastic tomato cutter. (I had heard that Blood-Smith, the solicitor, was moving from overhead and I did not blame him.) The Frenchman – he wore a black beret, had a waxed moustache, a blouse and cravat, and black hair à la the Laughing Cavalier – was directing the erection of an OPEN-ING SOON banner on which was emblazoned ' Pierre's Unisex Salon'. But he was no Frenchman. 'Fuck me pink, bollix Kelly, back from blighty!'

'How are you, Charlie, what are you up to?'

'Pierre, if you please, Pierre. The music business is fucked, hard rock, heavy metal – Jesus, Johnny Skaw, will you look what you're doing, the fuckin' thing is upside down – the Hoedowners are splitting up, hey, look at Yendall, hey, Yendall, come in on Monday, have your hair cut by a bird, Francoise, formerly Mary Murphy . . . '

I closed the window and withdrew, but I could still hear him shouting to Kelly about Simpson's Great Escape, and they 'have niggers working there now'.

Without Simpson as my mentor I was not up to date with

the doings of the underclass, so I had to wait to be informed by my newspaper that James Kelly was elected as a member of the Trades Council in an ex officio capacity stemming from his appointment as assistant secretary to the number two branch of the Transport and General Workers Union. Kelly, according to the news item – which of course I understood would have been supplied by Kelly himself – had been a tireless worker for some years in London on behalf of the exploited building fraternity, and had rescued hundreds from the tyranny of the lump and afforded them the sanctuary inherent in membership of a union. He had now returned to place his expertise at the disposal of all those on the bottom rung of the ladder. Regretfully, the news item concluded, his breach with the Labour Party remained unhealed, and he was convinced that the socialist future lay in the growth of the National Democratic Socialist Party. And for all that I knew or cared, he may have been right. Socialist future!

In this regard I missed Simpson: He had been a buffer softening the blow of bad news. He had interpreted the march of time for me by keeping in touch, however tenuously, with the scum, and to an extent forewarned, I was forearmed. Now so much came as a shock. It was natural that I should muse on his plight over tea and biscuits. I knew where he came from. Where was he going? Where, for that matter, were we all going? About his private life now, I knew little, and suspected that was all there was to know. I am hardly the first married man to ponder the lot of the celibate – of those days; one gathers now that every Tom, Dick and Harry is having it off as suits his timetable. But back then, what did Simpson do when the lure of women called? I had no idea. Certainly I never heard him mention going to the dance hall. Hard to imagine him there any more than myself, if the town crier, Halvey, could be credited. 'Hey, Wank, I saw you at the Stella last night, d'you get the ride.' Simpson was an only child. He had neither an older brother nor friends of his own cut from whom he might have inherited a formula to guide him. And, had he an easy grace, it would have served him poorly, as the rubrics of courtship among his own class were founded on crudity and shame. Perhaps he was just not bothered at all, or was too busy to notice. There was Mr Sloan himself, so long celibate now. How Simpson – or Mr Sloan – fended the call of nature I simply did not know. And other than limited speculation on my part in that regard would have been unhealthy.

CHAPTER 12

The Society of Bellringers

The blessing of Rome came through. We had a full house at the Saturday night peal. Sam had sent out postcards referring to 'tidings of great joy'. I recognized Clancy's authorship there. A few hundred yards from the church Charlie caught up with me.

'Sam Bollix Brown delivers this by hand to the pub this morning. If it was to save a fucking stamp I'd understand, no, to order me to dress properly. I said what's the tidings. He wouldn't tell me. Wait for the official announcement. Official. Did you ever hear such bollix of a word, Harding? What's going on, do you know?'

'I know. But I won't tell you. Because you're not dressed properly.'

'Fuck you too.'

He wore a pair of those unaccountably fashionable Doc Martin boots so useful for kicking people to death. Black jeans with the bottoms turned up. His sheepskin coat was unbuttoned. I could see his white braces, black shirt and white tie. And he had the golfer's hat with the tassel on top. Going in the door of the tower we were joined by Brock who had come through the church. I said: 'Goodnight, Father.'

'Goodnight to you.'

At the foot of the stairs we stood back to allow Brock to precede us. He clutched the rail with his right hand and every step of the stairs he pressed his left knee to spring himself forward. We went up so slowly that Donat, last to arrive, came through the trapdoor immediately after us. The other ringers were dressed in suits. Donat quickly took off his jacket and called the team. Charlie sat it out in his sheepskin coat.

So seldom did we have a full house that I had only seen Charlie sit out a peal three or four times and he always fumed, his face toxic with hatred. It was never a pleasant occasion. All the other ringers knew Charlie's omission was Donat's manifestation of his loathing for Charlie. Tonight, with Clancy sitting beside him and Brock on the other stool, Charlie bore his humiliation well. Half way through the peal Clancy turned to him and smiled and Charlie had no choice but to smile back, but when he looked over at me he lifted his eyes. The peal finished, everyone looked at Sam, who stepped out to the middle of the floor.

'Reverend Fathers, fellow ringers, I want to thank you all for coming tonight at such short notice. We have good news to announce but it was only confirmed on Thursday morning. And straightway let me stress that the good news is thanks to Father Willie and thanks to him alone. He is not with us long, but he spotted that some of us are long in the tooth. He noticed that some of us have been ringing here for over thirty years. And he decided to see what he could do to honour our long service. Those involved are Sam Brown, Dr Donat Cagney, Charlie Halvey, Midge Malone and Finbar Power. And of course Jack Molyneaux. If we forgot Jack, he'd bury us upside down. Father Willie went directly to the top. He wrote to the Pope – we are to receive papal medals.'

That was the end of the formality. They rushed at Sam. They cheered. They said: Jesus, the Pope! Charlie turned to Clancy and shook his hand. The rest of them gathered around Clancy, beaming at him for a change. I slapped Sam on the back and shook hands again with Clancy. Brock stayed sitting, unmoved. Donat stood by his bell.

'Order,' Sam called. 'Order, please. We'll have a word from Father Willie.'

Applause for the word from Father Willie from all except Donat and Brock.

I sat down anticipating a long speech invoking God and His Blessed Mother and the rest of it, and to watch the recipients-elect trying to look modest. Clancy came to the middle of the floor, clasped his hands, and bestowed a pulpit gaze of benevolence all round.

'My dear men. I thank Sam for his kind words. Yes, there is credit due – but not to me. There is credit to yourselves, your very good selves. You must not hide your light under a bushel. This is an occasion when you must be seen to have done good work – as a good example to others. And what better stage for the presentation – sometime in the new year – than after a concelebrated high mass after a Sunday morning peal.' Here, Clancy turned to Donat for a plaudit. 'The Bishop himself will preside, Doctor.'

Donat nodded. He had not yet put on his jacket. He did so now. He walked to the trapdoor. 'I'm very much afraid that is not quite my style. Young Harding can collect on my behalf.'

In the silence we listened to Donat's agile descent. Clancy's grin collapsed slowly. Sam Brown was stupefied staring at the trapdoor. His forehead crinkled in pain.

'I'll say goodnight to you all myself,' Brock said, and the best construction I could put upon it was that it was his abdication speech. Once his head was under the floor George closed the trapdoor. 'What in God's name made Donat say that?' he demanded, but not of any of us directly. Sam's stature was reflected in the fact that everyone looked at him.

'Tim, you said he doesn't practise, it couldn't be that, could it?'

'Who doesn't practise?' Paddy demanded.

'I don't know, Sam.'

'What are you saying, who doesn't practise?'

Clancy echoed: 'Doesn't practise, Sam?'

'Tim, you said he didn't?'

'He doesn't.'

Finbar burst out: 'What the hell has that to do with it? That shouldn't stop him receiving his medal, should it? Should it, Sam?'

I noticed Charlie kept his big mouth shut. He had stopped practising at ten. I grabbed my own jacket and flew down the stairs. I ran after Donat and caught up with him as he entered Sexton Square. I pulled his sleeve.

'Did you have to be so churlish, did you?'

He stared at my hand on his sleeve until I let go.

'That man has put a lot of time and effort into this. On your behalf. I know. They let me in on it from the beginning.'

'Nobody acts on my behalf. So, you were in on it. Do you see me up on the altar on display? Do you? With any gummy scivvy in a scarf who chooses as part of the audience? Do you see – ME! – joining in single file to have my name read out and have that bishop put the bauble round my neck and thrust his ring at me navel high to be kissed?'

'You don't have to look at it that way . . . '

'Goodnight to you.'

All five tables were occupied in the Draper's Club. Waiting for Charlie, I watched his mates, Simpson, Phil Thompson, Wally Kirwan and Butsey Rushe playing a four-hand. They were on the table nearest the bay window where Yendall brooded. He must have had a dog's life with Charlie. One of Charlie's ventures, back when men wore their hair long, was a Unisex Hair Salon which he called Pierre's – after himself. He showed me a photograph in which he was dressed as a Frenchman. He told me the only work he did – apart from bringing the lodgements to the bank – was to hold a mirror behind the victim's heads and inquire: Is Sir pleased? He liked to stand outside the door greeting the customers with *'allo, allo, bienvenu, bonjour Monsieur*. Across the street in Montague's, Yendall frowned on Charlie's enterprise. One morning going in to work, Charlie had shouted at him, *'Bonjour, Monsieur* Yendall, come over and have Francoise blow-dry your langer.'

Even as I was thinking of Charlie shouting at poor Yendall I heard Charlie: 'Out of my way, make way for Chevalier Halvey, I'm getting a medal from the Pope!' as he came down the hall towards me.

'Harding, you black English Protestant, I've been collecting slops . . . '

'. . . at a ha'penny a bucket since you were ten, what else is new?'

'I got paid for it. A ha'penny. But I got paid for it. They used to laugh at me. I had a nickname for a while. Slops. Fucking slops. Till I learned the Queensbury Rules. A kick in the bollix and run away. Everything I did I got paid for. I've more money than sense now, thank God or whatever prick is watching over me. I only stayed in the bells 'cos Dr Bollix couldn't stand me. And now I'm getting paid for that. A medal from the globetrotter, pipple of Ireland I luff Charlie. I went straight down to the pub to tell Hannah, fuckit if only my mother was alive. Hannah respects me now. All over a fucking medal. Hey, Yendall, I'm getting a medal from the Pope, congratulate me, look at him, he doesn't believe me, sour bollix, your nibs is below, Sloan's daughter, don't touch me, hey, Harding, where, c'm'ere, hey, Harding, our game, you bollix come back . . . hey, Butsey, guess who's getting a medal . . .'

She was wearing a fawn raincoat with a buckleless belt and a scarf emblematic of scenic Ireland, the Blarney Stone, Killarney's lakes, a round tower, Kate Kearney's Cottage. She was smoking, her glass of whiskey on the counter, legs crossed and visible just above the knee, one of her high heels dangling by the toe.

'Isn't it divine? I've decided on Timothy. It's so in keeping with our delicate courtship, don't you think?'

I had no experience of such a woman. Longing for her for eight weeks I stood there like a gawk. She finished her whiskey, stubbed her cigarette and slid off the stool.

'Come on.' She stood at the door until I played my part as a gentleman.

'Down the docks, Timothy. Tonight I am going to allow you to kiss me.' Outside she held my hand.

'Cecelia . . .'

'No, Timothy, don't talk. Not yet, you'll spoil the image.'

The river is just a block from Charlie's. She stopped at the first bollard and sat down. 'Stay standing with your back to the estuary. Now put your left hand over your heart.'

I put my left hand over my heart.

'Don't look so indulgently. Formal. Be formal. Right hand down by your side, loose fist. But not quite so stiff, left foot slightly forward. Very good, Timothy. Now raise your chin.'

'Cecelia . . . '

'Don't speak. You've moved your left hand. Back on your heart. Right hand down. Left leg bent, forward. Chin up. Higher. Don't look at me, look over my head, look towards the top of the cliff . . . '

'Cliff? What cliff?'

'Sorry. Just look over my head. That's perfect! I can see him. I can see him!'

I spoke over her head. 'See who? How long do I have to keep this up?'

Looking down my nose I saw her stand and come towards me.

'Timothy, put your hands on my shoulders. Just bend the elbows a little and hands on my shoulders. You may kiss me. You may kiss me chastely, Timothy. Be good now. Remember, chastely.'

I kissed her and it was chaste. It was short, yet long enough to get the taste of a chaste kiss and it was a sweet taste, not one that I had forgotten, one that I had never known. She took my hands from her shoulders and pulled me with her as she stepped backwards to sit on the bollard. She held my hands as she explained, looking up at me: 'I'm sitting on a ledge at the Diamond Rocks in Kilkee. Everybody walked out there at night. Originally it was to watch the sunset but somebody once sang a song and it became a tradition. Try and imagine all the rocks populated with ladies in summer dresses and emergency cardigans on their laps and the gentlemen in sports attire. Formal sports attire, not going around in rags like everyone does now. My father stood where you were, the calm Atlantic and the sunset at his back. He wore a blazer and slacks and a cravat. His left hand on his heart and his left leg bent forward and his head raised in song. My mother sat on the rocks and fell in love with him while he was singing

'Absence'. He was between a baritone and tenor and he had the purest and most beautiful voice and I have never heard him sing in my life. But everybody said he was beautiful. There was a character used to come into the shop when I was a child, Sir Thomas Ainsworth: "Blast you, Sloan, I haven't had a good cry in ages, come out and sing for me." And Mr Yendall, the book-keeper in Montague's, he would ask me if my father ever sang at home. I would tell him no. He'd shake his head. Timothy, he never sang after she died. But he must want to sing. I know he must want to sing. Everybody wants to sing . . .'

My response surprised both of us. I dropped to my knees and put my head on her lap and my heart wept. Not for Mr Sloan and not for beauty and romance or sadness, even though I knew beauty, romance and sadness to be the verities of life. Cecelia had held my head as a mother would a child's and I hungered to celebrate her figure of authority. She would orchestrate our lives. I would look up to her as I had not done to my mother, who was no match for a Fulham Cosmo hustler, and as I never would to a stone like Donat. She held my face between her palms and kissed me on the forehead. 'Isn't it divine? Absolutely wonderful, Timothy? Sitting on a rock and falling in love with him while he sang a song of love. That's the world we'll live in, a world of love.'

I pressed my hands on her thighs to help me to my feet and I could feel the frisson between us – so much so that I lifted her up and put my arms around her and pulled her close and kissed her and put my hand under her coat and around her backside. It was a long kiss and a lovely feel but when we stopped for breath she pushed me away. 'No. Too soon, Timothy. Another minute and we'd copulate on the bollard.'

'Cecelia, let's copulate.'

'When we're married.'

'Let's get married tomorrow.'

'Hold my hand and walk me home, Timothy – I love you, Timothy.'

'I love you, Cecelia.'

We walked along the quays, up the steps and across the bridge to her house. Our chaste and romantic courtship was saluted all the way by my erection. I could not stop myself telling her.

'Cecelia, my prick is standing.'

'Of course it is, Timothy. I would be quite insulted if it weren't. What do you do at Christmas?'

'I usually go to my grandfather in Kent.'

'Wonderful. I'll be here. We'll be apart, isn't that divine?'

'I can go anytime. I'll go before Christmas, grandad won't . . .'

'You will go at Christmas as usual. We must be apart, don't you understand? It's the only way to contain ourselves. Now, here we are. You must write to me, a long letter telling everything about you. And in return I'll send you my curriculum vitae. You may kiss me goodnight, Timothy. Chastely.'

I led her inside the gate and nursed her between an oak tree and the garden wall for privacy. Her acquiescence made me see the green light. I did give her the chaste kiss to get my foot in the door and then I worked her lips open and backed her against the oak. I slipped the belt of her coat loose and brought my hand up under her skirt. She slurped my lips and clamped her thighs around my hand and tightened her fist on the back of my hair. She started to groan 'Oh Timothy' and I could feel her about to go under.

'Cecelia? Is that you, Cecelia?'

'Oh Jesus. Yes, Daddy, I'm just coming. Timothy, goodnight. Get lost Buster.'

Donat punished all of us by his absence from the Sunday morning and evening peals. During the week I only attended the tower once to ring the chimes and so I was unaware of Clancy's plunge into introspection. It was a busy time of the year for me at Fagenders. People were trying to give them up to save a few pounds for Christmas. I was occupied writing my curriculum vitae for Cecelia and the stumbling block there was my parentage. I plumped for the revisionist stance –

erased Donat from my history and replaced him with a father who was a clerk in Peacock's Hardware in Faversham where my grandad did work. Now I had to kill him off in a car crash or give him a bum ticker. This was differentiation, I thought, mathematically. I reverted to integration. I wrote Cecelia the truth. I was busy too in the Drapers' Club. Every dog in the road reaches for his cue on the long, dark nights. I drank heavily in Charlie's to help me sleep and not lie awake dreaming of Cecelia.

On Saturday night Clancy brought something wrapped in brown paper to the peal. We had nine yet he declined to ring. 'If Dr Donat will forgive me I'd like to sit one out. I'm a little tired.' I noticed Donat made no rush to examine him. During the peal, when a change was called and I had to follow a higher bell, I could see Clancy with a loving grin fixed on Donat.

And after the peal, while Donat put on his jacket, coat and scarf, Clancy's hungry eyes never left him. There was nothing unusual about Donat's abrupt departure but Clancy bolted after him. Clancy must have been half-way down the stairs when we heard him call: 'Dr Cagney.' When I reached the tower door I saw them stopped in the middle of the yard. Clancy slipped his brown paper parcel under Donat's elbow. Donat went on across the yard to Brock's. Charlie came down and persuaded me to trounce him at snooker and then I went to the Professional Club. The parcel was open on the table in front of Jack Molyneaux and Donat. Jack was chuckling. Donat greeted me with: 'He said it was something he "happened upon as he was going through his library". He thought I might "find it interesting".'

I picked up the book. It was Newman's *Apologia Pro Vita Sua*.

'That was thoughtful of him, Donat.'

'I shall return it unread in the morning. That is, unread on this occasion. Bloody fool!'

And so he did. We all saw him hand the parcel to Clancy after the peal. 'I found it interesting. Thank you.'

But Donat was not to escape Clancy so easily. Clancy said – and again all of us could hear the invitation – 'I wonder, Doctor, I wonder if I could have a word with you?'

'Yes?'

'When the men have gone, Doctor.'

In obedience to the hint, Sam led the charge to the trapdoor. Donat caught my elbow and held me beside him. 'Yes?' he repeated to Clancy.

'Of course Tim may stay, Doctor.' Clancy produced a pocket watch from under his garments and offered it for Donat's inspection. 'It was my father's, Doctor.' Donat dutifully examined it. He allowed the watch to weigh heavily in his palm and then delivered the sarcasm: 'I'm sure it hasn't lost a second in fifty years?'

'A first-class timepiece, Doctor,' Clancy boasted, accepting the watch. He then pressed the winder and the back of the case flew open. 'Do you not marvel at the intricacy, Doctor?'

'Splendid craftsmanship, I have no doubt.'

'How much more intricate is the universe, Doctor, the galaxy.'

Donat looked at his own wrist-watch. 'I have a call to make. Good day to you.'

'Doctor . . .'

But Donat was already pushing me ahead of him. Going down the stairs I could hear Donat muttering behind me: 'Damn imbecile. Damn bony head. Wretched creature.'

Leaving the tower Donat looked at me. I smiled.

'I didn't find it amusing.'

'This Clancy is looking up, Donat. I hope he keeps at it.'

'You do, do you? As it is I shall have to mention it to Brock.'

'You wouldn't do that, Donat?'

'Come with me and hear for yourself.'

Brock was surprised to see us on a Sunday morning. He offered the bottle but we declined. He poured one for himself and settled down to listen. When Donat finished Brock chuckled, just as Jack Molyneaux had done. As I did. But then Brock said: 'Leave it with me.'

102

'I don't want you to get involved. I can deal with the fellow myself. But I thought you should know.'

'Fuck you, Cagney, I'm not thinking of you. I'm thinking of him.'

'So am I. But if you say anything he'll think I came running to you.'

'I shall make it plain that you didn't.'

'I don't see how you can do that.'

On Wednesday night I was in the tower with Sam and Clancy. I alternated with Sam while Clancy remained seated with his hands deep in the pockets of his soutane. There was no mistaking it now, he was down, no grin, no zest. So much so that I asked: 'Are you all right, Father?' He did not hear me. I asked again.

'Sorry, what's that, Tim?'

'I said are you all right, you look preoccupied.'

He assembled the grin. 'It's our duty to be occupied, Tim.'

Sam grimly rang the chimes. When we finished Clancy stood up. 'Goodnight, men.' We let him go. Sam lit a cigarette. I took out my Gold Flake.

'You smoke, Tim?'

'An odd one. To help me stay off them.'

'Tim, does Dr Donat go to his club Wednesdays?'

'He goes every night. Why?'

'I want to see him. Can a non-member go in there?'

'Come with me. He won't be there for another hour at least. You want to go to Charlie's for one?'

We had two pints in Charlie's and Sam needed them.

'I don't want to go there,' Sam said, 'but somebody's going to have to do something.'

For once Charlie was solicitous on Sam's behalf. 'Sam, take my advice. Don't go near that bollix. If you have half a fucking brain don't go near him.'

'Charlie's right, Sam.'

'Somebody has to do something.'

I brought him to the Club. Jack Molyneaux lived in the

103

place. He was delighted to see Sam, insisted on standing a round while we waited for Donat. Just as Sam was saying 'good luck' Donat came in and went to the bar. He always drank with Jack. I could read him. He was allowing himself a retreat. When he joined us he remained standing, resting a hand on the back of my chair, addressing Sam and Jack: 'Two more and we could have a peal.'

'Donat, I'm here about the tower. I hope you don't mind.' It was an understanding affectation of Sam's to drop the 'doctor' outside the bells.

'What about the tower?'

'Father Clancy.'

'Yes?'

'Father Brock's been on to him. Father Brock told him that the watch trick is rather common when dealing with someone of your calibre. He told Father Clancy to lay off, that you will return to the fold in God's good time.'

'I see.'

'Father Clancy's in bad shape, Donat. Tim saw it tonight. It's the first time I've seen him down in the dumps.'

'Am I to understand you wish me to look at him in my professional capacity?'

'He's a priest, Donat. It's his job to try to land you. Look, it wouldn't kill you to go through with the ceremony.'

'I don't do things simply because they do not kill me.'

'It's none of my business whether you practise or not but this is outside of that . . .' Donat continued to look at Sam as though Sam had yet to make his point. I was sorry for Sam. He was outclassed as Charlie and I had anticipated. Sam showed it now: 'I honestly don't think you should have gone to Father Brock about him . . .'

'I specifically asked Brock not to dress him down. This is just a lunatic crusade of Clancy's that could lead to another crack-up. And it is Brock's responsibility. Not mine . . . And not yours.'

Sam stood up and prepared to leave humbly. His last lame

statement was: 'Father Clancy doesn't know I'm here about him.'

Donat flexed his forehead to show his indifference. I left with Sam.

CHAPTER 13 .

The House of Montague

On the second day of the new decade Lady Ainsworth called into the shop and tapped her delicate knuckles on my open door.

'Good morning, Lady Ainsworth. A happy new year to you. And to Sir Thomas.'

'Thank you, Yendall. Not so happy, I'm afraid. Tommy's had a stroke. Could I have a chair, Yendall, please?'

'Lady Ainsworth . . . ' I rushed to give her mine. 'I'm so sorry. Can I get you something? Tea? Perhaps send Gabrielides round the corner to Arthur Skee's?'

'No thank you, Yendall. I'm quite all right. I have just come from the hospital. The prognosis is that Tommy will not walk again and his speech is impaired.'

'Lady Ainsworth, I'm so dreadfully sorry . . . '

'Dr Cagney is disconsolate, but of course it is no fault of his. Tommy was always so stubborn, wouldn't take the tablets. As far back as last May he was warned off the flask but you know Tommy, Yendall, he has a colourful vocabulary . . . '

'Invariably cheers us all up, Lady Ainsworth . . . '

' " . . . can't get pissed, Cagney, with Ascot coming up? . . . nonsense . . . " ' Lady Ainsworth's tender spirit broke through the brave mimicry as she reached into her bag for a handkerchief.

'Please let me get you some tea, Lady Ainsworth . . . '

'Thank you, Yendall. No. Down to business. I have to face it, from now on I must take charge of his affairs. I thought, may as well begin at Montague's. Send me his account, Yendall.'

'Lady Ainsworth, we've never sent Sir Thomas an account,

he wouldn't hear of it. He loved to come in, flush from a joust with the bookmakers, and rib me. "Thought I'd scarpered before the bumper, eh, Yendall? Never fear, Honest Tommy Ainsworth always pay up." He had his own way with him. Loved a jest. I would press him to read the account, but no, Lady Ainsworth. Sir Thomas would scold me, though with a twinkle in his eye. He would say: "This is Montague's, Yendall, not the corner shop where I've been ticking sausages and rashers all week."'

Lady Ainsworth smiled, yet her eyes brimmed. She took her cheque book out of the handbag. Among her pearls she fumbled for the cord from which her reading glasses depended and with a patrician flourish wrote us a blank cheque.

'Send me a receipt, Yendall.'

Sir Thomas's affliction, at the dawn of the year, was Shakespearian in its presage of the collapse of all that had been monumental. I had become inured to Halvey's barber shop for pansies across the road. Now, three doors up the street on our own side, Carroll's, the stationers, closed. The lease was up. I read in the weekend paper that Carroll's would reopen as a Wimpy Bar owned by 'a consortium of businessmen'. I ruminated and deciphered: a school of sharks. I could not distinguish the sexes parading to the latest Mecca, and every morning I found the pavement littered with chip and burger wrappers. What was happening in the schools? There seemed to be little now in the weekend newspaper but revelations of the plague. That James Kelly announced that he intended to stand in the next general election. My reaction was to look to the top of the page in the hope of reading 1 April. No such luck. He promised to publish his manifesto 'in good time'. I came across a fullpage advertising feature for Pierre's Unisex Salon Mark II. Halvey was opening a second front, mercifully five blocks up the town in what had been a decent tobacconist's. But I was disappointed to see a four-inch double column in support from Simpson captioned 'Best of Luck to Charlie'. Soon after, Simpson himself opened a second shop and this time he bought the building. Again I thought the street a bit off. But he had a spacious ground floor, almost as large as our own, and he had as tenantry a chiropodist, an insurance broker and, on the top floor, a flat leased to a married couple. We saw the announcement and a photograph of the building in the paper. On the fascia over the sunshade we read the script: 'Simpson's Second Shop'. Mr Sloan summed up: 'Such vulgarity.' The cloud creeping over us all must needs have begun to engulf me by then since I thought it damned clever of Simpson while at the same time his prosperity was beginning to stick in my craw. Of course Simpson could not be in two places at the one time and needed an assistant to be where he wasn't. He advertised and one of the replies – the most suitable – came from our own Mr Gabrielides. In his straightforward way Simpson called on Mr Sloan. They sat in my office, Simpson in his morning coat and striped trousers as he had worn with us.

'Mr Sloan,' he began, 'I hope you appreciate this is a decorum I scarcely anticipated having to observe. Mr Gabrielides was the last applicant I expected – I want to do right by Mr Gabrielides, but much more so I'm obliged to do right by your good self.'

It was the Simpson style. Mr Sloan took off his glasses and put them on my desk in front of him. He drew his palms from his forehead down over his closed eyes and then glared over the tips of his fingers at Simpson. He looked tired, weary of Simpson.

'What guarantee of secure employment can you offer him, Simpson?'

Simpson smiled in the way of one who had a tender regard for Mr Sloan – now that Mr Sloan was turning crotchety. Simpson said, and I noticed he tried to put a wink into his words as he opened his hands, 'Mr Sloan, who promised us tomorrow?' I was surprised by such *lèse-majesté*. Mr Sloan came straight back with the chill: 'We can do without the messenger boy aphorisms if you don't mind, Simpson.' I was beginning to find the whole business unpleasant but it seemed to go over Simpson's head. Or so he let it appear? I would have been unhappy to think him devious.

'I have been prudent, Mr Sloan.' This was a shaft difficult for Mr Sloan to parry, having taught Simpson his financial wisdom. And though we recognized little prudence in the wages Simpson offered – significantly higher than what we were paying Mr Gabrielides – we were obliged to remain non-committal. We were intelligent men in our own way, Mr Sloan and I, and it was impossible not to be conscious that Simpson was representative of a new age. Mr Sloan caved in quickly. 'Very well, Simpson. I will have to have a word with Mr Gabrielides. We saw ourselves to an extent *in locum parentis* but now it seems the chap is no longer happy here. I can think of no objection to your taking him on if you feel he will be suitable.'

'Thank you, Mr Sloan. Mr Gabrielides was honest with me. He will only stay a year to two at the most. His intention is to go home eventually and open his own shop in London.'

The whip-around for Mr Gabrielides was modest. Nothing came from the factory. Mr Sloan delegated to me the honour of making the presentation.

Of course we could keep up with Simpson by reading his full-page advertisements in the weekly newspaper. But there was so much more we might have noticed. We might have reflected on our own changing custom, or taken alert from the wan figures in the overall Montague statement of accounts. We might have caught ourselves turning the wireless knobs lower as the music sounded louder and louder. We might have questioned how chaps in waistcoats came to play snooker on our coloured television sets.

The Lyric cinema closed leaving Wally Kirwan beached. Phil Thompson continued as a full-time idler. I trusted he would share the secret of his success with Kirwan at the open air seminar outside our door at Butsey Rushe's news-stand. Less and less of our stuff was now made at the factory. At Simpson's Mr Gabrielides wore an ordinary three-piece in testament to the modern casual manner that was also mirrored in the variegated hues of the up-to-date shirts, socks and pullovers in Simpson's – and to an extent now – in Montague's. After a visit from Mr Dobson we prepared to stock denim. Mr Sloan was inspired to a bitter witticism: 'A bolt from the blue, Mr Yendall.' Mayhew's Medical Hall had not been the only long-established premises to change hands. The once familiar streets bawled awake every morning with a new birthmark. Basements came to life. Boutiques flourished. Security took to the high road after corsets and crinoline. Again Mr Dobson came over from London. He visited both of Simpson's shops. We had the carpenters in and conducted 'Business As Usual During Renovations'.

At our tea and biscuits one morning Mr Sloan aired his domestic life, something he had never done before. 'I'm worried about Cecelia.' I could not imagine him ever having to fret there. Cecelia had been an adorable child. She was educated by the Faithful Companions of Jesus and there is no better education for a young lady.

'If I can be of help, Mr Sloan . . . '

'She's not going to university.'

'I'm sorry. The points system is ridiculous.'

'It's not that. She has enough points to pick her faculty. She wants to travel. Sister Catherine is livid, Cecelia was the star pupil. I was an hour up at the FCJ's last night. Sister Catherine is livid – with me.'

'You can't be blamed, Mr Sloan. You see it all round you, this generation is an independent one.'

'No. Sister Catherine is angry because I don't want Cecelia to go either.' This was a Mr Sloan I had not met before. He was not a smiling man – not since he lost his wife – but he was smiling now, mischievously. 'Cecelia wants to walk to Greece. Work her way across Europe. Hitch-hike. She wants to go to the university of life.'

I knew where I had heard that expression before. From that unhinged Pierrot across the road. Down the years it seemed I could not open my window for fresh air without him bellowing through cupped hands that he had collected slops at ten years of age from the lanes for a ha'penny a bucket and adding 'you should have gone to the university of life, Yendall'. Accompanied by the usual expletives peculiar to such graduates.

'I can readily understand your concern, Mr Sloan,' I commented, yet I detected a manic exhilaration about him.

'I am worried in exactly the same way I would be if she did go to university or across the road to buy perfume. She is doing the right thing, Yendall, and I just hope she is doing it for the right reasons and not because it is fashionable.'

'You wouldn't prefer if she had a degree first? She would then have a sense of security.'

Mr Sloan thought about that as I expected he would. It was a good point. He took a long time to reply as he looked past me out the window. And then he shocked me. Dreamily – for he must have been in a stupor of sorts – he said: 'Mr Yendall, who promised us tomorrow?' Then he returned to his work.

CHAPTER 14

The Society of Bellringers

For the first time since I had joined the bells I was heavy-hearted next Saturday night on the way to the tower. I was not looking forward to a lugubrious Clancy mourning the loss of Donat's soul. I walked slowly and slower still up the steps. Yet, when I came through the trapdoor, I was greeted by a beaming Clancy. 'Goodnight, Tim, a fresh night, thank God.'

'Goodnight, Father.'

There were seven of us there and behind me I could hear Donat's steps. Everybody was stripping to ring, including Clancy. He was euphoric and that was good enough for the rest of the men. But I noticed another parcel on the stool under the hook where Clancy hung his collar. He had found the will to carry on his ministry. After the peal he immediately offered the parcel to Donat.

'A Don Camillo, Doctor,' Clancy explained and he stood his ground, prepared to be stoned. Donat simply nodded.

'Thank you.'

Sunday morning Donat returned the book and drowned Clancy with courtesy. 'I did so enjoy it, Father. I thought I was familiar with the entire canon, but I found so much I must have forgotten.'

Donat had decided to suffer Clancy – for Clancy's sake, I decided. Or else he would not convey the dignity of an adversary on Clancy. Sunday night produced Ethel Mannin's *Late Have I Loved Thee*. Again Donat accepted with polite thanks. But he did not return the book the following weekend. He told me: 'I read it. Or waded through it. But the longer I am in possession of that chap's library the less opportunity he will have of molesting me.'

And so it went on. A Chesterton followed; a Belloc; and Donat was tickled by his luck – Graham Greene. That brought us up to Christmas. There was a feeling in the tower that Donat was coming around to recognize Clancy's essential good nature, to see the humour of the situation. The little game of suspense they were playing was entertainment to the rest of us. Donat would yield, he would collect his medal. I wasn't so sure but my uncertainty was comfort in itself. Having taken a stand, the Donat I knew would jump off the tower before bending to someone like Clancy or to anybody at all for that matter.

I was going to Kent for Christmas to see my grandfather. At my last peal before leaving Clancy gave every one of us a small present. Those who smoked received cigars, and the rest pen, pencil and biro sets. I thought it odd that he omitted Donat. There was a momentary atmosphere. It was unthinkable that he would not have something for Donat. I could see Donat was confused, that anyone might suppose he could be chastened by omission from such tawdry largesse. But Clancy suddenly stood on a stool and from the window ledge hidden behind the photograph cabinet hauled out the mystery gift.

'For you, Doctor.' Another parcel, larger than usual.

'Please open it.' Butler's *Lives of the Saints*. 'It's a gift, Doctor.'

'Thank you. That's most generous of you.'

Later on I went to the Professional Club to wish Jack Molyneaux a happy Christmas and found Donat in a foul mood.

'When I came out from Brock's there was Clancy patrolling the yard, pretending to read his office. A perishing night, the fool blue in the face. As though he's surprised to see me he says, "Ah, Doctor." And then he asks me if I have thought any more on what he called "our little chat". I told him pointedly, with respect to him, that I did not wish to hear further from him on the subject. There was pain on the

113

fool's face. Hurt. And I told him: no more books. I have a decent library of my own.'

'What did he say to that, Donat?' Jack Molyneaux asked and I could anticipate the response myself.

'Nothing. Just looked at me lovingly with that inane grin. That's how I left him.'

My Dearest Timothy,

Imagine! Donat Cagney's bastard! How wonderful! How absolutely divine! And your mother. What a heroine! Oh God, how lucky we are. To think I almost married Jack. Tell you about him later. Not that much to tell really, about me I mean. Compared to you! Let's see. I went to school to the lovely nuns and simply sailed through. They said be a good girl and go home and study so I was a good girl, I went home and studied. No childish bullshit about not being a swot. And every night my father was there, coming in after his walk and drink in Arthur Skee's. He would sit by the fire reading and just loved to be interrupted when I needed help. I was a good daughter. I'd ask him about his day and he'd tell me everything about Montague's and Mr Yendall and the rest of them. Of course I went to dances and that but I couldn't meet my intellectual match which was what I needed then but don't need now. Ha! Then the most amazing thing. I'd studied and studied and when uni time came I just knew I didn't need to study anymore. It would be bad for me. I just knew! But how could I tell him? How could I tell Sister Catherine!! But I did tell him. And I couldn't have picked a worse time. They were changing the shop and had lost Mr Gabrielides to Simpson – Simpson started at Montague's as a messenger boy, worked his way up, left to open his own business and was replaced by the first black man in town – Paki actually. And what does Simpson do? Thrives. Opens a second shop and swipes Gabrielides from under Dad's nose. All the old custom was dying off and they were having to move with the times. Can you imagine my father moving with the times. And Mr

Yendall! But I waited until after his constitutional and malt in Arthur Skee's. I had his slippers ready and the cup of tea. I told him straight out that I didn't want to go to uni and waited for him to explode. But no. He sits there sipping and nods. And what would you like to do, Cecelia? I can't believe he's taking it so calmly. I tell him the truth. I tell him I don't know. I just don't want to study anymore. I mean study formally. I wasn't going to become a Philistine. I tell him I want to travel, be footloose for a while, I didn't just want England and America as my mentors, I wanted to see Europe. Timothy, it all gushed out of me. He nods away and smiles, really smiles like I have never seen him do before. But then he becomes paternal again, grave in the face and I think he's been indulging me and I'm waiting for the 'let me tell you what's what, young lady' bit. Timothy, listen to this: 'Cecelia, I see an impediment' – pause – 'how are we going to tell your aunt? And Sister Catherine?' I leapt upon him, kissed him and hugged him, oh Daddy, Daddy, Daddy. But here's the most amazing part. When I said 'I thought you'd be mad', he just smiles again and says the most uncharacteristic thing you could imagine. He says, 'Cecelia, who promised us tomorrow.' He went to the convent and put Sister Catherine in her box and he appeased Auntie. And I was off, up, up and away.

You louse, Timothy, with your birds and booze at Trinity. I will not be a doctor. I will be an axe murderer but I will not be a doctor. Timothy, that was romantic. And touring America on a debating jaunt, that was romantic. And going back when you qualified to work for that gangster getting people off the fags, that was not romantic. Now if you and Professor Bedford Rowe had helped to *start* people smoking, that would have been romantic. Donat Cagney is romantic. Do you know he doesn't recognize medical cards? When a poor person goes to him and takes out a medical card he says 'My fee is twelve guineas, if you can afford it settle with my receptionist, if you can't then consider it my treat.' Isn't that style?

115

I'm not a virgin. That's not romantic. But what could I do?
In the seventies? I love to think of you ringing bells. It is so
Franz Liszt. And your unashamed passion for snooker.
What a man! I reached Greece and was on my way back
unscathed when I fell in with the folk crowd in Brittany –
no, I was not a groupie, as a matter of fact I'm not musical
at all despite my beautiful name, I'm a sucker for the old-
fashioned singing voice. 'Absence'! A busker, well he's
probably completed his studies and is a brain surgeon now
but anyone could twang a chord then and he twanged mine.
Only once. Don't think I was the type to shack up. I have
my modesty. No, it was very rarely I did it three times with
the same man. I preferred one night stands, I doubt if
there's been more than twenty. Still love me? But to work:
there is absolutely no romance attached to working in a
canning factory in Amsterdam. Or waitressing in Munich.
Teaching English in Spain is the white-collar equivalent of
navvying. Look where I ended up. Sister Catherine was
right. I should have gone to uni and got my degree. Six years
ago I thought about going back as a mature student after
temping all over London for a year. Fuck the women's
liberation movement, a woman isn't a woman until she has
a husband and there was no sign of a really terrific prospect
anywhere – who would have me I mean – and worse, I
knew I was the type who would hold out. Then the agency
sent me to William Blake. Publisher! Magic word. I would
meet writers! Publicity assistant! No degree needed, no
pussy demanded. Art, why had I ever forsaken thee. I didn't
even hear the wages – in my right mind I'd have needed a
hearing-aid. Ninety-eight quid and your chances. And the
offices! Two rooms on the third floor of a three-storey
building in Hammersmith, sharing a loo with a loan company while the staff agency beneath us and the ground floor
betting shop had their own. William Blake had the oddest
policy, he would only publish good books. By that he meant
only fiction well-written. So the firm was and is and always
will be broke. When the accounts are audited every year he

goes to his bank manager – with whom of course he went to Oxford and then – and only then – he comes back and announces that we have broken even. By the time I recognized this I'm hooked – who could desert such a ship? Any time we have an author in town whose work sells and must be entertained I receive instructions to take him to afternoon tea in the Ritz – it's cheaper than dinner any place. This is no problem with Americans, and the couple of Irish on our list are too gauche for anything but a gallon of beer to help them conquer a ham sandwich in the local pub. But the home-grown trendies won't be fobbed off and dinner it has to be inclusive of the costliest plonk. Those who don't sell are treated by William himself in his cubbyhole. He shares a teabag and offers one of his Players Number 6. Now, contrast all that with the agency of one of our American high-flyers, the crowd Jack works for in Regent Street. They own the building. You sink in carpet. Jack's own office consists of two rooms, one of which has bathroom en suite and a third room shared by his three secretaries. Jack's forty-six, divorced, the most charming man I have ever known. He is a gentleman, takes me out to dinner, buys me presents, lends me money when I'm stuck, and chuckles when I attempt to pay him back. His divorce was in his twenties, clean cut, no children, she ditched him for an army officer. He wants to rescue me from William Blake, give me a job in the agency at an astronomical sum and he wants to marry me. How I resist him I don't know because he's just perfect in every way – or was until I saw you, Timothy. Romance, romance, we will have it, my sweet.

CHAPTER 15

The House of Montague

S ir Thomas Ainsworth and Dr John Cagney died within a month of each other. Mr Sloan and I had gone to see Sir Thomas in the hospital and found him a wretched sight. He was slumped in a wheel-chair beside the bed, his entire right-hand side immobile. His face was contorted from futile efforts at speech. His head lay on his shoulder while he grunted like some untamed beast: 'Aaagh, aghhh.' Mr Sloan and I were at a loss. Manfully, Mr Sloan recounted news of Montague's, of Cecelia's travels, but Sir Thomas shook his deformed head, raised his eyes and his left hand in rage at the heavens to take him. Then he collapsed briefly into a serenity and pointed a finger towards Mr Sloan's top pocket. Mr Sloan quickly understood and offered the pen to Sir Thomas who had a writing pad littered with scribbles. He scrawled a word that was indecipherable to me and looked at Mr Sloan with pleading eyes. Mr Sloan turned to me: 'I wonder, Mr Yendall, if you would leave us for ten minutes.' I went downstairs and sat in the waiting area, feeling somewhat spurned, I must admit. Mr Sloan came down before I thought of going up again. He did not comment and I knew enough not to pry. We did not see Sir Thomas alive again. He died at home two weeks later and Lady Ainsworth gave us all to understand it was a merciful release. They came from all over England and Ireland for the funeral and unfortunately they also came from underneath my window and from across the road. Naturally I would have expected Simpson, but Halvey, Rushe, Kirwan and Thompson polluted the attendance. They walked boldly up to Lady Ainsworth and shook her hand. It seemed nobody was to die in peace while those ghouls were at large. Leaving the cemetery I was with Simpson for a few strides. I indicated Halvey. 'Simpson, tell me, what morbid fixation has that fellow to turn up at so many funerals?'

'Underneath it all, Mr Yendall, Charlie has a big heart. He told me they went out to see Sir Thomas in the hospital. They couldn't understand a word he was saying at first but eventually they were able to pick up the odd word. Do you know Mr Sloan sang 'Absence' for Sir Thomas? It must have been very moving.'

When a fortnight later Dr Cagney died in his sleep I was conscious of the end of an era. And I braced myself to suffer Dr Donat accepting the condolences of Pierre and company. By the mercy of providence not one of them turned up. There was after all one occasion when they knew their place. Young Dr Donat was a striking fellow, lean from his travels, but now home to preserve the decorous continuity in Sexton Square.

A shopping centre opened on the outskirts complete with a vast car-park. Simpson took a unit and christened it simply: 'Simpson's Third'. Mr Sloan did not mention it and neither did I. We did not talk about Simpson at all now. But I did not have Mr Sloan's character. After a month I called out to see Simpson. He brought me for coffee to an adjoining restaurant called 'Snacks'. People were ashamed to put their names over their doors now. Mr Gabrielides was now supervisor of the two town shops with a couple of young chaps under him. And by now Mr Gabrielides was not the only coloured chap around.

'Mr Yendall, would you credit I had applicants who scorned the wages? I showed them the door. I had one man who seemed all right but when I told him he would be addressed as 'Mister' he burst out laughing in my face. I had no choice in the finish, Mr Yendall, but to hire a sleepy slouch unworthy of any less peremptory a title than his blunt surname. And as you saw here I have a girl working in the unit.' He was boasting. Anyone would do now, no matter how much he was paying them, labour was cheap because values were cheap. The shopping centre itself was an affront to me.

119

From what I saw the customers were zombies. They wandered round the place as though in a maze, and turned into every unit apparently because they were not in a street and in danger of being run over. Metaphorically their hands were raised: take the money out of my pockets, please. At the butcher's they did not instruct him to cut off the fat. They bought anything that was at a 'bargain' price whether it was a dog food or a shirt manufactured in Brazil, and everything was at a 'bargain' price since the price it never was was written above it and crossed out. That class of cheap trading. The customers did not know how to read between the prices as their mothers did. They did not feel the material, did not extract from Simpson or his girl an affidavit that they were getting a good buy. I found the shopping centre a depressing place. Who wants to have the smell of food in his nostrils when he is being measured for a suit?

For the first time in our history we had to let men go at the factory. It was an unpleasant experience – for Montague's. The men fought to be first out, thanks to this lunatic redundancy business. I thought they were damn lucky to get the statutory, but who arrived on our doorstep to negotiate on the men's behalf but the bold Kelly with his trade union vocabulary. I sent him packing. He went up to the factory and in ten minutes had them all out, every one of them bar Russell. Mr Dobson flew straight over from London and I had to sit there twiddling my thumbs while he succumbed so pusillanimously to Kelly's extravagant demands. Mr Dobson had brought his instructions with him. He assured me that we were well out of it in the end. It was the latest fashion, buy them out. Once out, they couldn't come in again.

We off-loaded twenty this way and could continue to meet our orders. Which showed how we had mollycoddled them down through the years. And we weren't alone. The streets were full now of able-bodied men strolling around during the day. Fellows taking dogs for a walk who had never owned a dog let alone a ball to throw and shout 'Fetch'. Kelly produced the long-awaited manifesto. He was for: ABORTION (in certain circumstances – after rape, and where a child was likely to be born handicapped); CONTRACEPTION (in all cases); NATIONALIZATION OF BANKS and the usual left-ish claptrap. After the election came the bad news that he saved his deposit. He received two and a half thousand first preference votes and five hundred more in transfers. Ours is a five seater and the last candidate was elected with four thousand eight hundred without reaching the quota. On the Sunday morning before polling day, the bishop's pastoral was read out in all the churches exhorting the electorate not to vote for any candidate who was not Pro Life – an obvious thumbs down for Kelly, but why his lordship did not come out and name Kelly I will never know. After all, the electorate was comprised of every Tom, Dick and Harry. Still, where did Kelly get his two and a half thousand first preferences and what asses gave him transfers?

The Drapers' Club has long since been swept clean of any lingering drowsiness, but at least I can say I made a stand. Because of the snooker boom manifested by those jumped up gentlemen on television we were always full, a regular going concern. Outside of our committee a draper was almost a rarity on the tables. What invariably accompanies such sudden prosperity is greed and we were no exception. It was John Moore of Cannocks' department store who brought it up, Moore whom I had always thought reliable. Cannocks sold every damn thing besides drapery, from children's bicycles to women's knickers. It was galling to bend the knee to such a representative. Moore proposed that the wall to the table tennis room be knocked down to accommodate three extra snooker tables. I was outvoted in committee. It was put to me: Who plays table tennis now, Yendall? I threatened to resign. I did resign. But they pleaded with me to reconsider. I did reconsider. Damned if I would walk away and leave it to them. Someone had to stay on and fight. In vain. Where once the antiquarians played bridge, we now sell coffee and minerals and sandwiches and peanuts.

Even with the five tables there was usually a waiting list for a game. We were no longer confined to members. Anyone could walk in off the street and put his name down. And anybody did. We were making money. I was brooding one night at the bay window when Simpson came in. It was years since he had played. He did not know anybody so I obliged him myself. After three-quarters of an hour he beat me on the pink in a game where I was content to address the red nearest to me. But Simpson played as if for his last sixpence, tense and bursting into relief when we finished. I was irritated and then amused. After the game we sat down again by the bay window. I had my pipe. Simpson did not drink or smoke. He was still exhilarated with his victory.

'God be with the old days over the shop, Mr Yendall,' he smiled at me, as though the flea pit had been a bond in common. I didn't carry much weight physically – or figuratively now – but Simpson was ageing in the well-fed aldermanic style.

'All that tosh about wasted youth,' he went on, 'the game is certainly respectable now, Mr Yendall. Did you see that Hurricane Higgins was fined a thousand for urinating into an aspidistra? A thousand is nothing to them. I was watching Steve Davis last night in the Consolidated Laboratories Classic. He cleared the table in seven minutes and then sat down without sweat to sip his glass of water.'

'I believe they use talcum powder, Simpson.'

'Just imagine it, Mr Yendall, before the last world championship in Sheffield, Davis hired a suite in a hotel where he installed every make of video game to pass the time between rounds.'

'Look around you here, Simpson. Every young fellow has his own chalk – in the pocket of his waistcoat. Waistcoats! On children. They dress to the nines and stand straight in emulation of your Steve Davis and that other urinating artist. They want to be a credit to the game!'

'You don't approve, Mr Yendall?'

'One weeps.'

'Come now, Mr Yendall. Isn't it good that the four minute mile is no longer a target? And these young lads, isn't it good that they don't have to worry about the price of the game like we used to?'

'I don't know, Simpson. As for your mile, of whatever duration, all I read in my paper now is kilometres.' I was crusty. But I could give him twelve years. He hadn't time to think with his empire. He couldn't see things. He was smiling at me, showing forbearance, and I didn't care for it one damn bit. I said: 'Well, Simpson, I'm happy everything is going splendidly for you. I take it your mother no longer turns shirt collars.' But he was not to bruise easily.

'Only for a few of the old neighbours who haven't a gift with the sewing machine, Mr Yendall.'

I left him soon after that, ashamed of myself, angry with him. I felt damn less than a gentleman. He brought the worst out in me, I thought. I had to blame somebody.

CHAPTER 16

The Society of Bellringers

The community dinner was usually an ordeal I suffered on Sam's behalf. We were the poor relations in the attendance and Sam would not have forgiven a defection. Donat likewise for his Burlington Bertie. Apart from our contingent there were present the choir, confraternity secretaries and trustees, pillars of the city and financial backers of the church, Brock, Clancy, the spiritual directors of the confraternity and novena, the choir chaplain. In all we numbered almost one hundred. We had minestrone, turkey and ham, creamed potatoes, Brussels sprouts, trifle, pudding and tea or coffee. There was no shortage of drink: brandy and spirits bummed from every publican in the vicinity and a half dozen barrels on tap courtesy of Guinness. Cigarettes all over the tables, it was the one time of the year I was supposed to 'break out'. After dinner we had the speeches. Every section was spoken for through its representative. Brock acted for us. He may himself have been in a state of unbelief, but he knew how to preach what he did not practise. We went to the yard for ten minutes' fresh air while the plates were cleared, and then went back in to entertain ourselves at the piano. We were supposed to mix yet I found myself with a group that included Clancy. He pissed me off. 'And how is Tim, did you have a congenial holy season?' The choir provided most of the singing, one of them leading off with 'The Holy City' and the rest of us coming in with the chorus. I don't sing but what can you do when strangers and friends thump your shoulder and order: sing up? 'The Bold Gendarmes' followed, complete with action and gesticulation. Then the Master of Ceremonies called for a contribution from the tower. Dr Donat. We'll have

Dr Cagney now, please. Order for Dr Cagney. Order please. Shhh. Shhh . . .

> ' . . . I walk down the Strand
> with my gloves on my hands
> and I walk back up again with them off.
> I've just had a banana with Lady Diana . . . '

He had a cane and bowler and white scarf while he promenaded. It was a performance to disarm his worst enemy, and I thought I understood why he revelled so in the part. It was a turn we would not see any more, Donat's annual act of defiance, as indeed were the entire proceedings, given a one-day parole every year and then returned to the custody of mothballs. We were all proud of Donat, we could show the choirboys we also had a trump. Even Charlie applauded. Every year Charlie said: 'He may be the biggest cunt unhung but Dr Bollix is the best Burlington Bertie I've ever seen.' Our friend Clancy beside me clapped on his own when the general applause subsided. His eyes protruded with immoderate excitement, orgasmic territory, that made me loathe him and for a moment sympathize with Donat. I noticed too that Brock was flushed with appreciation. Of course he had a half-empty bottle at his hand.

A confraternity trustee who was old enough to have more sense of dignity, press-ganged a few of his colleagues into sitting on the floor with him while they sang the 'Eton Boat Song'. There was a call then for a volunteer from the religious as there was every year and no takers on the couple of times I had been present. So I was surprised to see Brock push back his chair and cough into his fist as he came up to the piano. He put one hand on the piano and another on his heart just as Cecelia had described her father's stance. Brock sang 'On The Road To Mandalay' and a good job he made of it as testified by Charlie's approval. And damn it, I began to enjoy myself as I had not done in other years. The drink, the Victorian innocence and Cecelia's Romance, Romance echoing made me wistful. Graciousness had not after all been stamped out, even if it was only hanging on by its fingernails. I began to glow.

Although all of them could do a turn the choir did not want to be seen monopolizing, and the Master of Ceremonies invited all factions to contribute. But outside of the choir there was only so much talent. Out of the tower locker all we could furnish was Midge Malone, who sang 'Beautiful, Beautiful Munsters', the anthem of a rugby team associated with the one-time slums of the city. And so the night went on. When the tower was announced again we reneged, but the Master of Ceremonies chided us: 'Come on men, don't let the side down.' We all volunteered someone else's name but with no result. Of course everyone knew by now who could and who could not entertain after so many dinners over so many years. The Master of Ceremonies turned in Donat's direction: 'Let's have Dr Cagney again. You'll oblige, Donat?' With what Donat would have obliged I'll never know. Into the breach stepped Clancy. He muttered something to me . . . 'must do our duty, Tim . . . ' and walked up to the MC. Their heads were together. Then: 'Father Clancy says he can't sing but he has a recitation. Order, please.' I was squirming even before he began.

> 'The Old Priest Peter Gilligan
> Was weary night and day;
> For half his flock were in their beds
> Or under green sods lay.'

He read from a sheet of paper.

> 'Once, while he nodded on a chair,
> At the moth hour of eve,
> Another poor man sent for him,
> And he began to grieve.
>
> "I have no rest, nor joy, nor peace,
> For people die and die."
> And after cried he, "God forgive me!
> My body spoke, not I!"'

126

Clancy paused and looked around the room to see that his audience was with him. I could see Brock uneasy in his seat. Donat had the knack of banishing any possible interpretation of his emotions but I knew he must be suffering. Charlie looked at the floor.

'He knelt, and leaning on the chair
He prayed and fell asleep;
And the moth-hour went from the fields,
And stars began to peep.

'They slowly into millions grew,
And leaves shook in the wind;
And God covered the world with shade,
And whispered to mankind.'

Our crowd, Sam, Midge Malone and the men, were rigid with attention. On with Clancy and the doggerel.

'Upon the time of sparrow-chirp
When the moths come once more,
The old priest Peter Gilligan
Stood upright on the floor.

"Mavrone, mavrone! The Man has died
While I slept on the chair;"
He roused his horse out of its sleep
And rode with little care.'

Midge Malone inched forward on his chair – with excitement.

'He rode now as he never rode,
By rocky lane and fen;
The sick man's wife opened the door:
"Father! You came again!"'

Clancy turned over his sheet. He looked around again. He did not want to go too fast for us in case we missed the message.

'"And is the poor man dead?" he cried.
"He died an hour ago."

127

The old priest Peter Gilligan
In grief swayed to and fro.

' "When you were gone, he turned and died
As merry as a bird."
The old priest Peter Gilligan,
He knelt him at that word.'

Without recourse to his paper Clancy now recited the last two
verses. And I thought he directed them at Donat.

' "He who hath made the night of stars
For souls who tire and bleed,
Sent one of his angels down
To help me in my need." '

I wondered, did he write the thing himself. And I saw Midge
Malone draw his index knuckle up his cheek to dam a tear.

' "He who is wrapped in purple robes,
With Planets in His care,
Had pity on the least of things
Asleep upon a chair." '

Clancy bowed. Except for a few of our 'men' – Midge Malone
almost broke one of his hands off the other clapping – the
applause was hypocritically tumultuous. 'Marvellous, marvellous,' the Master of Ceremonies declared, 'now a bit of
community singing; altogether lads, "In the evening by the
moonlight . . . " '

Less and less attention was paid to the singing now as we
got drunker and jokes were told. At twelve o'clock we sang
the national anthem – everybody but myself – and we began
to disperse. Donat was saying goodnight to some of the choir
and moving off with Jack Molyneaux when Clancy sprang
from our group and went over to him. Clancy held out his
ballad sheet. 'Doctor, if you would accept it as a memento of
our lovely night.' With so many witnesses Donat nodded,
accepted. I was going out the yard with Charlie on my way to

get Kentucky Chicken to absorb the booze when Donat called. He was linking Jack Molyneaux. I went back to hear: 'I'm going to see Brock tomorrow night. I'd like you to come with me.'

Charlie and I fingered our snack boxes at a table while the drunken queue filed past. 'He made a prick of it all right,' Charlie summed up, 'Jesus, how he digs 'em up! Yeats must have been on opium.'

'Yeats?'

'Yeats wrote that. There's one for you. The Ballad of Father Peter Bollix. I hope he can hold himself together till I get my fucking medal.'

I was used to lying awake dreaming of Cecelia or plunging straight to sleep from drink. But that night I sat up smoking for hours and all I could see was Clancy and his manic grin. I thought of Cecelia and Donat and myself as part of the same beautiful world, the world of Romance and Style and the Done Thing, a world polluted by the cadaverous clodhopper, Clancy. My long resistance to Donat collapsed. I was pushed into his arms in recoil from Clancy. An oaf had stumbled through the french windows and assassinated the Victorian evening. When I tried to think of Cecelia I saw Clancy's face. My coach was a pumpkin again. The white scarf, cane and bowler were abandoned in an attic cardboard box and nobody heeded Bertie on the road to Mandalay as he mumbled 'spare a copper, guv'nor'. I went to the sink and threw water on my face and shook my head and spat my cigarette spit and Clancy was still there, a spot before the eye. There were only two worlds now, Clancy's versus Donat's/Cecelia's/Mine, and I was ready to settle down and accept my inheritance. I would be at Donat's side when he saw Brock.

Donat did not attend on Sunday morning but he was pacing the yard when I came out after the peal. After a community dinner we were always lucky to get six. We had eight and that was due to the long service men keeping in touch with their medals. Clancy looked drained from his ministry. He rang badly, missed a change, but now he had the ability to recover.

Donat did not mention the quality of the peal. I fell in with him and said: 'Yeats?'

'Yes, Yeats. Even Homer nods.'

Brock was surprised to see us. His fire was not yet lit in the study. He plugged in the electric and the three of us sat around the heat. It did not need to be said: none of us was able for the bottle. Donat took out his fags and Brock and I joined him. Then Donat went straight to the agenda.

'This is not to be construed as a tale out of school. I don't deal with the mind but I want you to understand my opinion is not entirely raw. I think this fellow is going to crack again.'

'I wouldn't be surprised, Cagney. Do you know when I was a seminarian I used to recite Peter Gilligan myself. The innocence of it.'

'Look,' Donat was impatient, 'if it's any help to you I'll go in to church and accept the blasted trinket.'

'No. It wouldn't do any good. Not in the long term.' They were both professional men dealing with the case. There was nothing I could offer. There was this to be said for Clancy: because of him Donat had lost his grandeur. In fact I thought both Donat and Brock were rattled. As a shield, Donat tried: 'How is your own faith?'

'Never better. I still believe in fuck all.' Brock spoke gruffly and revived Donat. 'Your language is quite ridiculous.'

'Tell me, Cagney, if the Holy Father himself came over here with the medals, would you tell him yours would do nicely in the ringing chamber? Or that you send your proxy?'

'When he was here on his tour of the country he held his show out in the racecourse. A quarter of a million with their folding chairs turned out to see him. I watched on television. With their sandwiches and flasks they thronged the place fifteen hours before he was due. Relieving themselves through the night in temporary conveniences. Three race meetings had to be abandoned the course was in such a mess. I tell you if you had posited Christ himself I could deal with it more easily. This Pole is formidable. At first I thought he joined the papacy to see the world. Roncalli going down the road to the prisons was only testing the water compared to this fellow. Now that he has seen the world though, he has the good sense to want to turn back the clock. And I'm with him there I can tell you. It may yet be possible to worship again without some peasant stretching out his paw in the sign of friendship. Friendship, by Jove! And I see he gave it to those Uncle Sam pluralists. And about bloody time, I say.'

'He's flogging a dead horse, Cagney. The women are only in it to see how they look in a mantilla on Sunday morning and John Paul wants them to use the rhythm method. As for the men, look at Reagan, petticoat government, matriarchal society. But fuck that. This Sam Brown, could he help us with Clancy? Has he – dexterity?'

'He's a Christian Brothers' boy.'

'Bony head?'

'I can't help seeing people as a compound of the miserable circumstances of their environment.'

'We're a bit snobbish, Cagney.'

'Of course we are.'

'Look, bring the secretary along tonight. Let's not leave a stone unturned.'

I was deputed to collect Sam. Donat did not even bother turning up for the peal. Sam was an excited man going across the yard, his first time in the lair. He did not know why he was summoned. When he asked me I said: 'I'd prefer if you heard it from Father Brock.' The fact was I did not want to influence Sam one way or another. Brock did not produce the bottle though he did offer Sam a chair.

'Dr Cagney tells me you have a good working relationship with Father Clancy?'

'We all do, Father.'

'Good. Good. Maybe you could do a better job of sorting out this contretemps than I can. You know Dr Cagney does not practise?'

'I was surprised to hear it, Father.'

'Now, this business of medals. Father Clancy has exceeded himself. He presented me with a fait accompli. Personally, I don't mind him going over my head – at least he went through the bishop – and what he's done is of course not in itself harmful. But we're worried. You understand this is confidential?'

'Yes, Father.'

'Father Clancy does not know his place. He's a zealot and a fool can see what that can lead to. What it has led to in Father Clancy's case up the country. Bluntly, I don't want another breakdown on my hands.'

Sam was nodding in agreement, waiting for more.

'So now, Sam, the question is: can you be of help?'

'How can I help, Father?'

'I'll tell you. I was thinking, if it came from you – going back as far as you do in the tower with Donat, and considering how well you work with Father Clancy – if you were to put it to Father Clancy that the doctor is a fierce, stubborn fellow, that Father Clancy is driving him away from the church by his persistence, you have the idea? Tell him the doctor is above authority but that if he's left alone he's far too intelligent to stay out of the Lord's embrace, he'll come back in his own time. Then you can go ahead with your ceremony and give Donat his medal in the belfry. Tim here will stand in for him.'

Brock was saying: Sam, here is a big chance for you. Execute my orders with finesse and there may be a chance you will be offered a bottle next time. Sam thought on the request. He let us see that he was thinking, struggling. Then he said, and I think it took courage on his part: 'I don't understand why Donat can't go into the church if Tim can. Tim is a Protestant, he's not afraid he'll catch a disease going in there . . .'

'I'm not concerned with Dr Cagney. I simply want you to help me with Father Clancy.'

Sam did not have the experience of denying authority. And it was not given to him to understand that he, Sam Brown, Christian Brothers' boy, conveyed authority on those above him. He saw authority majestic, without tributaries. But he had a savage sense of what was right and what was wrong. His voice shook: 'I'm sorry. I can't help you.' I thought now Sam should have done as he was bid. Brock did not push him. 'Very well. Thank you for coming to see me.' We were dismissed. Sam did not say a word as we walked out the yard. There had never been a silence between us. I broke it. 'Sam, why wouldn't you chip in like Brock asked you?'

'I don't see why I should interfere with a priest in the performance of his duty,' he snapped at me. Then he stopped in the middle of the yard. 'To hell with Father Clancy, what about us? What about the tower, for Christ sake? Donat is the one bit of real class we have in the bells, do you think it would be the same for the rest of us without him? For fuck sake, what's the matter with him, people of all religions and none go into each other's churches today. Every night Midge Malone or Paddy or George or someone asks me: What's wrong with Dr Donat. They all think he's off his rocker. And tonight I'm asked to try and stop Father Clancy from trying to get Donat into the church. If you ask me, if anyone needs treatment it's Father Brock.'

CHAPTER 17

The House of Montague

Arthur Skee had two sons who grew up on the premises. I remembered them as agreeable fellows, well-mannered and deferential to Sir Thomas and Dr Cagney, Mr Sloan and the rest of us. Arthur Skee himself had been apprenticed at fourteen years of age to a strict house in Dublin and after the fashion of such self-made men he spared no penny to give his children the opportunities denied himself. But whatever malady had infected our educational system I regret the two young Skees graduated in a faulty condition. On leave from university they attended behind the bar and on my rare visits I thought I detected an air of familiarity about them with which I was far from pleased. I went there with Mr Sloan one Saturday evening after work and having ordered I had to answer a call of nature. It was traditionally a busy hour at Skee's. Just as I came back to the bar after washing my hands I heard: 'Whose are these?' And the reply: 'They're Yendall's.' I was disturbed. But a beloved voice from the past – that of Sir Thomas – consoled me: 'Dash "Sir Thomas", Sloan, when you come out to sing for me call me Tommy in front of the servants. God only knows what they call me in the pantry.' I let it go. But I was more and more in need of the skin of a Sir Thomas as the decade progressed.

As with so many men who work hard on their own Arthur Skee had married late and was well into his sixties when the sons graduated as Bachelors of Commerce and Art respectively. The commerce lad was a teetotaller and the art fellow compensated for his brother's abstinence. Mr Sloan gave me the news at our elevenses.

'Poor Arthur's down, Mr Yendall.'

'What bothers him?'

'Neither of the sons is interested in the business. One of them is content to teach commerce, wouldn't worry if he never saw the inside of a public house for the rest of his life.'

'I dare say that is not the case with the other bucko?'

'No. He told Arthur that he knew which side of the counter he was destined for. He is by way of being a bit of a Bohemian.'

'A bit of a fool more like it. Arthur has built up the finest trade in town.'

'His heart's gone from it now with none of his own to carry on. He's thinking of selling.'

I was not a *habitué* of Arthur Skee's. I had always used the Drapers' Club and only went to Skee's with Mr Sloan on an occasional Saturday or at Christmas. And I had seen many places close, many change hands. But now I was visited with gloom. There is something solid about a long-established licensed vintners. Arthur's was a landmark. People arranged to meet outside Skee's just as outside Montague's was a hallowed place of tryst. I felt an ache at the thought of another name above the door.

'Maybe one of those young fellows will come to his senses.'

'I doubt it, Mr Yendall. I doubt it.'

Mr Sloan was right. I was smitten by the photograph in next weekend's auctioneering pages, which formed a bulky supplement to the paper: we were in a recession of our own making, giving government money to unmarried mothers and deserted wives and professional idlers like Phil Thompson. Yet some good came out of the bad times, I thought, when I saw that Halvey was selling both of his nancy-boy shops. In the slender midweek edition Arthur's was there again but overprinted SOLD PRIOR TO AUCTION. And I was not surprised. Somebody recognized a good thing when he saw one. Bought in trust. But we were not long in suspense. The glad tidings were revealed to me by Butsey Rushe: 'What about Charlie buying Arthur Skee's, Mr Yendall?'

Arthur sent over a note inviting us to a night. I was reluctant to go, thought Arthur should have held on for the auction, found a more salubrious client. The place was filled with ghosts for me. I could not enjoy myself. I thought of Sir Thomas, Dr John Cagney. We had songs but I thought the singing insipid. The young Skees created the most dreadful racket with something called 'Brown Girl In the Rain'. They were the only words I could pick out. Mr Sloan declined. It was a wake, a shadow of the past. Arthur was bountiful. I had one or two more than was good for me and went home almost in a lachrymose state. I mourned for the past, for taste, manners and the gentility that once graced our days. All of a sudden every chip of disappointment I had known in a quarter century was pressed into a cross and flung on my shoulders. I despaired.

I did not have to suffer the sight of Halvey's name over the door. In vulgar neon three-quarters of the sign contained the enigma, THE STATUE OF LIBERTY, and the remaining quarter the brand of a cigarette company. Going into the shop next day I met Simpson at Butsey Rushe's stand. He was full of the excitement of Halvey's purchase. I confess I was unable to contain myself. I inquired the provenance of Halvey's legend.

'It's the proclamation of his policy, Mr Yendall. He has a big sign inside that says THE MANAGEMENT RESERVES THE RIGHT TO SERVE EVERYBODY. Charlie says he's going to serve all the misfortunes barred from other pubs, he'll give them all a chance. I said it before, Mr Yendall, Charlie has a big heart behind it all.'

Butsey Rushe nodded at this quaint interpretation, forcing me to show my teeth bravely, to mask my outrage. As I was about to leave them Simpson said: 'How is the form upstairs, Butsey?'

'We hardly go up there anymore.' I dawdled to listen.

'Oh,' Simpson said.

'Tinkers, riff-raff, it's gone to the dogs. There's language up there now you wouldn't hear from a sailor. Young fellas that should be in jail, barred from every place else.'

'You don't go in there at all?' Simpson persisted.

'Once a week at the most. It's all new faces, they'd take a knife to you, some of 'em. Wally doesn't have the money anyway half the time. Although his brother-in-law is trying to get him into an electronics factory in the industrial estate.'

'And how is Phil?'

'Phil's the same. No fear of him.'

For the price of my newspaper I was up to date. Then I heard Simpson: 'We have five tables in the Club now, Butsey, why don't you get the lads and drop in, it's open to everyone.'

We. I moved off.

I was in the Club that night. They all came in together, Rushe, Thompson, Kirwan and Simpson. Mercifully they sat away from the bay window. As Simpson was putting his name down he waved to me and rejoined his heroes. I watched them watching the young sharks play. When a table came up – second next to the bay window – they went into action in a four-hand. Butsey Rushe gathered the balls and set up the reds without using the triangle while Thompson spotted the colours, all done with the causal manner of old hands. Every one of the four of them looked down the house cues sighting for warp. There then ensued nonsensical *badinage* over what number of points separated the respective partnerships, five, ten or fifteen. They may as well have arrived on penny farthings or heralded their approach with the honk of a Model T.

Simpson broke the balls and came down between the pink and blue off the side cushion to rest behind the colours staffing the baulk line. He was satisfied with the traditional shot. Wally Kirwan went in next, a Woodbine at the corner of his mouth. He nicked the reds and came straight back down the table. Near me I heard one young fellow exclaim to his companion: 'Christ, grinders!'

'Mind your language there, please,' I shushed them and I suspect they sniggered behind their hands. When the game reached the colours after forty minutes' tense play, quite a few of the youngsters waiting for a table had gathered round to pay loose attention to the close battle. Someone whispered:

137

'Who's got the bottle,' but Simpson and company were oblivious to the unsolicited witticisms. They were playing for a quid a corner. Then I heard a familiar voice barking before he had the door closed behind him: 'Who's ahead lads?' Halvey had landed in the Drapers' Club. The game finished with Simpson and Thompson beating Rushe and Kirwan on the black – a tap in for Thompson left on by Kirwan – to a derisive cheer from the onlookers . . .

That was how they came back to the game. They always tried to play on a table furthest from the young lion nexus – nearest the bay window – and they were left to themselves unless the place was overcrowded when they might be encroached upon and I might hear a young voice say: 'Let's watch the geriatrics.' Halvey played his cards cutely. Standing outside his public house, he might still bellow an invitation to 'Come in and let your hair down.' But in the Club he was careful to control his tongue. It was 'Goodnight, Mr Yendall.' He was afraid of being thrown out. What could one do in face of such a chameleon? I seethed in my impotence.

CHAPTER 18

The Society of Bellringers

The January weather brought the usual coughs, flus and bronchitis. There is no better climate to inspire people to try and give up the cigarettes. I was as busy as Donat himself. As was the case with Professor Bedford Rowe in New York, country people had an innocent faith in city specialists. My small ad in the weekend newspaper attracted good custom from the county. I saw most of them on Saturdays. And again as with rural people everywhere they had the grace of the tenth leper, they came back to give thanks. As well as my fees paid in advance, I received 'thank you' mass cards, gift tokens, letters of gratitude from the wives of men no longer coughing and spluttering all over the house and in bed. Less often I had a visit from the cured themselves.

From three o'clock on Saturday afternoon I had eleven appointments and I waded through them with increasing shame – Cecelia had banished the picaresque from my trade. At quarter-past seven when I thought I was done a lady came in bearing an apple tart. She had been in town shopping and remembered me. Her husband was the only one in the family who had not caught something. His eyes were clear again, he could breathe, he was a new man. All thanks to me who had transformed a physical wreck. Under my desk I glanced at my watch fearful that I would miss the bells. I could not interrupt her or hurry her on. She had a litany of so many things he could do now in contrast to his debility before he came to me. I suspected he was coming up trumps in bed. I heard the peal begin just as I was showing her to the door. In the hall were the chairs I had borrowed from an office across the way to improvise a waiting area. Before returning them I needed to go back in and have a cigarette. I was on my second draw when I heard: 'You prick!' It wasn't Charlie. Mulcahy burst in. 'What are you? You're a prick. Jesus, you're smoking. What goes on here?'

Trained under Bedford Rowe, I let him settle in his seat. I didn't speak. Mulcahy did his best but he didn't know how to be angry. It's an American thing, anger. Upset an American and he'll call you motherfucker and hit you or shoot you. Americans have loud voices and shout at each other all the time so they are in a constant state of readiness to fly off the handle. That's one of the reasons why I love them, why I don't have the talent to be a snob.

'You're smoking, Harding. What gives? You prick, answer me, why are you smoking?'

'That's not relevant at the moment. Have you a problem?'

'I looked in here six times this afternoon and every time there's a gang of people waiting. And you're sitting there smoking . . . my wife found out I'm screwing my secretary . . .'

Bedford Rowe's axiom was: whatever bothers them don't let it bother you. But I wasn't prepared for this. I nodded. 'I see.'

'You see, do you? I know what I see. I see you smoking. When you're tempted to have your first fag of the day do something else. Screw your mistress. If she's your secretary. Look at your credentials on the wall. Read your bank statement if it's healthy. You fucking sicko, Harding. I'd never noticed my secretary before. I go into work, take out the fags and then I hear you. Do something else. I have one cigarette out of the packet, fingering it while she's standing by my desk reading out from her telephone pad and I don't hear a word. Watching her tight blouse, tight skirt. My hand goes out, kind of pats her backside, half-encircles her and she doesn't stiffen. Smiles. Then I keep looking at her until she stops smiling, and she's nervous, wondering what the fuck I'm up to. Three minutes later I'd fucked her. Harding, you prick, you god-damned prick.'

140

I stubbed out my cigarette, a deliberate action. Mulcahy watched the forgotten rite. 'Your wife found out?'

'This morning. You know how it is with sex, most of the fun delaying the action. Saturdays became regular, no one else around. I always caught up with my work on Saturday. That's to say I'd come in and read the papers and do the crossword and sit around in casuals. I never worked a Saturday in my life. And never had a secretary in. Your system works, Harding. You prick. I haven't longed for a fag. Every time I'd even think of thinking of them the thought wouldn't even come to my mind. Because my mind was full of fucking a young one. Tight piece of meat. Harding, I never looked at another woman in my life. I'm happily married. I love my wife. She adores me. Did. Until this morning. This morning she goes to the library as usual to get out four books written by women. She only reads women writers. She gets her books and goes to the counter and it turns out her subscription is up. She gets out her purse. Then they notice she's had a book out over two years that she hasn't returned, she's had a hundred reminders. They won't let her take any more books out until she returns the one she's lost. Her mistake was telling them it was at home some place, she'd make a big search. But they won't let her have any books until she finds it. What if she can't find it? She'll have to pay for it. How much is it? Nine-fifty. She takes out her cheque book. No, she must go and search. Or some such fuckology. Jesus. She gets into a war of words with the assistant. Both dig in. She decides to call me to see if I have finished any of my books, then she can go back and get her Fay Weldon on my ticket. I do all my reading in the office – when I'm not fucking my secretary to keep me off fags. She has a key to the front door. She goes up the stairs and hears as she approaches my door: That was wonderful. She looks in the keyhole. Sees me with my shirt on, pulling up my cords. Sees my secretary pulling up her tights. When I go home she retails the whole business of the library, ignorant librarians, etc. And I'm half listening until she gets to the bit about deciding to call to the office. She tells me she was really angry with the bureaucratic bitch at the library. She tells me so matter-of-factly that I'm praying she'll say next that she changed her mind, cooled down and went home. "So I called to the office, Ted, and just as I'm coming towards the door I hear your voice, Ted, saying that was wonderful. And I know in my heart and soul that the words 'that was wonderful' can only refer to one thing. So I look through the keyhole and saw you pulling up your trousers and madame pulling up her tights." Jesus, Harding, she said it as if she's seen me practising putting, but she was cracking up inside . . . do me a favour, tell me why the fuck you're smoking, my mind can't leave that, why you're smoking . . . '

For the first time in my life I felt grotty. I was spiritually in the gutter, but luckily I had the wit to realize that the only way out was up. A man can only do something he doesn't believe in for so long and then he can't do it any more. No matter what the benefits, money, women, fame. I was well off, had Cecelia and a cynic's healthy disrespect for celebrity. But where was the peace? Where was Donat's composure? Where was my style? Up to now I had blundered through life, taking whatever turning the next signpost indicated without ever questioning who authorized the direction. Regardless of how peripherally I was responsible, I could not duck the guilt clinging to me for Mulcahy's unhappiness.

I told him the truth. 'I don't believe in it any more, Mr Mulcahy. I like cigarettes. They compose me. I like sucking in the smoke, exhaling.' The poor fellow nodded, swallowed. I took out my packet. 'I started again with the ones you left here. Have one?'

I took a cigarette for myself and offered the packet. 'Jesus,' he almost whispered and grabbed the packet out of my hand. I gave him the matches. He took a long draw, sat back on the chair, his head raised. He let the smoke out slowly through mouth and nostrils. 'Fuck cancer . . . how did you get into this racket, Harding?'

'When I was at Trinity I was picked to go on a summer debating tour in the States. We came up against Harvard in a

142

televised joust. You know how good they are? We were better. Destroyed them. That This House Supports Nonsense. A Celt's delight, we had some right nuts on our team, I was the soberest speaker of the lot. Yet next day there is a telephone call for me in the hotel. Who could possibly be ringing me? Professor Bedford Rowe. He had a proposition for me, would I call to see him in New York? We were going there anyway. He was impressed by me on the television. For a mad moment I thought I was about to become a film star. So I went to see him. Professor Bedford Rowe, Therapeutic Counsellor, on the glass of his office door. It was the Englishness of my voice that attracted him, that and the fact that I was goodlooking and could bullshit. He was only starting to explain the business to me when a client arrived, a woman, from Hoboken, who had broken out again. This is my colleague, Dr Timothy Harding, he says, and goes straight into telling her that she doesn't drown by falling into the water, that she climbs back out on to dry land, isn't that right, Dr Harding? That's right, Professor, I say. I'm hired at five hundred dollars a week into my hand for a month, the last two weeks of which he's taking a holiday. He has one stipulation: I'm not to fuck any of the clients. He has a booklet of soothing catch-phrases, think you can handle that, young man? I'm young and unsure, I demur, I'll have to think about it, Professor Rowe . . . Call me Maurey. Maurey Taylor . . . after the month he begged me to stay on, offered me a grand a week . . . it's a great country, Mr Mulcahy.'

Mr Mulcahy was smiling, yet shaking his head. 'That's how I end up fucking my secretary?'

'I'm sorry. Please believe me, I'm very sorry. It's out of the book of catch-phrases. If there's anything at all I can do to help, just tell me. If you'd like me to see your wife and explain the situation . . . '

'Thanks. It's okay. I came to you because I had to tell someone. She looked at me when she'd finished. Just looked at me. With the same honesty we've always looked at each other. I don't come from a long line of solicitors. My father was a carpenter. The bank owned me for five years and my wife was

143

with me all the way. I felt such a shit. I didn't know what to say. She was able to stand there looking at me, with a faint, quizzical smile, and I had to turn and walk out of the house, I couldn't bear to see how hurt she was. I drove fourteen miles out the road and stopped by the lake. I put my forehead on the steering wheel and cried like a child . . . '

'I'm so sorry . . . '

'It's okay . . . it's okay. It's going to be all right. I've thought it through. I'll tell her the truth. It won't excuse me but at least it will be the truth, she might understand. You know what? I feel like a millionaire just because you've given me a fag. Because *you've* given it. So it's all right to smoke?'

'If we bear our long illness bravely they might find a cure for it. And as for coughing and spluttering, remember: non-smokers fart.'

'Harding, you're some sicko. I'll see you.'

Walking up the block to the Drapers' Club I was depressed thinking of Mulcahy. I imagined his wife having Cecelia's face. Throwing the leg over at random is the very stuff of sport yet in certain marriages it is not done. Mulcahy's marriage was like that. Mine would be. I was confident Mulcahy would mend his domestic fences. They could move the piano all they liked to hide the cracked plasterwork. They could fool their guests. But Mulcahy and his wife could not fool themselves. They were moderns now. Their Romance was dead.

All the tables were occupied in the Drapers' Club and Charlie and Sam were sitting by the bay window.

'Why weren't you at the bells?' Charlie greeted me. 'Look at Yendall over near the door, he's kicking himself in the bollix for being late and finding me here in his seat. Brock chawed the balls off Clancy. Where were you anyway?'

'I was busy at work. What about Clancy?'

'Work? Jesus, I thought I was good in my day, you've it sewn up, Harding. On no account, Clancy was ordered, on no account was he ever to approach Dr Bollix again. Right, Sam?'

Sam nodded. He was watching the game on number five

144

table, Phil Thompson's crowd. 'It's over now, Tim. Christ, it was awful to look at Father Clancy tonight.'

' . . . don't mind your green, pot the fucking black, Simpson, take a chance for Jesus's sake . . . you should have seen him, Harding, the eyes were popping out of his head even while he was ringing . . . go way, Simpson, I'd have put it in with my tool . . . when he got Dr Cunt in his sights I thought his tongue would stretch across the floor to lick his arse . . . good man, Butsey, step in and clear the table . . . Harding, quick, look at Yendall, look at the face of that, I'm going to come here wearing my medal, ha, up his arse . . . '

We had to go through a rehearsal in midweek. Jack, Midge, Finbar, Sam, Charlie, and my good self standing in for Donat. Brock was there as he would be on the following Sunday. On the big day Clancy would be on the sideline but at rehearsal he stood in for the bishop. My presence did not mean we had lost all hope of Donat changing his mind. Where the men were concerned Donat was a busy doctor of the calibre who could be expected to go through any ceremony without rehearsal. And from our dry run a fool could have gone through with it off the cuff. The bishop would deliver his homily, after which a recipient's name would be read out by Brock; the recipient would leave the pew, walk up, kneel, kiss the ring, rise; Brock would take a medal from an acolyte, hand it to the bishop who would place it around the recipient's neck. There was little episcopal about Clancy, and Brock was impatient with the whole business. But the men – including Charlie – were acquiescent in abiding by directions. Charlie was wearing his usual clobber. Going out of the yard Sam said: 'What are you wearing on Sunday, Charlie?'

'What I'm wearing now.'

'No you're not. Turn up like that and I'll kick you – in your favourite word, the bollix.'

'I'm doing it for the Pope, Sam, not you. I'm hiring a suit from Rent-A-Thread.'

All eleven turned up for the Saturday night peal. Donat picked

Clancy before Charlie but he declined. He was decisive. 'Charlie must ring, in honour of his great day tomorrow.' Hungrily, when I noticed him during the peal, Clancy's fixation caused his lower lip to droop under the wilting grin as he devoured Donat. When we finished he remained sitting, staring pointedly at Donat, braving a last rebuff. I wondered: would Donat bring the light back into Clancy's eyes and the bounce back into Sam Brown? No. He hurried to put on his jacket and crombie. But not before we heard the death rattle:

'The eleventh hour, Doctor,' Clancy pleaded. Donat ran for the trap-door. I rushed after him. I didn't want to have to look at Clancy. Downstairs I said: 'Going to Brock's?'

'Not tonight. I'm due at Jack Molyneaux's for dinner and I must dress. The Molyneaux's are fond of formality. Goodnight, Tim. Represent me with style tomorrow.'

I went to the Drapers' Club, put my name down for a table and waited for Sam and Charlie. Again the place was full. Again Phil Thompson's mob were playing a four-hand. Yendall was in rightful occupation of the bay window. There were so many names down before me that I would not get a table until the second round. Charlie and Sam came in and sat beside me. We watched the games. It was commonplace pool hall chat, Charlie surmising that table three would finish first and the sharks taking it then would clear the balls in fifteen minutes. He was right. They were on the colours on number three and we were next. I was letting Charlie play Sam first, and I would play the winner. Charlie and Sam took off their jackets.

The tenor bell dropped.

The three of us looked at each other, listening, amid the clatter of the snooker balls. We were not so much listening to the tenor falling as listening for an interpretation of why it was being dropped. And by whom. We read each other's minds. Sam put on his jacket again. I led the charge out of the Club. I won the race to the tower and stood panting, waiting for Sam and Charlie. Sam switched on the downstairs lights and took the steps to the ringing chamber three at a time. Behind him, I saw him pause as he pushed up the trapdoor. He turned on the light in the ringing chamber. And then he said: 'Jesus.' I shoved him on ahead of me.

Clancy was hanging from the tenor rope, his black shoes three feet off the floor. His head was cracked open and the neck was, I hoped, mercifully broken. Blood was spattered all over the place. No ringer would have difficulty reconstructing events. Clancy had tied the rope around his neck. He must have tugged the sally with force for the rope to shoot towards the ceiling yanking him up with it, breaking a stay. The tenor bell weighed twenty-four hundredweight and a quarter. Clancy's head would have pounded the ceiling just after his neck broke. The body would have come down again, the feet hitting the floor. Not that it mattered, his head would not have reached the ceiling a second time, his weight dropping the bell. Up and down until the rope's orgasm had stilled. The body would have swayed for a few minutes until it finally steadied. Charlie said: 'Holy fuck.'

I couldn't tell yet how Sam was taking it. He was in shock. I caught his arm and led him to a stool. I said: 'Take it easy, Sam, I'll go and get Brock.' He didn't answer me. I looked at Charlie: 'Hold the fort.' I knocked on Brock's door and pushed it open. He was sitting by the fire, reading, a glass by his side.

'Father Clancy's dead. Where can I use a phone.' He stood up and preceded me to the office. He stood by me as I rang Donat. My report to Donat was explanation enough for Brock. Donat said: 'I'll ring Jack and I'll be there directly. Keep everybody calm.' Neither of us spoke going across the yard. Brock panted to keep up with me. I let him take the stairs first. He could not improve on his usual measured ascent. With only his head clear of the trapdoor he was able to take in the scene, Clancy grinning lopsidedly in death, hands hanging, his head in the noose as though in the stocks, the toes pointing to the floor.

Brock dragged a stool close to the body, stood on it and said an Act of Contrition into the dead ear. Charlie's irreverence was curbed, frozen. He was sitting down, opposite Sam, his eyes flitting from Brock and the body to me to the floor. Brock sat on the same stool as Sam's but a few feet away. I sat down beside Charlie and took out my cigarettes. We waited in silence for Donat.

Donat's steps on the stairs were restrained. He was wearing the dress suit. We all stood up when he came through. I helped him pull the stool over to the body. He said: 'Loosen the noose.' He put his arm round Clancy's backside and lifted the body clear. Closing my eyes to the skull I held the body under the arms, as we laid it on the floor. Donat turned to Brock: 'It would have been swift.' Donat almost put the inanity as a question. He was down on one knee looking at Brock who was nodding in agreement. They remained like that, looking at each other, for half a minute, while the rest of us stood around mesmerized. Professional men must have some code. Brock said: 'Could it have been an accident?'

Donat understood. He stood up, turned to Sam. 'Sam?'

Sam looked at him, puzzled, coming out of a reverie. 'What?'

Donat said: 'Could it have been an accident?'

Sam broke out of his shock, all the bitterness coming through. 'Yes. It's part of the art of ringing that we tie the ropes around our necks and pull the sallies. How do you mean, could it have been an accident?' Donat shrugged at Brock. I could read the gesture. All very well giving the fellow a chance to shake off the carapace of bony-headed conformity, we're going to have to work harder than that, if we're not to have our condescension churlishly spurned. Brock stood up. He walked over to Sam. 'If you insist he hanged himself we can't dispute it. I only ask you to reflect, what good will come of it?'

'It's the truth,' Sam said. He was crying. Charlie's tennis eyes were darting. 'It's the truth,' Brock pressed on, 'that Father Clancy was a sick man and not everybody was aware of it. It's the truth that his mother still lives.' He turned back from Sam. 'Donat, *could* it have been an accident?'

'It was an accident. Tonight he might have said to us, "You go along men, I'll lock up." He stayed behind to look at the photographs as he liked to do so often. Tomorrow would be the culmination of his efforts to honour the tower, he was basking in the achievement.'

Donat stopped down and opened one of Clancy's shoe-laces.

'He tripped ten or twelve steps from the bottom, went headlong –'

'*Shut up*! For God's sake, stop . . . '

Donat sat down beside Brock, took out his cigarettes.

' . . . we all know how he died. You killed him, the two of you . . . that's what happened . . . Jesus, Mary and Joseph . . . '

Even though Charlie and I were flanking him in an arc Sam stood isolated in the middle of the chamber. He was over-wrought from confrontation with a suicide and who could blame him? He wasn't a professional like Donat or Brock. He had no training for the occasion. He walked around the room, running his hand through his hair. He stopped and looked down at the body.

'It would help things along if we knew what we were about, Sam,' Donat persisted trying to embrace him as a confidant. 'That's Jack now.' We could hear a commotion downstairs and Jack Molyneaux ordering: 'Go on up, go on up.' Four of his men stampeded up the stairs before him, two of whom I recognized as his sons from the Professional Club. One of the others carried a rolled sheet. They saluted Donat and stood around waiting for Jack who took an age climbing the stairs. Jack came through and sat down to recover his breath. He sat staring at the body until he was fit to stand up. He clicked his fingers at the one holding the sheet. They had the body down the stairs so quickly that I found myself deprived that we no longer had a body in the middle of the chamber as a focus. Jack's only words to his men were: 'Come back and tidy up here when you're done.' He indicated the blood. When they were gone he let the trapdoor fall.

'Jack, this is Father Brock. Jack Molyneaux.'

They shook hands. 'A sad business,' Jack decided, 'you have no idea how much of it is about. Poor fellow, a novel method, I must say.'

The three of them – Donat, Brock, Jack – might have traded anecdotes. All the ears into which Brock had whispered Acts of Contrition, all the hearts Donat failed to hear beating, and all the hasty bodies Jack oversaw removed in sheets. And before Jack's dinner party the three of them might have crossed the yard to Brock's and entertained themselves with death and whiskey. But there was Charlie . . . and there was Sam . . .

'It has its advantages,' Jack said, 'only you four in the know.' He meant Brock, Donat, Sam and Charlie. I was an appendage of Donat. 'What I always find the bane is this rushing to the police and the newspapers when the body is certain to be found in one of the popular spots of the river within a few days. That type of thing. Just imagine the mess if it had not been Sam and Charlie and Tim here first on the scene. Some hotter head rushing screaming into the street. Sam, you did well, though you look pale. Understandably. Did Donat give you anything?'

'Sam doesn't need anything, Jack.'

'Of course, Donat. You know your business. Father Brock, please accept my sympathy. So sorry to meet you under such circumstances, perhaps another time, Donat's mentioned you often. We like to talk shop. Dinner calls, Donat?'

'Not for me, Jack. We have work to do here. We have ten bells to muffle.'

Jack looked around at the rest of us. Then he summed up like a man talking to himself. 'Yes, yes. Following an accident . . . Donat, perhaps you would get the necessary from Father Brock, for the obituary notice? And I do take it the show must go on, it was surely what he would have wished . . .' That was that. Nobody was going to argue with Jack's venerable authority.

'Goodnight, Father Brock.'

'Goodnight, Mr Molyneaux,' Brock answered, with appreciation.

'Tim,' Donat took over, 'see Jack to the door. And hurry back.'

I went down the stairs with Jack. He had brought his car. Yes, he could manage. When I got back up Donat had taken off his jacket. He began to drop the number nine bell. Sam capitulated: he started to drop the treble. Charlie and I mucked in. In five minutes we had the nine bells dropped and while I was doing my share I thought morbidly of how Clancy had contributed by dropping the tenor. Brock studied us. When we finished Donat dragged the box of mufflers from under the cabinet.

'Is there anything I can do?' Brock offered. Here Donat played his master card. He checked his answer and deferred to Sam. Sam was obliged to answer. 'We're going up to muffle the bells if you want to come.'

Donat led the way with Sam. Brock followed. Charlie and I brought up the box of mufflers. Attaching a muffler to a bell is a simple enough operation. But matching the correct size muffler to the correct bell was time-consuming without the benefit of daylight. Sam, because he had done it on his own so often, knew the bells and the mufflers as well as his own children. He was in command handing them out. He gave one to Brock to fit. We were all in it together. When we had done Sam checked them all, including Donat's. By the time we climbed back down, one of Jack's men had returned with cleaning stuff and went to work on the blood. His presence was a blessing in that it afforded Donat the opportunity to leave on a formal note. 'We'll want to be here early tomorrow to put up the bells and comfort the rest of the men.'

I left with him. Sam and Brock were staying to see Jack's man off and I could trust Charlie to look after them. Out in the yard Donat rested his elbows on the bonnet of his car. 'You bore up well, Tim. As I would have expected. Blast Jack, I'll have to go on there for a while. When I do they'll all gather round me, see Clancy as a bereavement to me. I tell you

Clancy's name will not have been mentioned in such good company before. And I will have to prepare myself for Sam Brown's apology tomorrow.'

He sat in the car. 'You want a lift any place?'

'It's okay, I'll walk.'

'Tim, you won't take it too hard if I deprive you of the honour of being my proxy tomorrow?'

'You're coming?'

'No reason not to now.'

CHAPTER 19

The House of Montague

One did not need inordinate percipience to be unsurprised when the sweepings of the city rallied to mine host Halvey's clarion call. In three months Arthur Skee's was a knocking shop. I saw every variety of scum cross his threshold. Where once Rushe, Kirwan and Thompson would not have walked on the same side of the street they now established themselves as Halvey's flagship cadre of customers. Inevitably the next tent on the horizon was that of the art crowd who had at last reached the promised land. What better catwalk to flaunt one's patches. Simians running in and out from the betting shops, criminals, musicians, so called *characters* – unfortunates who were apt to urinate in public, talk out loud to themselves, lie stretched in alleyways clutching cider bottles – they came from all over to do pilgrimage at the shrine. Once Halvey's new broom had swept away the last trace of Arthur Skee's ethos the ladies of the night realized they now had a roof over their heads and forsook the docks. I saw Kelly the office seeker going in there. On Friday evenings I spotted a few young solicitors approach the place – but as far back as Al Capone you always had an element of the respectable attracted by the low life. And to my absolute stupefaction Mr Sloan continued to bestow his patronage. I put it to him.

'You still go to Arthur's?'

'Old habits die hard, Mr Yendall.'

'The custom's changed, I imagine?'

'Yes. Unrecognizable from the old days. But they don't interfere with one.'

Mr Sloan was blind to so much. He was determined to live his own life in his own way as he had always done and stubbornly excluded falling standards from his consciousness. All very well but impractical. Negligence of the inch lost the foot – the adage was damned prophetic there. The day would come when they would take the body.

Approaching the first Christmas of Halvey's reign Mr Sloan anticipated – correctly – that I would prove obdurate to an invitation to celebrate in a pigsty. He put it thus: 'Where do you think we should go for our Christmas drink, Mr Yendall? Do you feel Arthur's might be too nostalgic?'

'I agree. A clean break I should think.'

'Where would you suggest?'

'Heavens, I have no idea. I propose we enlist one of the assistants.'

We went to a public house a little further up the town. We were well received. The place was clean, a comfortable lounge. Spacious, modern upholstery. I was not at home. It was not the same. Like so much that was not the same. But after a few drinks I mellowed. I kicked myself in the shins. I told myself: grow up. Snap out of it. Get into the spirit. We talked a lot about the past, all of us. Russell was there from the factory, we always let him come along, not least for his fine voice. Mr Sloan brought me up to date on Cecelia. She was settled down now, working with the gentleman publisher, William Blake. That added to my little contentment. The pub began to fill up and we were less dominant in the lounge, a trifle hemmed in. Women drank freely now, the snugs were all coming down. At last Mr Sloan called on Russell to give us 'Moya, My Girl'.

'I will, Mr Sloan, if you'll give us "Absence".'

For a moment I hoped. But no. 'I can't promise that,' Mr Sloan said, and his flicker of sorrow was enough. Russell did not push him. Russell cleared his throat.

I was settling in to enjoy the beautiful words and Russell's pure voice when we were interrupted.

'I'm very sorry, gentlemen, but no singing allowed. Rule of the house.'

We were not a long session group at the best of times. A

154

couple of hours. We chatted and we sang a few songs and went home. That was our humble form. We accepted the authority of the manager – the pub was owned by a building contractor, his diversification accounted for by the catch-all desire for 'cash flow'. What riled me more than anything else was our being reprimanded in front of the world and his wife. In contrast to dear old Arthur Skee's where a cough elicited a 'Silence, please' from Arthur when Russell or anyone else was singing. We had one more round so that we could leave under our own steam. The manager thanked us for coming and invited us to call again. Not for the first time nowadays I walked slowly home. There was so little left that was sacrosanct.

The day came, Mr Dobson flew over from London to inform us personally. We brought him to lunch at the Royal George which was under new ownership and would henceforth be known simply as The George. They were dropping the word 'Royal', from what scabrous motivation I hesitated to conjecture. I mused on the symbolism: the House of Montague was to close, the factory, shop, the lot. Mr Dobson was staying over for a few days for redundancy discussions with the union. He was content that Kelly would be amenable on the workers' behalf. So it proved. At any rate there were no sit-ins or any of that nonsense. Things would have been damned different had I a say in affairs. Mr Dobson gave them the key to Fort Knox. Neither myself nor Mr Sloan came out so handsomely.

We announced a Closing Down Sale. It was an unimaginable mortification. I bore up myself by watching over poor Mr Sloan who was less able to deal with the blow. The man refused to show emotion. 'All good things come to an end, Mr Yendall,' was all he would say, a messenger boy aphorism if ever I heard one. He was in shock. After the first notice appeared in the newspaper I found myself looking at the telephone, thinking of Simpson. I avoided the Drapers' Club. I thought of Simpson searching his soul for the etiquette to deal with our calamity. It was without precedent: how would he react? I dreaded that he might rush in with his sympathies and embarrass the fastidious Mr Sloan. Yet neither would it be in good taste on Simpson's part to stay aloof and ignore the closure. Three days passed. I speculated that this inaction proclaimed indifference. But I knew that would not be Simpson's form. I was not that poor a judge of character. On the morning of the fourth day one of his assistants arrived and handed me a note addressed to Mr Sloan, Esquire. Mr Sloan read the note in my office and then handed it to me without comment. He looked out my window at the street while I read:

' . . . with deep sadness and sincere regret that I have received the news of Montague's imminent closure. I am ever mindful of and grateful for the start in life afforded me by your good self in your capacity as the very personification of the House of Montague.

I would esteem it a signal honour to be allowed to call on you to offer my formal commiseration and, dare I be so bold, perhaps for old times' sake, share a last tea and biscuit on the premises . . . '

I loathed Simpson then. Never before had I felt such anger, such resentment towards a fellow being. Mr Sloan looked out of the window. I let the note slip from my fingers on to my desk. What I had bottled up by keeping a weather-eye on Mr Sloan's stoicism burst forth now. 'Impudence,' I spat. And then I just waited for Mr Sloan to conquer the nausea he needs must have been suffering. At length Mr Sloan coughed into his fist, turned round and simply pointed at my stationery. 'Dear Simpson,' he dictated as I uncapped my pen, 'Dear Simpson, Thank you so much for your concern. Please feel free to call at any time. Yours, etc. G.H. Sloan. Sign it per pro.' Without another word he walked out of my office. This was Friday morning. Simpson had the good grace to spare us a visit on Saturday. As I expected he came on Monday morning.

'Let me take your hat, Simpson,' Mr Sloan entertained

abruptly while I spooned the tea into the pot. He took Simpson's coat and scarf. 'Kettle almost boiled, Mr Yendall? Sit here, Simpson, make yourself comfortable.'

'Thank you,' Simpson said, gravely. He was himself. I was less sure about Mr Sloan.

'No need to ask how you're faring, Simpson,' Mr Sloan battled on, 'that shopping centre taking off, is it?'

Simpson lied: 'Not quite yet, Mr Sloan, but once the parking advantages are recognized . . . '

'Ah, here we are. Good fellow, Mr Yendall. Never felt the need of a car myself. Sugar? Best help yourself, Simpson. Take a biscuit.'

Mr Sloan bit a plain biscuit and sipped his tea. He chewed with his mouth closed in the refined manner. Simpson sat in my chair. Mr Sloan stared out the window over Simpson's head. I realized it fell to me now to search for a platitude but Simpson suddenly took off: 'Was it,' Simpson fondled the word, 'sudden? Or did you know for some time, Mr Sloan?' I thought for a moment that Mr Sloan had not heard the question. But after silent consideration he let loose with zest: 'I imagine the dogs in the streets knew before we did.' He stood up, walked away from his cup of tea, turned his back on us, looked out the window on to the street. I could see his jaw ripple. I was helpless. I knew enough to stay silent. But Simpson did not enjoy my privileged position. He had come with good intentions and was obliged to persevere. He stumbled on, now talking to Mr Sloan's ramrod back. 'Mr Sloan, that's if I'm not intruding, I'm sure they've seen to it that you're coming out, that after all the years I mean, I presume that you're well looked after, in the outcome, that there isn't any question of not receiving your due . . . '

I glared at Simpson to shut up but I don't think he was aware that I was in the room – my own office. Mr Sloan turned round slowly. He sat on and gripped the sill with both hands. In his travail he armed himself with the sinew of war peculiar to his age and station – controlled hysteria.

'A pittance, Simpson. On a par with the pittance I've had

here all my life. It is long since that I discovered lorry drivers are more deservingly remunerated.'

How would we rid ourselves of Simpson now? Mr Sloan looked down at the floor, bravely prepared to acknowledge whatever further condolences Simpson brought with him.

'If I may say so, Mr Sloan, I consider that to be an absolute disgrace.'

'Well, Simpson,' I recognized the hollow cheer, 'you were wise in your time. I didn't have energy in that direction myself. But it has been good of you to drop in. Learn from the experience, Simpson, mind your business. No profit sitting here is there? Must get back out myself. They paw everything now . . . ' I thought: good on you, Mr Sloan, hasn't been such an ordeal after all. But then: 'Mr Sloan, I was wondering, if you wouldn't think I'm taking a liberty . . . '

'What is it, Simpson?'

'On Saturdays. I'm usually in the shopping centre on Saturdays and Mr Gabrielides is most dependable . . . ' I wanted to jump on Simpson to stop him. ' . . . this is only if you might be interested or felt you had the time . . . ' I let my eyes fall on my saucer. ' . . . the fact is, Mr Sloan, it's next to impossible to get somebody these days, I mean somebody who knows the business and can act in any situation and at the same time has the right presence . . . what if you'll pardon me suggesting is that if you could spare me a Saturday, if otherwise you'd be at a loose end, it would mean so much to me, we could come to an arrangement that would be mutually . . . '

'I'm afraid not, Simpson.' I looked up. By a miracle Mr Sloan was screne. He was smiling at Simpson.

'I thought . . . '

'No. I'm sorry to be so direct, Simpson. But you see, I've had time to think my position through. This is a part of my life I have done with.' He waved his hand to encircle the House of Montague. 'I have places to see, things to do, I haven't had the opportunity up to now. As for – despite the – shall we say their munificence, despite that, I've been a reasonably prudent fellow and no, Simpson, I am sorry. But you will find somebody. Hold out and you'll get what you're looking for, you'll see.'

We had surely come through. And now that we were safe I saw the good in Simpson. He had come to offer Mr Sloan the run of one of his shops. He looked relieved. Mr Sloan would be bad for his business. I say that with pride in Mr Sloan. Mr Sloan would not have had a way with the modern shopper – for that Mr Sloan deserved honours. Mr Sloan had not moved a second in forty years. But if Mr Sloan were to bankrupt him in one of his old-fashioned seconds Simpson yet had an obligation, moral, binding. He had done his duty. He could relax now. Mr Sloan had a flourish: 'And by the way, Simpson, thank you. Thank you indeed. I'm flattered you should think of me. But as I say, that chapter is closed.'

And so too was Simpson's visit terminated as Mr Sloan straightened and gave Simpson his hand. We both walked Simpson to the main door. 'Sharp,' Mr Sloan said, sniffing the weather. I watched Simpson go up the street. When I turned round Mr Sloan had his hands clasped behind his back in the old authoritative way. His jaw was working and he was crying. I have never seen a sight as sad in all my life.

CHAPTER 20

The Society of Bellringers

I went to the tower half an hour early on Sunday morning but even before I got there I heard the muffled bells being put up. Charlie and Sam were there before me. I joined in. Donat came just in time to put up the last bell. We had twenty minutes before the peal. Donat, Sam and I all went for our cigarettes. It was an awkward moment. Donat could not be fazed and Charlie was a survivor. It was awkward for Sam. How had he got through the night? He was short odds to break the silence and he did it quickly.

'I didn't mean what I said last night, Donat. It was the shock.'

Donat slackened his fist and punched Sam tangentially on the shoulder. Sam went on: 'I'll have to see Father Brock, I owe him an apology too.'

'You'll do no such thing. I'll talk to Brock. He'll understand.'

Then came the first footsteps. They could only have been Jack Molyneaux's. He was being honoured. That might have – but not necessarily – accounted for his presence. I thought he was there to lend authority to the fiction. The first of the non-conspirators, Midge Malone, came next. 'Muffled?' he asked, 'for who?'

Whoever answered him would have to carry on with the explanation. We all looked at Sam. 'Midge, sit down. We have bad news. Father Clancy died last night,' Sam began.

'Good God . . . '

'A tragedy, Midge,' Jack Molyneaux put his hand on Midge's shoulder, 'tripped ten or twelve steps from the bottom . . . '

160

'Good God!'

'He died instantly.' Donat.

'His shoe-lace was open,' Charlie put in.

'We're going ahead with the presentation,' Sam promised, and inspired Midge to the predictable unfounded assumption: 'It's what he would have wanted.' More steps on the stairs, Paddy and George. When the last man came through, Finbar, it was Midge who greeted him: 'Father Clancy's dead. He fell down the stairs and cracked his skull.'

'Tim,' Donat called. I was about to take off my jacket. 'Jack, we'll ring on eight, all those to be honoured.' Curiously, I had speculated earlier that Donat might for once include Charlie in the light of Charlie's compliance and I rejected the idea as being unDonat. Even this eight to be honoured lark was unDonat. Everything about him that morning was unDonat. As I sat out the peal I noticed two groups in the tower – those who knew the truth and those who didn't. They stood out from each other as though painted black and painted white. I was at home with the innocents. I thought them real. Their faces were suitably grieved. Some of them had also an eye on the medal. That was natural. When I looked at any one of them I was at ease and when I flicked on to one of us – even Sam – I saw a mask. I thought of Donat playfully absolving Sam with that uncharacteristic punch to the shoulder. He felt guilty.

We had no time for talk after the peal but going down the stairs the men muttered to each other. 'When I heard the bells going up I thought that was odd, but when I realized they were muffled . . .'

The ceremony neither took from nor added to my irreverence for the religious way of life, and I saw in the prelate no more an imposing figure than I had ever seen in Brock or Clancy or anyone else dressed differently to the layman. Yet I could not but be impressed by the men embodied by Charlie in his Rent-A-Thread suit. It struck me that the man was not born who could turn away from praise. We are feeble in our need of

161

human respect. A riband to stick on our Rent-A-Thread coat. I longed to be up there with them.

After mass the men were all going to the nearest pub. Donat held me back: 'Brock's invited me to his den. I want you to come. I'll have to give him a lead,' Donat explained, 'enlist his opinion of the East African situation. Anything that remains to be said about the Clancy business belongs to the realm of gossip.'

We had lingered in the yard for no more than fifteen minutes while people came up to congratulate Donat and the men. Now we intruded on Brock busy writing letters. Or, as I deduced, being seen to be busy writing letters.

'Ah, Donat,' Brock greeted us. Not 'Cagney'. 'And Tim. Sit yourselves down, I'll be just a second.' He wrote an address, licked the envelope, affixed a stamp. He took the bottle from the bureau and placed it with only two glasses on the table.

'Help yourselves.' We did, Donat acting as mother. Donat did not comment on the missing third glass – the missing second bottle. He raised his own glass to me and said: 'Good luck.' He sat back, at ease.

'As you may notice, I'm not joining you,' Brock told us. Donat held some of the whiskey in his mouth before swallowing. He nodded at Brock as he let the whiskey down his throat.

'My masturbating days are over,' Brock went on, 'and I have no more use for that other word. So what do you think of that?'

'One suspects one is being invited to congratulate you.'

'It didn't affect you at all, Donat, did it?'

'I was always interested in how you were lost, not how you were found.' Donat finished his drink and stood up.

'You're going?'

'I never drink alone. Should you ever feel the need again, shout. It has been enjoyable.'

Brock left it at that. I trailed out after Donat. I certainly had no business there on my own. Donat fumed. 'Such bad taste, I must say. Affected by dramatic circumstances, by Jove. His own business is his own business but how crude of him to

162

question my reaction. Does he not understand I would not dream of ever seeing myself as others see me. Not a glimpse.'

'Donat, how do you see yourself?'

'I see myself as my father's son at all times but now we are beginning to die out. Jack Molyneaux is at the tip-head. We're outnumbered at the Professional Club, indeed we were out-numbered the day we let one who was not our own in. The country is run by rabble, society infested with it.'

'That's snobbery.'

'You want your egalitarian arse tanned, young man. Brock has been such a disappointment. It won't be long now, Tim, and I'll be alone. The last . . . snobbery? You can be damn sure it's snobbery.'

Clancy was brought to the church on Monday night and entombed in the crypt under the main altar on Tuesday morning. We rang a muffled peal prior to the obsequies. Charlie got full value for his Rent-A-Thread fawn suit. Sam cursed. 'It's a funeral, Charlie, for Christ's sake, not a wed-ding.' That was the only note of normality. 'What do you want me to do, die the fucking thing black?' During the funeral rites and solemnities the only people comfortable in their bereavement were the ringers who thought Clancy tripped over a shoe-lace. I did not want to look at any of the rest of us. I did not want to look at myself. I concentrated on my beloved Cecelia. Our romance was real. The burial, shaking hands with Clancy's mother, was all a mockery. Better – or worse – was to come. In the weekend issue of the newspaper I read:

Late Father Willie Clancy

Our dear friend Father Willie slipped away from us recently, but did so gently and quietly albeit unexpectedly. 'It was the way he would have wished it himself' someone remarked at his funeral, and indeed it was.

Father Willie had that sense of individuality and tranquil temperament which people who aspire towards fame and fortune rarely acquire. He was very much his own man, gifted with a singular mode of expression, tinged with a modicum of eccentricity which endeared him to his many friends in the community.

Though he did not fortify himself with the odd libation, being a lifetime abstainer, when in the company of those of us who do succumb to the occasional dram Father Willie was never a wet blanket. On the contrary, Father Willie could change gear upwards a notch or two with the best of us and on these occasions his innate sense of humour manifested itself.

Those of us who knew him in the short time he minis-tered at the tower will remember him in many ways, notably his sense of pace. He never got ruffled or excited. His patience and sincerity will long be remembered.

> When mine hour has come
> Let no teardrops fall
> And no darkness hover
> Round me where I lie.
> Let the vastness call
> One who was its lover,
> Let me breathe the sky.
>   A.E.

The light of Heaven to his soul.
                          J.M.

It was one of Jack Molyneaux's fill-in-the-blanks obituaries.

The days crawled by until I would see Cecelia again. In a premeditated putsch to decontaminate myself of the doleful influence that would linger for some time in the tower, I set out to distract myself by practising for a couple of hours at night in the Drapers' Club against the top talent, afterwards drinking heavily in Charlie's salon of democracy. And I received a boost to my self-respect at Fagender's. He was a client who only thought he wanted to give up the cigarettes. Up to now when I had a ditherer I washed my hands. So many are half-hearted or pushed into it by nagging relations. 'You want to smoke, that's your business,' I told them, 'you want to stop, that's my business.' But now I shook off the passive.

Mr Dunmore was a successful businessman. I knew of him without ever meeting him from reading the newspaper. He had his own office equipment outfit, was active in the Chamber of Commerce, and was president-elect of the Rotary Club. He was a golfer and also gregarious in the cultural life of the city in that his photograph turned up often at first nights of plays and art exhibitions. Just recently, wearing his Rotarian hat, he had received much praise in the papers – in the letters column and the editorials – for his sub-committee's promotion of the resurrection of grammar in the primary schools. Thanks to Mr Dermot Dunmore, and editorial eulogized, fewer people would grow up boasting of 'what we done'.

'Well, young man,' Mr Dunmore greeted me with a smile, waving his cigarette, 'is this my last?' I shook hands with him.

'Take a seat, Mr Dunmore.'

'Dermot. Call me Dermot. I've heard a lot about you, whatever it is you do, you must do it well.'

'Thank you. I don't do that much, Dermot. People come to me who want to stop smoking. I let them.'

'You're too modest, Tim. I was with two of the cured last night. In the golf club. They've been trying to wear me down for over a year. Lifelong smokers, both of them. And they don't miss it. I can tell. They don't miss it. They're still civilized. Except one of them has a notice in his car forbidding smoking. I don't travel with him anymore.'

'He didn't get the idea of the notice here,' I said.

'I'm glad to hear it. Well, young man, what can you do for me?'

'Do you want to give them up?'

'To be honest with you: no. But it's addictive and I wouldn't be the first addict not to be able to see clearly. I've been involved through Rotary in various projects helping AA and GA. And I've seen so many give them up without a bother.

They're still good company – except for the bloody notices.'

'How many do you smoke?'

'Forty. I know about your fees, that's okay by me. The fee is reasonable if you succeed.'

'Succeed in what?'

'Making me stop.'

'I don't want to make you stop.'

'That's your business, isn't it? At least I was given to understand . . . '

'Not if you don't want to, Dermot. I'd much prefer to help you be comfortable with the habit.'

'Do that, young man, and I'll buy you a drink.'

'All right. You don't want to give them up to save money?'

'Check.'

'Health?'

'My doc says I'm sound. But he says I should give up the cigarettes. He smokes himself. He'd love to give them up. The health's fine. But I have the cough.'

'Dermot, what the hell is wrong with a cough? Isn't that how we can tell whether a sermon is good or bad? A speaker going on too long? You come across that in Rotary. If people lose the art of coughing the greatest bores and windbags will hog the pulpits and the rostrums.'

He chuckled. 'Very good.'

'Rotary. Very responsible people. Good image. Good example. Can't be going around with a fag in the mouth. People waving their hands when you light up over the coffee. They say, Dermot, when are you going to cop yourself on. Statistics prove . . . anti-social. In America now . . . day will come when it will be banned from every pubic place and proper order . . .' He showed he was enjoying me. I was enjoying myself. ' . . . can climb the top of that hill now without noticing it . . . eyes are clear in the morning . . . Dermot, fuck them all, as my friend Charlie Halvey says, a cigarette is the most relaxing experience in life, Kipling . . . '

' " . . . a woman is only a woman but a good cigar is a smoke . . . " '

166

'There you have it. What about a cigarette after a swim?'

'Nothing like it, old son. Heaven.'

We savoured the fag after the swim. 'We might die, Dermot but at least we will have lived.'

'Enough said. You've sold me, young man.' He took out his cheque book.

'Hold on,' I protested.

'They're all out there having paid you a month's smoking and they can't smoke. I pay you a month's smoking and I can smoke. I'm on a winner. Thank you, young man. I've been listening to lunatics.'

CHAPTER 21

The House of Montague

'*Mirabile dictu*'. My early retirement agreed with me. My eyes were lifted from the paperwork. House decoration, once a chore, I now thought a pleasant occupation. I soon had the garden in tip-top shape. Without the burden of the House of Montague no weed could grow behind my back. I was only uncomfortable in the early days after the closure when I was lumped with Simpson in the Club. Once I survived the first wave of humiliation of course I went back to the Drapers'. I was not going to skulk. With Halvey ensconced it was my duty to protect what was left of our institution. Fellows like that worm their way into position, and while you're tying your shoe-lace they're suddenly running for president. Not so fanciful, given that Kelly was elected on the slogan 'Fearless and Unafraid – The Man Who Stuck To His Manifesto'. God knows the country deserves him. He would temper the wind for the shorn lamb. Abortion, contraception, divorce for dole fiddlers who hadn't two brass farthings to rub together. A galling aside, Kelly's union rented space in our old factory and there he held his clinics, bedraggled queues stretching round the corner, Kelly the friend of the bottom dog, relieving them of the fear of God, assuaging their hunger with condoms, family planning and access to cervical smear tests. There was nothing anymore that was not mentionable or at least there was always somebody who would mention anything – Kelly. For a vote. Men died for the franchise only to turn in their graves and see it exercised capriciously. Kelly was not a month counting his expenses when he called for a coalition of the left. He proposed to hold 'talks' with the Labour Party. Under the umbrella of a united front against capitalism, he invited the independents to forsake the political luxury of the prima donna and join him.

Halvey continued to harass me when I walked into town. 'Hey, Yendall, what about taking a cruise?'

In the Club Simpson was uneasy with me to the point where he claimed to envy my leisure, when I knew he was damned glad to have made the break and avoided my fate. He was solicitous as to an invalid, more assiduous than ever in his servility. He pitied me. He entrusted me with his regards for Mr Sloan. I assured him he had no need to worry about Mr Sloan. I fear I lied. Mr Sloan had taken to walking the streets, gloves, scarf, crombie, bowler. He watched builders at work, he had a lone coffee, he was disinterested at the scenes of car crashes. Any time I met him I was saddened by his manic jauntiness. But I knew he was lost. A wretched figure. He was fading on his feet from misery. All that he had was taken away from him. He had no authority, no position now. He could not walk the streets all day. He would have to go home, sit in a chair and be assailed by his thoughts. He did not go abroad that first summer. He went to Kilkee. I saw him sitting on the promenade wall eating periwinkles, his back to the sun. My wife and I stopped to talk to him. He was effusive in his celebration of the leisure at our disposal. My wife agreed he was putting up a front. How could he be content walking the streets reading the signs? Rich Bitch, The Edge, Ulysses, Rent-A-Thread, Swamp (where Woolworths once stood), Chapps, Clobber'n'Fodder and Deja-Vu – once the House of Montague. Could Mr Sloan look up from the pavement and not feel a pang?

I almost lost my temper with Simpson in the Club. My retirement opened my eyes to a lot that I should perhaps have noticed before. For instance the Club itself and the game. The modern young man did not fade into the Drapers' Club as Simpson had used to, nipping up to the hall over the shop in the old days. No. Your lad from the Comprehensive or Third Level or electronics factory breezed confidently up to the door, wearing his waistcoat with his chalk in the pocket, carrying his own cue under the arm, staff officer fashion. He was coiffed and body freshened. He had more 'disposable' income than most. I took chilly note of his efficiency. I arrived one night with Simpson in time to see Phil Thompson take on a young shark. The geriatrics' table – so christened by the younger blackguards – had come up while Thompson was waiting for his generation and the shark had suggested a game. As Simpson and I took our seats Thompson was setting up the balls. The shark flicked the score marker. He said: 'Take forty.' And then: 'Have something on it?' Simpson nudged me, a familiarity from which I shrank. He was trying to tell me that Thompson would teach the young fellow manners. 'A quid?' Thompson ventured. The shark rolled his eyes as though a pound was a shirt button. He then proceeded to destroy Thompson. Half-way through the game he shouted down to a confrère: 'Book number three next, I want that tenner back.'

Simpson sat on with me after the game. He harked back: 'Forty points, Mr Yendall. Nobody in the world in the old days could have gone into Montague's and given Phil Thompson forty points.'

I said: 'The game has changed.'

'Not that much, Mr Yendall. Phil should have been able to hit and run, a black or a blue on to his forty points and then kick for touch.'

'He tried, Simpson.' I was already impatient.

Simpson shook his head. 'He overdid it. There were pots there tonight that he hasn't the temperament or the ability to go for anymore. Shots I could have made myself.'

'It isn't as easy on the table as it is on the sideline, Simpson.'

'Mr Yendall, he didn't take the simple chances that would have built on his lead. He let the other chap chip away. Then he went reckless to regain ground and let himself open.'

'Just so, Simpson. But the young lad made two breaks over fifty. I don't see what Thompson could have done about that.'

'He should have played better safety, Mr Yendall. And scored more at the right time.'

He was emphatic. I was disinclined to argue against his sudden self-appointed authority. Indeed it was the first time I had known him not to touch his cap to my opinion.

The Society of Bellringers attached to the Redemptorist church has served the community in its own way without ever impinging on my humble bailiwick of instruction. Good luck to the Redemptorists – and for that matter the Christian Brothers – but their constituency thrives on a less subtle brand of indoctrination than I am comfortable with at the Jesuits. I accept the mob's hunger for rough theology and doff my hat to those who answer the call to provide the beads of solace to the lower orders. But what has baffled me as long as I can remember is Dr John Cagney's decision to sacrifice Donat to the leper colony of rope pullers – as they needs must be drawn from the area for whom they peal and represented as they are by Halvey, the campanologist. True, Jack Molyneaux, the undertaker, was also a member of the tower, but perhaps there must have been a different element there in his early days. Then again in Molyneaux's profession one is obliged to act the democrat more than one would wish – a coffin is indiscriminate in its choice of corpse. Halvey, young Donat and Jack Molyneaux were the only ringers I had heard of – one could only surmise in what circles the rest of them mixed. So I was shocked that from out of that belfry came a climactic thunderbolt in the person of Tim Harding.

Harding – I now know – was a couple of years younger than Cecelia Sloan and was brought to the tower as a protégé of Donat Cagney. He and another ringer, Brown, began to frequent the Drapers' Club – as a guest of Halvey. I am as good a judge of appearances as the next man and Harding did not quite seem to me to have the colour of a Halvey disciple, viz., a Wank Mitchell or a Johnny Skaw. Indeed Brown too looked respectable. Yet apart from the Drapers' Club I had also seen both of them patronize the Statue of Liberty as regulars. I thought of Sir Thomas's funeral: it may have been that Halvey's belief that he could mix with kings and princes and still have the common touch was so strong that he communicated his credo to his victims. I questioned Simpson.

'Tell me, Simpson. Those two with Halvey . . . '

'They're in the bells with him, Mr Yendall.'

' . . . just so. But don't they seem to you a cut above him – not that that would take much effort.'

Simpson smiled at me. 'Charlie has depths, Mr Yendall, that not many people know of.'

'Depths, Simpson, yes. I agree with you there.'

The draw for our Annual Handicap always ensures a full house. Simpson alone of his ilk entered. He pleaded with them to put down their names. Sitting in the bay window I listened to him. He offered to stake them to the fiver a head entrance fee. No. The money was no deterrent to a life-long newsboy. Wally Kirwan was self-sufficient again thanks to his job in the electronics factory. Phil Thompson showed his age and his philosophical vocabulary: 'No point pissin' against the breeze, is there?' They accepted that they were simply not good enough to put up a show. Not so Halvey and his friends from the tower. Harding was as good as any of the young fellows I had seen playing. Snooker to Halvey was just another aspect of his jack-of-all-trades, follow-the-band motley: he would as quickly have put his name down for bowls. And not Simpson. He joked to me later: 'Mr Yendall, I believe the boys have lost their – their bottle, Mr Yendall.' I did not find that funny. There is no more need to lower oneself in speech than there is to grow sideburns. Simpson thought he was amusing, thought his were the only antennae alert to the music of the young. I don't care for the pathetic accommodation of a language's massacre.

A few days before the draw for our handicap Halvey hit the headlines again. His photograph appeared in the paper, not as a singing cowboy, not as a French tonsorial artist, and not in his capacity as mine host of the knocking shop. No. This time Halvey was the recipient of a medal from the Pope. One pinched oneself. That pontiffs and potentates live lives remote from the rest of us has long gone unchallenged, yet how a pope through his hierarchy could convey such an honour on Halvey makes one wonder if there is any institution uninfected with ineptitude. Halvey's medal was for his long service of thirty years ringing bells. Did nobody think of giving him a medal for his thirty years standing on the pavement shouting obscenities? Or of giving me or Mr Sloan a medal for having to listen to him? And, I wonderd, would His Holiness have been gratified to learn through the ecclesiastical grapevine that Halvey – before the novelty wore off – took to wearing his medal while he wielded his cue against his fellow ringer, Harding, addressing him – out of his depths – with the affectionate: 'You black English Protestant, you've fuckall chance tonight against me medal. Rome Rules okay.' As I have long observed: as we sow, so shall we reap.

When the handicap card went up everybody gathered round and Simpson squinted through his reading glasses to see that he was given seventy points against a scratchman: T. Harding. Simpson could not control himself. He turned gleefully to Phil Thompson: 'Sorry now you didn't enter?' He came down the hall to join me in the bay window. 'Seventy points, Mr Yendall.'

'You feel the committee has been liberal with you, Simpson? I've watched Harding. He has style.'

'Mr Yendall, if I don't win the handicap with seventy points in every game all the way through then all I can say is I don't deserve to be called a snooker player. Charlie Halvey only got forty. He might give me ten, Mr Yendall. He could never give me thirty.'

For a few nights I abandoned the bay window and sat in the middle of the hall with an umpire's eye on the form of this Harding and of course on Simpson. Simpson slipped away from his empire early those evenings and played as many as five games a night. It did seem to me that Simpson was generously treated. Certainly had I been still on the handicap committee I would not have voted him seventy points. Perhaps thirty-five. But the committee was a youthful one, cognizant of the general form and perhaps had lumped the elders generally as supernumerary. Simpson was probably as good as he had ever been as a youngster. His style was rooted in Safety, the rust on which is comparatively easy to shake off. He played all games with a competitive intensity that I thought unseemly in a man of his age. That was also his style — he did not like to lose. But he was stiff in comparison with Harding who, if self-effacing in demeanour, was colourful and flamboyant in play. I would hear him declare in the middle of a break: 'Attacking football, Charlie, shove your medal.' There was no comparison between Harding and Simpson. Yet I thought: seventy points. And Simpson must have thought the same. He grew cockier every night. To my shame I looked forward to him getting his come-uppance.

It was the first game of the handicap and drew a huge crowd. All Simpson's old pals were there as excited as Simpson himself. Butsey Rushe, Wally Kirwan, Phil Thompson, Halvey. I wondered what camp Halvey followed. Dr Donat Cagney came presumably in support of Harding. It was ironic to think of Halvey and the doctor in the same corner. The other fellow, Brown, was there. Kelly, the politician, turned up and I winced to watch half the hall queueing up to shake his hand. The crowded hall combined to provide the right atmosphere for a handicap game. Before I left the bay window to get a suitable vantage point Simpson came up to me. 'Wish me luck, Mr Yendall.'

I said: 'Got your shoulder flash?'

He patted the pocket of his waistcoat. 'Mr Yendall, that's more important than the cue.' And he smiled. And I was struck then on the spot and changed from a churl to a partisan on his behalf. I did not want to remember how the night before I wished defeat on him. Dammit, in the realm of snooker we had soldiered together. I had no allegiance to the other fellow — I pressed Simpson's arm: 'Good luck, Simpson.' His decision to enter was vindicated it seemed when bets were struck. I heard clearly — as Simpson must have and been boosted by — Halvey's gauntlet: 'Tenner he beats you, Tim.' Harding put his thumb up in acknowledgement. All round me

I saw sums of money produced and entrusted to a third party. Gambling is forbidden by the rules of the Club. But what could we do – unless we wanted the lavatories clogged. Wally Kirwan acted as referee and some young lad did marker. Butsey Rushe, Phil Thompson and Halvey sat together close to the middle table where the game was being played. Dr Cagney sat on the other side, alone, aloof. Kelly had a prominent seat as befits such types. I moved a dozen yards up the seat from the bay window. They were playing best of three. Simpson divested for the occasion. He was in waistcoat even if it was the emblem of his era and not the topping off ceremony job that was the badge of respectability of the new crowd. Harding rolled up his sleeves and loosened his tie. I could not place him: he was not of the younger crowd, yet he was a far cry from the era represented by Simpson.

Simpson broke the balls. His white came back down the table in the orthodox fashion and rested up against the green ball in a Chinese snooker. Only one red had become detached from the bunch and that red was occluded by the blue still on its spot. The shot spoke for itself: what idiot had given seventy points to such an old hand? Simpson stood back from the table, pleased with himself. Harding walked round the table, studying angles, looking for the best approached shot, I calculated. His concentration was attended by a hush apart from the exhalation of cigarette smoke. Finally Harding disdained the oblique. I remembered his 'attacking football' philosophy. He raised his bridge and almost stood on his toes. He swerved the white round the blue, potted the red and kissed the black lightly, still in position.

The room applauded as I felt obliged to do myself. Granted there must have been an element of luck in Harding's actually potting the red but it was still a great shot. I glanced at Simpson. I saw him swallow. Harding swaggered down to pot the black and screwed into the bunch to release two more reds. Simpson stood by, helpless. I noticed he scratched his neck à la the nonchalant fashion, but I caught him as his thumb and forefinger slipped behind the knot in his tie to undo his collar button. I was on the road a long time. I knew the game. Harding put together a break of sixty-seven during which Simpson coughed into his fist, fingered the bridge of his nose between the eyes, licked his lips, sat on the edge of a seat, stood up again, looked at the floor, stroked his chin, folded, unfolded his arms. Harding's break was top stuff, almost faultless, only cut short by a difficult pink that wobbled. He received a well-deserved ovation, lacking only in warmth to the extent that we would not now have a contest. He had left a red on and it was Simpson's turn to step in. The red was an easy shot as was a black after it, whatever about going on from there. But then no one of Simpson's era ever thought beyond such accumulation. He managed the red but when he lined up behind the black it was straight. He attempted to roll it in but did not hit it full in the face. The black stayed up. Harding charged in and scored twenty-nine. I did not watch Simpson while Harding was scoring. I couldn't. He was in pain. Simpson did not pot another ball. On his next shot he went in off and no excuse for it either – he didn't cannon off another ball – just came back down the table in a safety shot and went into the right-hand baulk pocket. On the colours, from a handicap of seventy, Simpson needed a snooker. Harding potted the yellow, green and brown. The blue was safe. Harding hit it a box around the table in the hope of a fluke but it did not go near a pocket. He then looked over at Simpson. No one ever conceded overhead Montague's where when there was life there was hope. But now that belonged to a class of romanticism. Simpson spared us. He started to throw the reds on the table. On Harding's part it had been a performance worthy of television but I thought I sensed in our applause a pity that it had been against old Simpson.

We had a short break while Kirwan set up the balls for the second game. The game was played on number three and Simpson stood with his back resting against number four. I was only a few yards away but he did not acknowledge me. As I read him he looked confused between determination and defeatism. Wally Kirwan walked over to him: 'Stay cool, you'll have him this time.' Simpson nodded. Harding was near the marker end of number three. Through the megaphone of cupped hands, Halvey stage-whispered loud enough for me to decipher: 'Fucking bully.'

It was Harding's turn to break the balls. He was young. The cockiness was there to be seen. He thundered the white down the table and scattered the reds in front of all pockets. Simpson had so many pots on that he walked round the table twice trying to make up his mind. When Steve Davis – or Harding – did that they were building a mental break. I knew Simpson's ambition was one red and one colour and then head for the hills. As, I might add, would have been my own plan of campaign. Harding sat down. Simpson settled on a red near the black spot that needed a tender touch of side for position. I suppose the pockets must have begun to look small to him at this stage. For – without analysing it to death – he missed. There was something of a collective groan from the hall. Harding shrugged at Halvey. Halvey cupped his hands again but I could not catch what he said. Most assuredly he did not quote from the *Pater Noster*. From what I had seen of his ability the game was on for Harding. Now, though I say it myself, I am a shrewd hawk at times. As he bent over the cue I noticed Harding's eyes lift and he must have taken in Simpson who was in his line, though standing far back. Poor old Simpson, as he must have appeared to young Harding. Youth – the flower of it – has its code. He straightened himself again and chose a different red. He contrived a pot that left him in bad position for the black. So he was able to miss the colour with a degree of authenticity. That was what I suspected and I was proved right.

Simpson was in again. But it was no use. He was a wreck from his desire to win, and if I could see it then it must have been more obvious to Harding and the cocky new breed. That's the – the 'bottle' they talk of. Simpson did pot a red but a colour was too much for him. He missed the pink for the centre by a good two inches. The whole table was still on. There was only so much a young fellow could do. Harding was not a combination of Steve Davis *and* Olivier. How many more in the hall had already spotted that Harding was trying to take a dive? Halvey would have. I was sure Dr Cagney would not have been unaware. Simpson was as yet seventy in front. Harding tore in and scored twenty-eight – three blacks and a green – before he overdid a miss on a red and was obliged to shake his head dramatically in case Simpson caught on. The pattern then ensued where Simpson missed and missed again, and Harding stepped in and out again with a display of controlled attrition worthy of a bad jockey stopping a good horse. And I began to realize: Simpson must have an idea now, if for no other reason than the old usually know when the young are telling lies. Maybe he did know just then but was driven on by rage for immediately he managed to pot a red and then a black and a second red and position for a second black. I sat up. So did the hall. But what we saw was Simpson's bridge shake at the prospect of scoring sixteen. It was embarrassing to watch his hand tremble. He missed, a shambles of an effort. Worse, by now he was only nineteen in front and Harding was faced by balls that he could not fail to put away. He took two pinks and a blue and went one in front. His attempt to fluff his shot on the next red was a desperate effort, so much so that if Simpson did not know now then he did not want to know. The boy was trying to carry him. The whole hall knew. I could read as much on the face of Wally Kirwan; the attentiveness of Butsey Rushe; the sadness in Phil Thompson; the raised eyebrow of Dr Cagney; Halvey's pleased grimace; the wide-eyed charitable wonder of the young sharks. I supposed Simpson, to retain a shred of dignity, to stop himself swallowing, to keep tears out of his eyes, I supposed he had to see Harding's misses as the product of tension. One behind now, the cue was slippy in Simpson's grasp. He wiped his palm on the thigh of his trousers. He loosened his tie – publicly. Because of the bad play the colours were all over the place, the pink waxed against the top cushion, the black in baulk and the blue hanging over the bottom right-hand pocket. They were on the last two reds.

Simpson played a shot that was intended to clip a red and bring the white back to safety but he was beyond control from the shakes. The balls double kissed and left a red on that Harding could not miss. Now everybody has his own chalk in his waistcoat pocket today. Harding did not have a waistcoat but he did have his own chalk. That does not excuse our obligation in the Drapers' Club to have chalk appended to each table. Harding turned his back on number three and used the chalk on number four. From where I sat I could see him. He pulled his palm across his mouth first, cogitative fashion, but he drew his index finger along his tongue. I spotted that. I think everybody else on my side of the hall concentrated on the layout of the balls. I watched Harding chalk his cue. I saw him wipe the chalked tip with his wet finger. He lined up to the soft red and proceeded to mis-cue in spectacular manner. Four away to Simpson, now three in front, the red still on, the blue a sitter, Simpson in.

There is this about the game: if you do happen to be playing Steve Davis himself and you are in and the balls are on, there is nothing Steve Davis can do but sit back and sip his glass of water. That is the theory . . . Simpson lunged at the red – and succeeded. He had poor position for the blue but the blue would have fallen in had he coughed. At least he could see the blue. He potted, he was nine in front, one red left. Now he had to wipe the sweat off his eyebrows with the back of his hand. A win was on. He craved the win and he could not hide the craving. I could sense the hall was with him. Only Harding was cool, impatient to have Simpson take his chances and then step in and take the third game after giving the old boy a run. Simpson bent over the table. His face contorted with concentration. He hit the last red. It went everywhere except where he intended. The hall groaned again. Simpson dragged himself away from the table. It was easy to visualize Harding finishing the game now. Simpson's brief was to stand there and await with dignity the discharge of the firing squad. Misery knows no dignity. His lips quivered with defeat. He was a bad loser. I have heard the cry: why should anybody be a good one? One red alone on the table, there was nothing left in Harding's locker but to pot the ball. He came down to baulk. He put in the black. Simpson only one in front. The yellow – and the table – were on. I looked over at Simpson and I could climb inside him. His throat was dry. His legs were weak with hope against hope. I looked at Harding studying the table. There was nothing to study. The balls were on. Harding, a frown on his forehead, glanced briefly in Halvey's direction. He could have put the yellow in with the back of his cue. He played the yellow slowly, slow enough to stay out of the pocket and sit there for Simpson. Harding jerked his arm and clicked his fingers, but I knew and anybody who wanted to know knew that he hadn't slipped up. Yet Simpson and the whole hall sighed with relief at the let off.

Simpson faced up to the yellow, never before so much the centre of attention. His stance, his bridge, the cue sliding between thumb and forefinger; his age; his old man's waist-coat; everything about him betokened the ham-fisted, the past, yesterday's man. He coped with the yellow and went three ahead. The green was not impossible for him but neither was it the snip it would have been to Harding. It would require a contribution from Simpson. And from somewhere he found the shot, though as he bent down his tongue slid out between his teeth and after hitting the white he jerked erect to send a prayer after the ball. He sank the green. Cheers and clapping greeted the effort. Partisan displays during the game are contrary to the spirit of the hall. Wally Kirwan called: 'Order. Order, please.'

Simpson could not stop himself smiling, happy like a child is happy. I was embarrassed at his nakedness. He was six in front on the brown ball.

For a moment Simpson was fresh with the relaxation of the reprieved. He looked almost authoritative as he took on the brown, a long shot for the left end pocket. The ball rattled the pocket, drawing me to lift off my seat but, as if on a roulette table, the brown changed its mind and finished resting an inch from the sack. There was a collective 'aw'. While Harding slapped in the brown and reduced the lead to two points, Simpson stood sick in his stomach, his smile, his child's pleasure snatched away. It was blue for favour. Harding sank the blue, defiantly, at odds with himself. Mind you he did it without getting perfect position for the pink. There was room for ambiguity yet. Nothing so captures the attention of spectators at snooker as a two for one situation with the outcome open. Harding dipped into his trouser pocket for his chalk and briskly caressed the top of his cue. He did not yet bend down. He was pricked to look around the hall. The bodies leaned forward in the seats, the faces intent. I could not see a happy or smiling face even among his own, even among those who had backed him. Again the shot needed no analysis yet Harding walked round the table to observe the line from the pocket. He must have observed Simpson standing there, choking his cue with the grip of his fist, his tie pulled loose from around his neck, his teeth clamped together inside his parted lips, sweat again shining on his face and the jaws working, a man trying desperately not to cry. The hall was frozen in silence. It was no easy shot to miss without being seen deliberately to miss. The white was half-way between baulk and the blue spot. The pink was diagonally three feet from the bottom left-hand pocket. Harding was up to it. He stabbed the pink and sent it narrowly round the angle of the pocket back up the table where it rested in the open. He shook his head openly, solemnly. He was improving as an actor.

The hall hummed. Simpson leaked hunger as he shuffled to the table. 'Quiet please,' Wally Kirwan commanded. Flailed alternately with indignity and exhilaration Simpson was by now unconscious of either emotion or rationale. But for all the coordination remaining in him he might as well have had two hands from a Montague's dummy. He did not have the nerve to deliberate and take aim. No sooner did his palm land on the table and assemble a hasty bridge when he let fly with a wild, hard shot. The pink travelled four cushions before finishing a middle distance half-cut for Harding. And that was it as far as I could see. Simpson dragged himself away to take up the last suffering vigil. I deserted him. I was ashamed of his pitifulness. I wished Harding would pot and have done with it, and let us go home and forget the whole business. Dammit, Simpson should have been able to stand up and take a beating like a man. It was only a game.

Back to Harding. We were aware of how valiantly he had tried to lose. We could hand him the greatest accolade of all: he had done his best. We could expect no more. And yet . . . he studied the ball. I studied his face. Where he was relaxed storming in and potting all round him now he was tense. He was determined: he was not going to win the game if it meant he had to go and throw his cue out of the window. He bent down and took careful aim and he did it. He cut the pink so much, so fine as to leave it on in a way that Simpson could not miss. I was too shamed myself now on Simpson's behalf to look at him. Instead I looked down at my shoes and listened to the expectant silence until at last I heard cheers and applause. Simpson had put in the pink – but of course without any attempt at position for the black. The white came to rest up against a side cushion with the black diagonally on for a corner pocket. It was at the same time a long table black and because of the position of the white a very difficult shot for a Steve Davis or a Harding. But what a shot to win a game! The flying header or overhead scissors kick of football, the stuff of fantasy.

The white was right up against the cushion making it impossible for Simpson to put his hand on the table. He would have to employ a bridge founded solely on the tips of his fingers and of necessity top the white ball – carrying the risk of a swerve that would militate against accuracy on a long shot. We were all conscious of his predicament. Outside of willing Simpson to win, the shot was intrinsically interesting to his entire audience of supporters – including Harding. In his whole life Simpson could never have been through as much as the last half hour. Such was his life. I noticed him pat his waistcoat pocket with his left hand. The shoulder flash. I thought: this shot means so much to him. I was back on his side. He took out his handkerchief and wiped his forehead and his eyes. He chalked his queue. He cleared his throat again. At last he bent down. But his attempted bridge, resting on the tips of his fingers, shook so much that he stood straight again and tried to compose himself. There were some gentle titters, not of mockery, but of understanding throughout the hall. 'Shhh, please,' Wally Kirwan whispered. Simpson attempted the second bridge but the shake was even more pronounced. A man with the shakes is a naked and shameful sight and no one was more aware of his condition than Simpson himself. He was choked with shame.

He raised the cue on his shaky, shameful bridge, sighted and topped the white. Too much so. He missed – missed the black ball completely . . .

The first outbreak of end of game applause is always for the winner. Simpson did not take part but I forgave him there. It was not bad losing. Quite simply it was obvious the poor fellow was too dejected to even think of form. When Harding went to shake he had to lift up Simpson's limp hand and let it fall back by Simpson's side. Harding called out: one for the loser. The applause was warmer, hysterically so, genuine sympathy for the old sod as the new breed must have seen him. But then the hall went quickly back about its business taking up all the tables. I watched Simpson put on his coat, take his cue apart and put it in the case. I waited to sympathize as did Kirwan, Rushe, Thompson. But, head bent, he passed down the other side of the hall and went out. I thought that graceless. But that was in character, like the day he came to condole with Mr Sloan, though he had meant well that day. That was it, I summed up, he had good intentions but no style. Then, suddenly, where were my own manners? Where was my style? I could not let him go off on his own. Kirwan, Rushe, Thompson, all shook hands with Harding. So too did that Kelly climb into the limelight. As I was rushing out after Simpson I saw Dr Cagney walk towards Harding with his hand out.

When I caught up with Simpson he had reached his car. His

elbow was on the bonnet and his forehead pressed on his elbow. I gripped his arm. I did not think he should drive – there are worse dangers than drink. I said: 'Simpson, come with me in my car. I'll take you home.' He allowed me to guide him away. My car was cold. Out of the heat Simpson's skin was dry after the sweat and he shivered and sneezed, too lost in himself to produce a handkerchief in time. He had to wipe the mucus off his lapel. Such was his introspection that he did not offer an apology. Neither of us spoke. I supposed he was replaying all the shots with a different result. I know the game.

Driving down the town I identified two familiar figures walking ahead of me on the footpath – Mr Sloan, linked with Cecelia. I had not seen him for some time. I stopped the car and got out to bid him goodnight – you did not honk your horn and expect Mr Sloan to bend down to your window. I said: 'Goodnight, Mr Sloan, Cecelia, lovely to see you.'

'How is Mr Yendall?' Cecelia answered, sparkling.

'Yendall, the very man. Please come and join us. Cecelia is announcing her engagement. Just a quiet drink. I'm meeting her fiancé and I need your support.'

'Cecelia, congratulations to you. Mr Sloan, I have Simpson here in the car with me, taking him home.'

'Simpson? I must have a word.' The word was a brief one. Mr Sloan tapped on the window, put in his hand, shook Simpson's. 'How are you, Simpson, everything goes well?'

'Mr Sloan. Very well thank you. Are you keeping well yourself?'

'Thriving. I'll let you get on with it, Simpson. I won't keep Yendall. Goodnight, Simpson.'

'Goodnight, Mr Sloan.'

'Now then, Yendall, put Simpson to bed then hurry along to join us at Arthur's . . . ' Mr Sloan smothered my reaction. ' . . . now, now I need you, Yendall. Don't you worry about Charlie. In my company he's on his best behaviour, is that right, Cecelia?'

'You will come, Mr Yendall?'

I was trapped. 'Delighted, Cecelia.'

CHAPTER 22

The Society of Bellringers

That night I was to ask Mr Sloan for Cecelia's hand in marriage. 'It will only be a formality, Timothy, but it must be done. Isn't it divine? Isn't it wonderful?' She was so confident in planning for both of us that I allowed my masculinity curl into a foetus and snuggle up to her protective wiles. 'First we'll go to the Statue of Liberty and let him have his constitutional because that's where we first saw each other, Timothy. Then we'll walk him home, I'll give you tea and withdraw and you can do your business. And then, sweetheart, we'll go back to your place and we'll put the romance aside with the false teeth and glasses and make love. Sexy love. Hot love. I'll bring the sweat out in you, Timothy . . . isn't it divine? Isn't it wonderful?' . . .

Earlier I had to play my first round handicap match against the old guy with all the shops, Simpson. Charlie told me Simpson started as a messenger boy in Montague's where Cecelia's father worked. Romantic. Until the handicap card went up, I hadn't taken much notice of him. He always played with Charlie's cronies on the geriatrics' table. But when I saw I was drawn against him I sneaked a look at his style. He didn't have any. I had to give him seventy points, but I could afford to attack knowing if I did leave anything on, Simpson would not be able to capitalize unduly on the advantage. Still, I had my long, hot bath as I always do before an important game. Snooker might traditionally have been seen in dingy settings but cleanliness brings out the bottle in me. Even on top – as I would be against Simpson – even playing Charlie or Sam, the adrenalin brings out the sweat no matter how coolly I can play. Cleanliness helps and would be no handicap to an orgy of sex with my beloved Cecelia.

In the afternoon I had gone to a jeweller's directly across the road from Deja-Vu, formerly Montague's. Cecelia had insisted: her father knew the old boy there. I went in feeling like a spare dick and must have created a world record for the speediest purchase. 'I want an old-fashioned engagement ring for an old-fashioned girl.' He recommended a solitaire diamond ring ranging in price from a hundred and fifty to five thousand. Give me, I commanded, one for a thousand. I was out in the street in ten minutes. I was chuckling in the bath, the old boy and his assistants staring after me, the shop cat safe from a kick in the arse for another day. Giving the old balls a good scrub with the sponge who should invade my sanctuary but Clancy. His death left the tower unclean. It would never be the same again. Cecelia would help me to shed my dependence on its society. Tonight I must tell Donat about Cecelia, I supposed I owed him that much, couldn't have him hear it on the street: 'Hey, Simpson, the fella that beat the bollix off you is knockin' off Sloan's daughter.' Bath thoughts. The proceeds from the sale of the house in Fulham were working day and night for me in a building society. My grandfather in Ospringe had promised I would be his heir. I would get his house and whatever few bob he had put by. As an antidote to my riches I realized I might be on to a good thing if I ever woke up poor. How would I ever go hungry helping people to stay on the fags? *Fagstart*. I prayed Cecelia would not make me teach maths. Fagstart was *romantic*. I really wanted to do it, tingled with the vocation. The bath-water began to cool, the bath thoughts evaporated.

I rang Donat. 'Donat, I have good news.'

'Good for you, Tim! Enlighten me.'

'I'm getting engaged.'

'Congratulations to you. Who is the lucky lady, not one of your pub fucks, I trust.'

How had I ever used the expression? 'No, Donat. Definitely

no. This is the most delightful vision removed from a – this is my dream girl, Donat. Cecelia Sloan. Her father . . . '

'The shop assistant's daughter? Not old Sloan's daughter?'

'Hardly shop assistant, Donat. He was the manager at Montague's.'

'Won't do, Tim. Totally unsuitable.'

'Donat, would you kindly fuck off.'

'How far have you gone with this girl? I'm telling you I won't have it, you don't know what you're getting into.'

'Donat, are you crazy?'

'When do you see her again?'

'We're announcing our engagement tonight.'

'Come over and see me right away.'

'Donat, I'm going out of the door to play in the Drapers' Club handicap. Then I meet my beloved. Talk to you tomorrow.'

'Hold on . . . '

'Goodbye, Donat.'

Donat aside – actually I found him amusing – I had my share of contentment going to the Drapers' Club. I was in love. I would have sex tonight with my sexy beloved. I was in top form and about to display my form against Simpson. I was comfortable with my age. The tower might never be the same for me again since Clancy's death, but I didn't think I needed the tower as much as I did before I met Cecelia. I had the engagement ring in my pocket and that is a pocketful for anyone. My life at that moment was one hundred per cent romance. Happiness thoughts: it was almost too much. I should feel guilty. I laughed. When we're happy we feel guilty that we're so happy. Simpson compounded my guilt.

Charlie, the fool, put a tenner on Simpson. The first game was over and I still had hold of my happiness. Then Charlie called me a fucking bully. I had destroyed Simpson in the first game. Confident as I was, seventy points is a sizeable handicap to chip away. But early in the second game I could not get Simpson out of my conscience. My cup floweth over and there was this old guy almost crying from misery because I was beating him. Every time I went to play a shot I thought of myself standing in Simpson's shoes. The hall was packed. Kelly, the politician, was there. All the trustee nobs of the Drapers' Club headed by Yendall. Sam was there to support me. All Simpson's old mates were up for him. Donat came, wished me good luck, adding: 'Tim, I want a word with you later.' I decided to let Simpson win the second game. I had no choice. I just couldn't beat a man without leaving him something. Then I felt better, noble. Cecelia would be proud of such consideration. But, Jesus, he wouldn't let me let him win. I knew bets were struck on the game and if I had lost the third – trying – I might have been thrown out the window or had my knuckles broken because Simpson was so bad, so riddled with nerves, I had to become more brazen with every bum shot to try and keep him with me. Somehow I brought him to the black. What does he do? Misses the fucking ball completely! But at least he had come that far. He was miserable while I shook his hand. To watch him crawl out of the Club left me feeling hollow in my victory. But when I was being congratulated I was able to shake Simpson off. I told Charlie and Sam I'd see them in the pub. I was looking forward to my engagement being a surprise to them. I relished their seeing me with Cecelia and her father. Donat congratulated me.

'Come on up to the house for a minute.'

'For what?' I was suspicious of him. It was difficult to believe he might have the neck to put me off Cecelia because she was 'a shop assistant's daughter' but Donat was Donat.

'I'll give you a drink.'

A drink was what I needed. We had only a block and a half to walk. Most uncharacteristically Donat, after a word on the game – he saw me try to throw the second – mentioned the clemency of the weather. We had our easy silences – but never the weather.

Donat took out his keys, opened the front door. He walked into the hall in front of me and stopped at the waiting room.

'Sit in there a moment.'

I waited two, three minutes, not sitting, standing, hopping

from one magazine to the next, smiling at the notice on the back of the door: patients may smoke if they wish. Then I heard his voice in the hall: 'Now, Tim.' I followed him up one flight to his surgery. Not the study, I thought that odd.

'Sit down, I'll get the drink.' He indicated the bloody couch. He went out and came back with the bottle and two glasses. We had our drinks, we took out our cigarettes.

'How long have you known Miss Sloan?'

'About four months.'

'You've slept together?'

'No.'

'No? Four months? Tim, I must have the truth.'

'Donat, what the fuck are you on about? As a matter of fact, no, we have not slept with each other. But we will tonight.'

'I beseech you not to.'

'Why?'

'She's not suitable for you.'

'Is that right? Because she's a shop assistant's daughter?'

'Precisely.'

'Look, Donat, you can't be serious. You're having your little joke, in a minute you're going to raise your glass in a toast – as I expected you would have done already.'

It was the first time I had seen Donat uncomfortable acting the prick. He was always so much at home. His old snobbery fitted him. But not tonight. Could he be cracking up? It was the type of thing that did happen, or at least one read about, fantasy taking complete control. He might really believe Sloan's daughter not good enough for his son. He was in *pain*, looking at me with what I could not but recognize as love. He looked at me for so long that I realized he was gone past looking at me, the pain and the love were there, but he was looking at something beyond me. I suspected he was looking at my mother. Our knees all but touched, we sat so close together, me on the couch, Donat in his professional chair. He started to shake his head slowly. 'I can't think of a way out . . . there is no way . . . no way . . .'

Suddenly he thumped his forehead and hissed: ' . . . Good Christ . . . '

'Donat . . . '

He stopped thumping and held out his palm to 'shh' me. I waited.

' . . . there is a diriment impediment.' He swung his hand around to his desk and lobbed a book in my lap. The Code of Canon Law. It was bookmarked. 'Canon 1091,' Donat said, 'It's underlined.'

I read:

Can. 1091. Marriage is invalid between those related by consanguinity in all degrees of the direct line, whether ascending or descending, legitimate or natural.

'Cecelia Sloan is your sister, Tim.'

'You sick cunt,' I shouted at him, throwing my whiskey in his face. I lashed out, thumped him on the jaw, then kicked the Code of Canon Law to clatter off the wall between the ceiling and the door. He was limp in accepting the thump and the spirit trickling down his face.

'If I had only known, Tim, if you'd told me when you met her first . . . '

'Sick, sick, sick, sick. I understand, Donat. Back in your horny days, no problem to you to drive around to Mrs Sloan – I know you'll tell me you were her doctor – while the old boy is behind the counter blissfully unaware you mounted his missus . . . '

'George Sloan is your father, Tim . . . '

'Shut up! You mad fucker you.' I grabbed his two ears and hopped his head off the back of the chair. 'Dr Bollix! Dr Cunt!' I was shaking. I grabbed the bottle and rattled the rim of the glass filling it to the brim. I tried to throw the drink back in one go, dribbling at the corners of my lips. Donat was listless, slumped in the chair and there was a tear or whiskey – I didn't know which – coming out of his eye.

' . . . I'm sorry, Tim . . . I'm sorry . . . '

'Donat, *persuade me*. You're my father, remember? That's

what you told me. That's what my *mother* told me. Right? Was she a liar? Well, was my mother a liar?'

' . . . Sloan was disconsolate . . . after his wife died, my father was concerned . . . Pearse Farrell . . . twelve months on, Sloan was a – a zombie . . . he must have loved her very much . . . he sent him, my father sent him . . . he sent him to your mother . . . '

'Donat, please . . . please, Donat . . . don't . . . '

'He never knew. George. He never knew . . . it was a disaster. My father didn't want him to know . . . George Sloan, he couldn't have coped with something like that, he didn't have . . . he didn't have . . . '

'Style? The style?'

' . . . call it that . . . call it what you like, does it matter . . . my father . . . he let me know in his will, he felt responsible, adjured me to keep an eye, keep in touch . . . I'd loved her once, it was initiation, but it was love . . . it was love, Tim . . .'

One image drained the fight out of me. I saw her again for the first time in the Statue of Liberty. My loins were girded up for the pub fuck yet I was distracted immediately Cecelia came into the pub. Because I was looking at something I had never seen in a woman before, something I could now identify. I was looking at the rest of myself, my armour.

'Donat, you're telling the truth?'

'As I have it from your mother and my father. For the past few years whenever I met George Sloan in town I would detain him. Before I saw you I would have passed on, a good morning, a good afternoon. But now I would stop. Ask about the shop, his daughter, his health, his retirement. And all the time I would study him, his features, his eyes, listen to his voice. Tim, I'm afraid it is the truth.'

I sprang like a cornered rat. 'Okay, it's the truth. But only you know it, Donat.' I pointed at the Code of Canon Law. 'Fuck the book, Donat. That's Clancy and Brock and a whole shower dressed in funny clothes, you don't believe in them yourself, paper never refused ink, something to keep them occupied when they're not wanking or guzzling.' Donat was shaking his head. I ignored him. 'If it's incest, so what? Only I'll know, Donat. You think it bothers me? It doesn't. As Charlie would say, fuck 'em all.'

Donat came out of his slouch. He stood up, stood on the chair, examined his top shelf of books. He brought down *Encyclopaedia Britannica*, Volume 5, page 32, underlined, 'Effects of Consanguinity':

' . . . A large proportion of offspring of consanguineous mating of the first degree die or have serious defects by six months of age. In the offspring of first cousins . . . '

While I digested the stark terror of those few lines Donat poured a second drink for himself. I closed the book, put it on his bureau.

'You would have to tell her, Tim. You know that.'

I cried, not a manly tear, but the last blubber of innocence. Donat sat down beside me on the couch and put his arm around me. I cried into his chest. He held me, took out his handkerchief and dabbed my eyes until I recovered. I went to his sink and splashed my face, soaped my hands, looked at what was left of me in the mirror. I could see Donat in the mirror, embarrassed to face him. He was not Dr Bollix after all. And without his father's sense of duty where was my life? Aborted. Or at best my mother caring for me without anyone on the sidelines to cheer her on. 'Your father was a good man, Donat.'

'I know that, Tim.'

'You're a good man yourself, Donat.'

'Thank you. I know that too, Tim.'

I laughed. I turned around. Donat watched me, looking for hysteria. Then he laughed. We both laughed. Both of us were treating the same case, steady now, steady, steady, Tim. We were able to look at each other for just a moment, until I could see in his eyes that he had confidence in me. I would do the right thing.

CHAPTER 23

The Plastic Tomato Cutter

I drove him home. Though neither of us spoke I could sense the humiliation burning him as he saw what I had seen earlier – an old, pink-faced shuffling figure shamelessly persuading himself that he wasn't clinging to the pity and charity of a young shark. When I reached his house and stopped the car he made no move. He stared out of the windscreen.

I said: 'We're home, Simpson.'

He was slow in turning towards me. He tried a weak smile. Humble. 'Mr Yendall, would you honour me, by coming in for a drink, a cup of tea, Mr Yendall?' Too damned humble. His old self all right. I was relieved. I said: 'Why, thank you, Simpson.' I thought it best. I would not sleep soundly unless I had seen him through his ordeal. It was a policy of mine, to see a thing through. Besides, I was not in a hurry to make my debut in the Statue of Liberty. There are delights one has the fortitude to postpone. Simpson opened the door and welcomed me in the hall. 'Mother will be in bed, Mr Yendall.' I nodded, understanding him to mean that I should forego my customary war dance. I refused a drink in his drawing room when he brought his hands together hospitably. All I could see were a couple of bottles, a whiskey, a gin – an abstainer's cabinet.

'Tea, Mr Yendall?'

'Now, Simpson, I've come for one of your famous tomato sandwiches, there's a good fellow.'

That pleased him. He would 'only be a jiffy'. But I followed him out into his kitchen. It was modern, fitted. The type my wife nags me to install no matter how many times I remind her that there are only the two of us, and that with a place for everything and everything in its place we are appointed as to our needs.

He was about to fill the kettle. I said: 'Let me do that, Simpson, you see to the sandwiches.' He set to and cut four slices of bread into diagonals while I plugged in the kettle, sought the tea-caddy and the pot. Simpson spread a ground-sheet of butter on each slice and then from the cutlery exhumed a peculiar yellow object. It was his famous plastic tomato cutter. He chopped two tomatoes into minuscule fragments. I could not help thinking: practice makes perfect. He used the cutter as a spatula to shovel the sliced tomatoes on to the bread. 'Do you take salt, Mr Yendall?' I said: 'The tenderest shake, please, Simpson.' He shook the cellar lightly over the tomatoes. Then he cut the sandwiches into triangles. I was happy now that his activity was soothing to him and of course my presence was an unexpected delight. I had been alarmist. He was over it. He idly gripped the tomato cutter as he turned to join me watching the kettle, waiting for steam to issue from the spout. Suddenly he burst out, an agonizing cry: 'Bottle! That's their word for it. No bottle!' He slumped down in his chair, twiddled his tomato cutter. 'Respectable! The game is – respectable – now. No pissing in the aspidistras!' he was bitter. Out of control. I am not a demonstrative man but I put a hand on his shoulder. 'You're to put it behind you, Simpson.' He leaned forward in the chair, clenching the plastic tomato cutter. 'Not to have entered . . . to be able to call back time . . . '

Steam began faintly to whiff from the spout. I waited until the lid began to dance on the kettle. Simpson was lost in his own maze of mist. I pulled out the plug and scalded the pot.

'There were no aspidistras overhead Montague's,' I heard him declare, still bitter, my back to him. And then I heard a crack. I turned round. Encircled by his four fingers and his thumb, the plastic tomato cutter had snapped in two. Simpson opened his hand and studied the remains. 'We used the toilet. A seatless closet. Coagulated shit stuck to the bowl . . . '

'Now, Simpson, please. I beg of you.'

' . . . all colours. Wormy. Yellowish diarrhoea. Unflushed sausage shapes from the healthy passages . . . '

'Pull yourself together, Simpson. Come on, tea's made.'

I put the pot and two mugs and the sandwiches on a tray while his crude nostalgia had its cathartic effect on him. I added the sugar bowl, milk jug, and watched him as his hand went slowly to the waistcoat pocket. He brought out the K.O.Y.L.I. shoulder flash.

'Nits, Mr Yendall . . . '

'Now, Simpson, you lead the way, there's a good fellow.'

I took the shoulder flash out of his hand and the broken tomato cutter and put them on the tray. He was obliged to open the door and lead me out. I ordered him into one of his own fireside chairs. I poured. I gave him his mug and sandwich and sat down to try and enjoy my own. But I had not succeeded in distracting him in the slightest.

'Nits . . . Faeces, nits, alopecia . . . Woodbines, consumption . . . '

'Please, Simpson . . . '

'One stick of chalk to serve twelve tables. They don't have nits now, Mr Yendall. They give more than the price of a game as a tip to girls who wash their hair at the Unisex places . . . '

'Delicious, Simpson. Quite delicious. I congratulate you. Now then, tuck in.' And it was quite delicious. But when had I a tomato sandwich last?'

' . . . when it went missing the caretaker held an investigation . . . '

'Do try to eat up, Simpson. Do you good, there's a sensible fellow . . . '

' . . . shop assistants yawn now. Yawn. Imagine it. Yawn. My father . . . when I think of Mr Todd coughing all those years and always at his post . . . lying dead, dead all by himself face down in the Rhine mud . . . without my mother, or even me or a neighbour or someone from the same job . . . just alone, his nose and his eyes pressed into the mud . . . '

It was difficult to enjoy bite or sup and be witness to such laceration. He had lanced a boil now and would not be content until the last ooze of pus was tasted, nay, relished.

'Even the picture houses gone, Wally Kirwan in that factory, Steve Davis plugged into his video machines, respectable, the game's respectable now, on television . . . sponsored . . .'

At last he lifted his mug and had a bite of his sandwich. I decided he was coming round. Dr John Cagney's words came back to me. 'Time, time is the fellow. We'll give it time, Yendall.' If such panacea was sufficient balm to Mr Sloan's loss then it would do Simpson now. And yet, to whatever melancholy I had succumbed myself, I did not want Simpson to bounce back abruptly. I wanted him to go on. It was music only missed when switched off. I was comfortable in the fireside chair with a good mug of tea and a tomato sandwich.

'Mr Yendall?'

'Yes, Simpson?'

'I was a fool, wasn't I? To enter, Mr Yendall, I was a fool to enter. Butsey, Phil, Wally; they all saw it a mile off. Those young fellows are in a different class. I was blind. I just couldn't see it, Mr Yendall. I was a bloody fool to enter at all.'

'No, Simpson. No, you weren't a fool. As a matter of fact I take my hat off to you. You were, if I may put it, gallant, Simpson.'

He smiled at me. 'Mr Yendall, you – you and Mr Sloan, you were always good to me.' I didn't protest. I just nodded. I hoped he wouldn't pursue the humble again. He seemed to drift off. He picked up the pieces of the plastic tomato cutter.

'Do you know, Mr Yendall, I always had some idea that plastic was unbreakable. I seems – it seems like only yesterday that the old enamel buckets were hanging up in the shops.'

'I suppose your mother will just have to buy you a new one, Simpson. I dare say the shopping centre boasts a choice selection.'

He shook his head, smiling. 'No, Mr Yendall. I still have the breadknife. Good old Sheffield steel, eh, Mr Yendall? Yes. I think I shall manage with the breadknife.'

He yawned himself now, a polite effort that he patted with his four fingers. He looked drained. I said: 'I'd better get along, Simpson.'

'Mr Sloan . . . I don't think there is a day, Mr Yendall, when I don't think of Mr Sloan . . . '

I could not leave yet.

'And there tonight I wanted to win, not only for myself, I wanted – I wanted to strike a blow for Mr Sloan. And Mr Todd . . . Butsey Rushe, Phil Thompson, Wally Kirwan, I was trying for them too. From the old days . . . ' Simpson dropped the pieces of plastic on the tray. He looked at his open hand. He picked up the shoulder flash and looked at it in his palm for a moment before putting the talisman back in his pocket. ' . . . they were pall bearers to the old days there tonight, Mr Yendall. I see that now. But it's just . . . do you know what I don't like, Mr Yendall? What irks me? The way they keep on insisting it's respectable now. As though we were – were – as though I don't know what we were supposed to have been . . . respectable . . . you'll laugh at me, Mr Yendall, I wanted to win for my father too . . . '

'No, Simpson. I won't laugh.'

'Yawn? If it only stopped at that! They skit behind your back. They jump off buses and crash into you and only half say sorry. They're so *confident*. Like Steve Davis. I don't know how they can be that way. Charlie – Charlie Halvey often shouts at me: "Simpson, smile and give your face an excursion." Charlie only jokes, Mr Yendall, but it's true for him . . . respectable . . . '

I could not stay much longer. It would be disrepectful to Mr Sloan. Yet I was loath to leave Simpson in his dejection. It was difficult to know what to say to him. I was not a Dr John Cagney. Sir Thomas – Sir Thomas would have banished such gloom with a sparkling witticism. I was not a Sir Thomas. I felt inadequate. Damn them all that a poor fellow like Simpson should not be content. I stood up to leave. Again I put my hand on his shoulder.

'Don't think of that fellow Davis, Simpson. And forget

about his disciples. Because you can take it from me, Simpson, and I'm sure I can speak here for Mr Sloan and for a good many more, sure of it, Simpson, you can take it from me that you were respectable when Steve Davis and all the rest of them, you were respectable, Simpson, when their arses were the size of shirt buttons.'

To be sure it was a messenger boy aphorism. But it met the case. Simpson was looking up at me and there was life in him again. I could see it in his eyes, shining. 'Mr Yendall, do you really believe ... ' He would have me stay up all night repeating myself. He would resume the humble until dawn broke. I cut him short.

'Goodnight, Simpson. Thank you for the sandwich. I'll see myself out.'

I did not give him a chance. I was in the hall when I heard 'Goodnight, Mr Yendall.'

I drove back to town and parked the car outside the shop. I sat there for a few minutes to compose myself, prepare a dignified entry into the Statue of Liberty. I would not depend on the asylum of Mr Sloan's company. I would take no nonsense in there.

From my years at Montague's, leaving my office and walking through the shop or spot-checking the factory, I was accustomed to moving through crowds without giving recognition to every individual face. It is the walk of authority characteristic of management. The packed Statue of Liberty would not intimidate me. But I was not in the shop, I was not in the factory and certainly I was not in Arthur Skee's. I opened the door and hit the back of what I took to be a Mohican, a tall fellow in a leather jacket, completely bald save for a crescent topiary of hair in the middle of his head stretching from nape to forehead. I said: 'I beg your pardon.' But I was literally talking to his back. He did not turn round. He did not move so that I could open the door fully and gain entry. I had to turn sideways and squeeze in. I could see Mr Sloan and Cecelia at the end of the bar by the fireplace. They were seated in the corner and opposite them on a stool at the counter I noticed Brown, the bellringer. The first cluster to whom I said 'excuse me' did not hear me and how could they? They were shrieking, the women showing their gums above their teeth, their rude companions with heads thrown back, laughing at some inanity. This gross novelty of course had been with us for some time but they had eyes, noise does not impede one's sight, they could see me, see I was desirous of progress towards my company by the fireside. Did they stand apart to let me through? Hold in their breath to give me an inch? They did not. 'Excuse me,' I tried again, this time emphatically, making quite sure I was audible to the deafest. Nothing. I had to push through them and they accepted that as the norm. And so on down the bar. Butsey Rushe, Thompson, Kirwan, and two criminals I had heard addressed on the street by Halvey, the Wank Mitchell and Johnny Skaw, were together at the counter in a circle. As I navigated to port I was greeted by the newsboy: 'Goodnight, Mr Yendall, move back lads and let Mr Yendall through.' He had learned something standing all those years at our corner. I touched my hat. I continued through the men wearing earrings, the women in denim. I was edging through a group in the middle of the bar when I heard my name called. 'Goodnight, Mr Yendall.' Halvey, from behind the counter, was greeting me wearing his wide grin under the tusseled tartan hat that he liked to affect when he was in mufti. I ignored him. I detected sarcasm in his welcome. Mr Sloan saw me now, rose, called: 'Here, Yendall.'

Cecelia stood up to let me sit down beside Mr Sloan. 'What will I get you, Mr Yendall?' she asked me. I said I'd have a whiskey, hoping it was safe, knowing the depredations a merchant of Halvey's ilk was capable of perpetrating. 'Daddy?' 'I don't know I should have a third, Cecelia.'

'Of course you will.'

Mr Sloan made a helpless gesture to me. Then he said: 'I think you should take off that coat and scarf, Yendall, you won't feel the good of it when you go out.' I knew that myself but I had hoped to escape *quam celerime*. The fire was warm, heightening the dinginess that assailed one. The only novelty of the place since Arthur Skee's day was the dirt – and the customers. I divested. Noisy as the pub was, Halvey rose above the din. I could hear him: 'You'll have to stand for it, Miss Sloan, the drink is on the shagging house so take it away. And you, Sam Brown, go down on that and have another, 'tisn't every night our black English Protestant gets engaged. Where is Harding, anyway?'

'He went off with Donat.'

I turned to Mr Sloan: 'Is that the lucky man, Mr Sloan, Tim Harding?'

'Yes. That's his name. I must say he's taking his time.'

'That's the chap who beat Simpson in the handicap tonight. A talented fellow.'

'Cecelia speaks highly of him. Here we are. Your good health, Yendall.' Cecelia handed me the whiskey. 'To your future happiness, Cecelia. And congratulations to you.'

'Thank you, Mr Yendall. I can't imagine what's keeping Tim, Daddy.'

'You will have your turn going up the aisle, Cecelia. Your mother kept me waiting twenty-five minutes.'

Mr Sloan spoke lightly. I had not heard him mention his wife since her death. But we were not in the shop now and he was on his third whiskey.

'Charlie stood us again, Daddy. Isn't it wonderful? Isn't it divine, Mr Yendall?'

'I believe I saw your intended tonight, Cecelia. He beat Simpson in our annual handicap. A good player. Good-looking fellow.'

'Oh, Tim is divine, Mr Yendall.'

'How is Simpson, Yendall?'

'Broken-hearted.'

'Broken-hearted?'

'Losing his snooker match. He takes the game seriously. Too seriously, I'm afraid.'

'Poor Simpson, wait until I see Tim.'

'Cecelia, you shouldn't have let Charlie stand us again.'

'I couldn't stop him, Daddy. He wouldn't take my money.'

Charlie. Dum dum dum dum dum dum dum. Lah lah lah lah lah lah lah. Somehow the group at the front of the bar near the door created space to encircle the Mohican who was gyrating, clicking fingers and thumbs while he and his ensemble chanted Lah Lah Lah Lah Lah Lah Lah, Dum dum dum dum dum dum dum. Having established tribal accompaniment Uncas was let loose on the solo:

> 'Show me the way to Amarillo,
> Everynight I'm huggin' my pillow.
> Dreamin' dreams of Amarillo,
> And sweet Marie who waits for me.'

Lah lah lah lah lah lah lah. Lah lah lah lah lah lah lah.

I could think of many ways to celebrate one's engagement. This was not one of them. I was embarrassed. I looked down at the floor. And I could see Mr Sloan tapping his feet. I thought, perhaps unkindly, of pre-senile dementia that has afflicted so many decent people in recent years. Yet that was such a palpably nonsensical explanation to entertain that I switched to self-pity. It was inconsiderate of Mr Sloan to drag me into this cesspit, this company of sweaty nightcaps, uninhibited in their vulgarity, their lack of courtesy, their savage exuberance. There was that idler, Phil Thompson, with his back to our end of the bar, slapping the thighs of his shiny trousers, never worked a day in his life, a pint in front of him, a butt at the corner of his mouth; Kirwan was vociferous in his contribution to the lah lah lah lah lah lah lah while Butsey Rushe played the drums with his fingers on the counter – behind which the maestro himself was playing the spoons, and exhorting:

'Lift it up, lift it up, for Jayses sake we're not at a wake!'

Cecelia was smiling at the madness and winked at me causing me to flush with shame that she should so imagine I was not being tortured, that she should think I could succumb to such a circus. Lah lah lah lah lah lah lah. Lah lah lah lah lah lah lah. For sweet Marie who waits for me. Monstrous

201

cheering and stamping of feet and wiping of sweat from foreheads. Ye Gods! How far we have come.

'I wonder what's keeping him,' Cecelia said. My glass was empty. I did not like to push Mr Sloan. But I needed another drink to brace myself against the surroundings. I said, pointing to his glass, 'Mr Sloan?'

'No, no, Yendall. Thank you. No more for me.'

'I insist.' But we were interrupted. Interrupted with the cry from Halvey: 'Give us a song, Mr Sloan. Sing "Absence", Mr Sloan.'

'Have one more, Mr Sloan,' I continued to press my hospitality. He did not respond to Halvey who nevertheless invited clamant assistance from his customers. 'A big hand, for Mr Sloan, let ye hear singing for once, real singing. Come on, Mr Sloan, don't let us down.'

'All right, Yendall, since you press me.'

I had hoped to get the attention of the woman behind the bar, Hannah, I heard her called, whom I believed to be Halvey's sister. But she was engaged and I was trapped by Halvey.

'What can I get you, Mr Yendall? Come on, Mr Sloan, give us "Absence".'

Where had Halvey heard Mr Sloan sing? He must have had the effrontery at some time to lower the tone of Arthur Skee's. It was no surprise to me that Halvey should think his enticement would succeed where better men – Arthur Skee himself, Sir Thomas, Dr John Cagney, Russell from the factory, my own modest urgings – had failed. He was immune to the refinements of life.

'Three whiskeys, please.'

He did not use a measure. 'Butsey, get order down there, Mr Sloan might sing for us.' He poured liberally into the glasses, double helpings. 'Now, Mr Yendall.' I took a five pound note from my wallet and placed it on the counter while I handed Cecelia and Mr Sloan theirs.

'Thank you, Mr Yendall. Daddy, go on. Please, Daddy. Sing for me. Sing for me tonight.'

'Thank you, Yendall.'

I turned to get my change.

'On the house, Mr Yendall. Cheers.'

'No thank you. I pay my way.'

'Not tonight. We're celebrating. Put your money in your pocket. My compliments, Mr Yendall. Come on, Mr Sloan, don't let us down.'

Doth not Brutus bootless kneel. 'May I have the change of three whiskeys, please. This instant.' I froze him. Wiped the smile from his face. He bent towards me with temper.

'For Jayses sake, Mr Yendall, wouldn't you let a man have the chance to be decent.' And so saying he stuffed the fiver in my top pocket. By his lights, intimacy now established, he enjoined me: 'Get him going, Mr Yendall, get him to sing for us.' I thought it best simply to walk away from the counter.

It was just then as I sat down that I noticed the quiet of the place. I looked down the bar to see the motley congregation intent in our direction. 'Come on, Mr Sloan,' Halvey persisted. And gently, Cecelia echoed: 'Please, Daddy.' Mr Sloan looked into her smiling eyes. He patted her knee. The observant hawk behind the counter cried: 'He's going to sing. Order now.' Mr Sloan stood up and stood with his back to the fire, resting one hand on the mantelpiece. He sang, not 'Absence', but Russell's favourite, 'Moya, My Girl'.

'Over the dim blue hills strays a wild river . . . '

To hear the voice again, after so many years, was such a joy.

'Over the dim blue hills rests my heart ever.
Dearer and brighter than
Jewel or pearl,
Dwells she in beauty there,
Moya, my girl.
Dwells she in beauty there,
Moya, my girl.'

Cecelia's eyes were brimming with pride. As indeed were mine – with longing for the graceful past.

'T'was on an April eve, that I first met her . . . '

Even among savages I could have closed my eyes and been wafted back to Arthur Skee's again.

'Many an eve shall pass e'er I'll forget her . . . '

Harding came in. Out of respect he remained standing by the door.

'Since my happy heart has been
Lost in a whirl,
Thinking and dreaming of
Moya, my girl.
Thinking and dreaming of
Moya, my girl.'

Such was the purity, the mellifluous sympathy of his voice that Halvey and his stones and blockheads and the rest of the ill-mannered rabble dared not breathe. Harding stood with one arm folded, his palm clenching his mouth, staring intently down the bar, riveted by Mr Sloan.

'She is too kind and fond
Ever to grieve me.
She has too pure a heart
E'er to deceive me.
Were I Tir Connell's chief
Or Desmond's earl,
Life would be dark without
Moya my girl . . . my girl.'

O hark, o hear, Sir Thomas.

I rose to my feet to lead the applause and search the bar to invigilate Mr Sloan's reception. He had charmed all. I had not heard such clapping greet a dulcet tone in thirty years. Mr Sloan bowed modestly. And we continued to clap him. Most moved of us all I thought was the young man, Harding. He applauded vigorously, yet even with the length of the bar between us and my fading eyesight I could see tears on his

204

cheeks. Did I not understand them to flow from ecstasy I would have conjectured that he was in pain. But I had seen Mr Sloan have that effect on Sir Thomas. Now Halvey stepped in with 'Encore. "Absence." "Absence".' And the mob, who love to follow anything, echoed: ' "Absence", "Absence", "Absence". We want "Absence".'

Cecelia threw her arms around Mr Sloan and kissed him. She turned and waved at Harding, blew him a kiss. Mr Sloan moved to sit down but Cecelia stood in his path. 'Please, Daddy. "Absence".' They – Cecelia, the mob – could not know what they asked of him. It was the song that brought him and his wife together. He had often told me so. She had first heard him singing at the Diamond Rocks and thought he sang directly to her, chose the words for her alone. For just a moment Mr Sloan covered his eyes with his hand. Then he smiled at his daughter.

'Quiet everybody,' Halvey the soothsayer foretold, 'quiet for "Absence".'

'Sometimes between long shadows on the grass,
The little truant waves of sunlight pass.
My eyes grow dim with tenderness the while,
Thinking I see thee, thinking I see thee smile.'

There was an eternity between the first and second verses. O gracious age, o times long gone, the gentle past, the tender, dear departed spirits, they were all with us again. How I rejoiced! But for Mr Sloan the memories were a cross and he had to steady himself to take another step.

'And oft'times in the twilight gloom apart,
The tall trees whisper, whisper heart to heart.
From my fond lips the eager answers fall,
Thinking I hear thee, thinking I hear thee call.'

Harding, he may have indulged curious consorts in Halvey and his brigade, he may have been a young man, but what soul must he have possessed. I do not think he could possibly have seen Mr Sloan through his tears. It was a show of emotion that

I could only term manly. Mr Sloan turned to Cecelia to give her the third verse. He held a delicate finger under her chin. He tried to smile. And he sang to her:

'God's blessing rest on you both night and day.
And guide thy footsteps lest that they might stray.
Until we meet on that eternal shore,
There we shall greet love,
There we shall part no more.'

I must confess I am not a sentimental man. Nevertheless, to see Mr Sloan in filial embrace as Cecelia once again fell upon her only parent was to cause one to resort to cough and handkerchief to camouflage the emotions. Perforce the motley applauded vigorously yet with temperance – none of the foot-stamping or finger-whistling appropriate to sweet Marie who waits for me at Amarillo. No. Mr Sloan elicited appreciation from a gentler plateau. Now young Harding, still clapping, made his way up to us through the off-duty phalanx. He stood patiently, had a word with Brown, until Cecelia and Mr Sloan were so recovered that they could acknowledge him in our midst.

'Tim! Wasn't he wonderful? Wasn't he divine? Daddy, this is Tim.'

Mr Sloan took a moment, but not so long as to excite the suspicion of bad manners, to appraise the young man.

'How do you do, Tim?'

'Pleased to meet you, Sir.' They shook hands formally. Yes, I could tell at once Harding was suitable. His respect for Mr Sloan was marked.

'Tim,' Cecelia continued the honours, 'this is Mr Yendall, a friend of the family.'

Young Harding smiled at me as we shook hands. 'Mr Yendall and I know each other from the Club.'

'Let me get you a drink,' I offered, 'you came in on my round.'

'Thank you, Mr Yendall. A pint please.'

While I ordered from Halvey I could hear Harding intro-

206

duce Brown to Mr Sloan and Cecelia. Waiting for the drink I insisted Harding sit in my place beside his future family. I nodded to Brown. He said: 'Wonderful voice.' I had such a proprietorial interest in all of Mr Sloan's virtues that I accepted the congratulations as though they were my own.

'Now, Mr Yendall,' Halvey said as he put the pint in front of me. Then he shook his head and waved his hands as I reached for my money. He walked away to roar at the group near the door who were about to launch some Eurovisionese composition:

'No more singing. Pack of insensitive sods, no one sings after *Mr Sloan*.'

I handed Harding his drink but remained sitting on a stool with my back to the counter. For the first time in my life I felt out of place; not out of place in the Statue of Liberty – I was happy to clash with my surroundings there. But in the company of Mr Sloan, Cecelia and Harding I was redundant. Indeed so was everybody else in the bar. I could not suddenly establish an acquaintance with Brown. Forced conversation may be the art of the commercial traveller. It is not mine. And Mr Sloan, Cecelia and Harding would have job enough on their hands to initiate the nuclear relationship without the impediment of my non-kindred interference. I thought it best to leave. The protestations may be imagined. The parting was accomplished by impeccable behaviour on all sides. Cecelia 'insisted' that I stay. Mr Sloan pleaded with me 'for old times sake'. And Harding: 'Do stay, Mr Yendall.' I suppose the young man could have done with some neutral agency to help deflect the nervousness that needs must attend one's impending betrothal. I could smile at that. 'No,' I told them, 'I must go. Thank you so much and congratulations again.' So they let me get my hat and coat and fight my way out of the premises.

CHAPTER 24

The Plastic Tomato Cutter

I never did wear an overcoat or a hat or use umbrellas. When it rains I get wet or get a taxi, go to my flat and shower or just dry the hair with a towel. Caught out, I sit in the pub or the tower and let it dry into me. On a very cold night I wear a scarf tucked into my jacket. Tonight was not a night in need of a scarf yet I was cold. I shivered and it was not from the elements. I was cold without Cecelia, frozen by the thought of the loss of her. Even though my new-found father, Mr Sloan, was insulation against the iciness that pursued me I was cold. I was undernourished cold, lonely cold, misery cold. How would I tell her? I stopped in the street and leaned against a pole and smoked a cigarette. Leaning against the pole, after every drag, I watched my cigarette smoke shoot out under the lamplight. It was a romantic stance that called for a king-sized cigarette, a fag long enough to allow me to lean against a pole forever. The worst part of smoking is having to stamp on the cigarette end – a man who would not hurt a fly . . . a long illness bravely borne . . . I laughed and walked on.

Crossing the road to the Statue of Liberty I heard first the lack of roaring in Charlie's. And at the door I heard the song. I stepped inside and saw him as my father for the first time, standing with one hand on the mantelpiece, singing. *Since my happy heart has been lost in a whirl.* I stayed where I was. *She is too kind and fond ever to grieve me. She has too pure a heart e'er to deceive me . . . life would be dark without . . .*

He did have a beautiful voice. My hands joined in clapping the man who was breaking my heart. He was twisting the knife in me and I was lucky to be at the back of the crowd where nobody could see me cry. They were roaring for an encore. Cecelia saw me, blew me a kiss, must have thought, did think, my tears were for a song. So they were. He sang 'Absence', the song Cecelia had waited for all her life.

Her fawn raincoat with the buckleless belt was piled on top of the coats thrown on the window ledge, the scarf hanging out of one of the pockets. She was wearing a bra and panties and a slip. They can take off the dress, blouse, skirt, jump suit, jeans and even the tights. But let me have the bra, panties and slip. I like to begin to make love while I am naked and she is still clad in something to slip my hand under. I am one of millions who can strip a woman with my eyes, ravish her and not give offence while some poor souls find themselves out on the pavement with a kick in the arse for doing the same thing, only letting it show through saliva at the corners of the mouth or not bothering to hide the bulge in the trousers. Because I could see the right thigh of her crossed legs through the slit of a tartan skirt pinned together by a huge safety pin I was blind to the skirt and to the bright red jumper laced at the neck by the collar of her denim shirt. I clasped a cheek of her arse through a fistful of silk and she smiled in her ecstasy looking up at Mr Sloan as he sang *Sometimes between long shadows on the grass, the little truant waves of sunlight pass.*

The anticipation of foreplay that I had for months deflected with romantic self-hypnosis breached the citadel and a horde of Charlies burst through chanting Romance, my bollix, led by the arch-Hun, my tingling prick. He would not be fobbed off with a wank. Take Monica Miller with her pair of knockers, behold, perfumes from the East. Golden goblets, excellency? *Virgo Intacta?* Mouth full of the grape: take them away. I will have one thousand and ninety-one. I must have one thousand and ninety-one. I am in the grip. One thousand and ninety-one.

Jekyll and Hyde moved down the bar together, Jekyll to greet his father with: Pleased to meet you, Sir, and Hyde to insist: I must screw her. This will be the fuck of a lifetime. My own sister.

Mr Yendall was in the company and bought me a drink.

From listening to Charlie and from being aware of his surveillance in the bay window eyrie of the Drapers' Club I had assumed Mr Yendall to be a cantankerous left-over from the past. Yet now I enjoyed exchanging civilities with him. He settled me. I introduced Sam. We were an enclave in the Statue of Liberty, at ease, cut off from the general bawdiness that flourished under Charlie's ethos. Sam, Mr Yendall and Mr Sloan were crutches to my better nature but Mr Hyde continued to feed gluttonously on Cecelia's thigh, to speculate on the red jumper coming off over her head, the denim shirt lifting out of the tartan skirt. He nuzzled his nose between her tits. I was not a third down the pint he bought me when Mr Yendall decided he had to leave us. I joined in the appeal for him to stay, knowing he was comfortable in Mr Sloan's company and that he was leaving out of propriety for our intimacy. But I saw him as an ally of mine, defecting, yielding room to Mr Hyde who already had the tartan skirt on the floor about her ankles.

'Well, young man, Cecelia tells me . . . ' Even if they did take place in the Statue of Liberty the exchanges were as predictable and traditional as in the millions of studies where fathers unlocked the chastity belts. Cecelia held my hand. With the nail of her little finger she drew a circle on my palm and prodded the circle. Mr Sloan had had four whiskeys and would not have another. It was way past his bedtime, he pleaded. We walked him home, Cecelia in the middle linking both of us. We were to go into the house and over tea I would formally ask for her hand. That was the plan. Romantic. But at the gate Mr Sloan unlinked Cecelia. 'Be off with you now. I'm tired and I'm happy and you have my blessing. Go on, go and enjoy yourselves.' Cecelia hugged him. 'Oh, Daddy.' He shook my hand. We stayed to watch him walk in the gravel.

On the way back to town Cecelia swung out of me.

'Timothy, what do you think of Daddy? Isn't he divine?'

'He's wonderful.'

'He knows we're going fucking.'

'He what?'

'I told him all about our romance and how it was so romantic and modelled on his romance with my mother and do you know it made him cry? He was so proud of us. But I explained that we couldn't last any longer, we were bursting, had avoided seeing each other, but now we were bursting. And he understood. We were sitting by the fire after tea and when I told him he said: "There is so much about today that is wonderful." He said it very sadly, Timothy, but it sounded divine to me. I said to him: "Tell me what's wonderful today, Daddy." He said that the clothes were wonderful. There was so much colour. People wore everything and anything and nobody minded and he thought that was wonderful. He said in his time the whole world was in uniform and the uniform was a strait-jacket. And earlier tonight in Charlie's he looked around at the crowd and he indicated Charlie behind the counter and he said: "Cecelia, there's a gentleman for you." He meant Charlie's sign, the management reserves the right to serve everybody. He said to me: Could Christ have put it better. He said he was at home in Charlie's because he felt that he was as entitled to be there as anyone else, and he said the only person he felt sorry for was Mr Yendall because Mr Yendall didn't understand the world and Charlie understood that Mr Yendall didn't understand the world and that's why Charlie was shouting at him all his life trying to save him. When we saw Mr Yendall tonight Daddy insisted that he came along. He told me he wanted Mr Yendall to see Charlie's, to see the world. Timothy, I never realized he thought so much like that. He was never stiff with me at home, he let me do anything I wanted to do and when I told him we were going to make love tonight he thanked me for telling him. "Cecelia, thank you for letting me belong," he said.'

We had crossed the bridge again and were approaching Montague's. It must have been an institution. Nobody yet referred to Deja-Vu's corner. Cecelia stopped to look at the building. 'If a man can't have one sort of life he is entitled to another. That's what he said tonight. Isn't it profound?'

'What did he mean?'

'He said he was lucky that he didn't understand that until after he retired otherwise his life would have been a misery. When my mother died he lost his sort of life and because he didn't understand he was entitled to another he made do. And then when they closed Montague's he was bitter. But gradually it dawned on him how difficult it had been to be romantic in his own time – the golden age of romance – and how things are so much more conducive to romance now. He said nobody cares what you wear now or what you do and that's the way it should be. He said Charlie must have known that all his life. Can you imagine how lucky I am, Timothy? We're going fucking and he knows it and gives it his blessing. I feel so free. Every time I was ever on my back I was haunted by something but tonight there is nothing to hold me back. You lucky man, Timothy, let me put my hand in your pocket.'

For two blocks going up the town Cecelia held my hard prick. I had to put my hand inside her coat and slip it under the red jumper and down her skirt. My flat was a basement entered through the long hall of an office building. We began in the hall the moment I closed the door. Cecelia kissed me and started to unbutton my trousers while I brought my two hands up under her skirt and kneaded the cheeks of her arse. Kissing and feeling we lurched along the hall and down the steps to the flat. Once inside she threw off her coat while I kicked off my shoes and began to open my tie. She had the jumper, shirt and skirt off and I was still in my shirt and underwear. 'Don't move,' I begged her. I pulled down my shorts and opened my shirt and took her in my arms and with my prick pressed against her aimed us at the bed.

I did with Cecelia all the things I had ever done with anyone who was game. When we had exhausted the interlocking legs, the kissing, the snaking tongues, the fingering, the upside-down contortions, Cecelia gasped: 'Put it in. Rest on your hands. Let me see it going in and out like a piston.' I reached out to the bedside table and slipped on the Johnny but when she saw it on she pulled it off and dropped it on the floor. 'Are you safe?' I whispered to her. 'Shut up, Timothy.' I thought I could pull out on time but the first exquisite squirt was loosed before I creamed her belly.

I had always anticipated lying there afterwards with my arm around her, having a fag, the post-coital companionship not possible after a pub fuck. Now I had to go to the bathroom and throw her a towel. She was frowning at me while she mopped up the semen. I turned away and pulled on my underpants and trousers.

'Timothy, why did you pull out?'

I took my shirt, tie, jacket, shoes and socks off the floor and held them to my bare chest. I was Dr Jekyll again, my sense of decorum intact, the beast fed and asleep. 'Cecelia, get dressed. There's something I have to tell you.' I went out of the bedroom. I was sitting by the gas fire, smoking, when she emerged about five minutes later. I gave her a cigarette.

'What is it, Timothy? Is there something wrong?'

'Did you know Donat's father, Dr John Cagney?'

'Yes, I remember him.'

'He was concerned about your father after – you were born. He sent him to London to my mother. He was there before Donat. Donat isn't my father.'

Cecelia made a mockery of counting on her fingers. She hammed the widening of the eyes. She came off her chair to kneel in front of me and rest her elbows on my knees and look up at me.

'My brother?'

'Your brother.'

'But, Timothy, this is divine, this is absolutely wonderful!'

I should have expected that. She took her cigarette off the ashtray and walked around with her arms folded, the fag poised, repeating 'divine' and 'wonderful'. But she was thinking. 'If a man can't have one sort of life he's entitled to another. He had the other life only he didn't know it. I can't wait to tell him. No wonder it was so good, the fuck. You sneak, Timothy, you should have told me first . . . '

'Were you safe? Offspring die or have serious defects within six months. That's why Donat told me. Were you safe?'

'It's in between time. I'll check it tomorrow in London.'

She stayed away from me, sat on my kitchen table, swinging her legs. 'Oh God, Timothy, now that I know, when will you be ready again, I want the thrill.' It was bravado, she was trying to fight being my sister. I couldn't let her stay. It was a fight she would win with my help as soon as I could be aroused. I got her coat and put it in her lap while she was still sitting on the table. 'I'll ring for a taxi.'

She was in a dream clutching the coat when I put down the phone. I helped her off the table, held her coat. I walked her out to the hall with my arm around her, our brotherly and sisterly cheeks touching. We both knew we had to part quickly. We looked at each for what I decided would be the last time as the taxi stopped. I said: 'I'll ring you tomorrow afternoon.'

I rang her from the airport. The test was negative. Once I heard that I cut us off. I was drugged with pain on the flight to New York but once there I recovered. You have to.

CHAPTER 25

The Plastic Tomato Cutter

The changeover to the lithographic process accomplished, our weekend newspaper escaped the restriction of having to print photographs in monochrome. Wearing a red velvet waistcoat, the foul beret, a yellow blouse and a red polka-dotted dickey bow and incongruously – although what could be congruous I hesitate to conjecture – pinstriped trousers, yellow socks of course and a decent pair of polished black shoes – Halvey's splendour was immortalized by the wonders of technology. The coloured photograph also hangs in our hall – of fame. The ensemble was topped off with his papal decoration. Vatican papers please copy. The photograph was captioned: 'Drapers' Club Annual Snooker Handicap'. And underneath, the information: 'At the presentation of the Montague Cup after the Drapers' Club Annual Snooker Handicap Final were, left to right, W. Kirwan, P. Thompson, S. Brown, Knobby Stevens (Runner-up), Mr John Moore (President, Drapers' Club), Charlie Halvey, holding cup, the winner, L. Simpson, Deputy James Kelly, B. Rushe and Mr H. Yendall (Trustee).' Mr Yendall, shove up a bit there and leave Butsey in. Everybody now, say cheese; Simpson, for Jayses sake, say cheese. Yes, it was a night to remember or rather try to forget. Halvey was drawn against Harding in the second round but Harding had scratched. He beat John Moore, who had only entered out of a sense of tradition, in the third round. Once into the quarter-finals there was no stopping Halvey with his forty points. He was a man who took his chances. He concluded his victory speech, during which he alluded to the lamentable absence of his late mother, to wit, 'top of the world, Ma', with an invitation to all to adjourn to

215

the Statue of Liberty where 'the piss-up was on the house'. He was cheered out of the hall by the greatest collection of riff-raff ever to hail a conquering hero. For myself, I was too lethargic to throw myself into the docks.

I first became aware of Harding's disappearance on the night that Halvey was granted the walkover. Then I realized that I had not seen Harding in the Club since the night he defeated Simpson. I beckoned Simpson to the bay window.

'Goodnight, Mr Yendall.'

'Young Harding's failed to appear, Simpson?'

'He's safe, Mr Yendall, thank God.'

'Safe? Simpson, what are you talking about?'

'When he didn't come in for a few days and wasn't in the Statue of Liberty either, Charlie went to investigate. He went to Harding's office and looked in the letter-box and saw the post on the floor. Then he tried his flat. And when he didn't show up at the bells Charlie was really worried. Any time Harding goes away any place Charlie always knows about it. So he couldn't understand Harding going off without telling him. They were talking about reporting him missing, but Dr Cagney told them Harding had gone to America on business. That's all we know.'

'My sympathies are with Dr Cagney. What right does that lunatic detective have to report people missing because they miss a few nights in his doss-house? And did they not consider Mr Sloan? Surely a communication to Mr Sloan – that is if they were entitled to make such a communication which is assuredly not the case – but did it not occur to them that Mr Sloan would know if his future son-in-law was missing?'

'I see what you mean, Mr Yendall.'

Cecelia's sudden engagement had been a surprise to me. But now I understood. With young Harding about to be called away on business – and nobody goes to America for a short time – they must have decided to bring forward the engagement. That too presumably accounted for the peculiar choice of venue. They probably had a more elaborate occasion of celebration planned. Good for Dr Cagney. Except for him

216

Halvey would have precipitated hideous publicity on Mr Sloan. Halvey should not have been at large.

I did not have a chat with Mr Sloan again for some time but that was not unusual. He walked around the town for his exercise whereas I preferred decorating and gardening to keep in trim. When I did take a stroll it was usually away from the city. Through the suburbs I carried memories of once-splendid thoroughfares while the burger parlours stole in behind my back. At night I went into town to the Drapers' Club before Mr Sloan set out for the Statue of Liberty and he would have been home and tucked in before I returned. At weekends our paths crossed often on the bridge but he or I might have been in company restricting us to the exchange of greeting each other the time of day. So it was that my next information of young Harding did not come from Mr Sloan. It was one of those mid-week mornings when I had to go into town early for paint and took my paper from Butsey Rushe.

'Great gas in the Club last night, Mr Yendall.'

'Indeed.'

'Charlie had a letter from Tim Harding.' There was this about Rushe that reminded me of Father Flanagan's famous dictum that there is no such thing as a bad boy. Rushe, I believed, had he not from an early age been obliged to mix with his class, might have amounted to so much more. He understood my affinity with Mr Sloan and that therefore news of Mr Sloan's future son-in-law would be palatable to me. 'We had a great laugh. Charlie says he's over in America teaching people to smoke and making a bomb out of it.'

'I'm afraid,' I spoke leniently, 'that Halvey – not for the first time – has misconstrued whatever intelligence fell into his possession. I believe young Harding helps people who wish to give up cigarettes. You have been a victim to a perverted sense of humour, I imagine.'

'No, Mr Yendall. We knew he did that here but over there 'tis the other way round. People go in to him who smoke but who're worried about it and he sets their minds at ease and then he charges them what they spend on smoking in a month.'

One Saturday morning, as I was about to leave the house for a dose of late spring sunshine, my wife stood in front of me in the hall and demanded that I look in the mirror. Yes, the collar of my shirt was frayed. She furthermore pointed out that I had let my wardrobe run down since Montague's closed. Muffled in winter scarf and overcoat one was not inclined to attend in idleness to the dapper figure of commerce. It behoved me to attend to the matter now. I could find no just cause not to go to Simpson. He was a good as any around. Certainly he could not have been worse. I had once been hypnotized by the masochist in me to look at the window of Deja-Vu's and observed *the boast*: 35 per cent cotton, 65 per cent polyester. So I took the bus out to the shopping centre where I knew Simpson presided on a Saturday. Who should I meet coming out of Simpson's but Mr Sloan himself. We decided to have tea in the adjoining restaurant which had been called 'Snacks' on my first visit to the centre but which now rejoiced in the equally self-explanatory: 'T'n'Tart'. We were served two cups of water each holding a tea-bag, with a string over the rim of the cup to facilitate its removal, thanks to somebody's thoughtful ingenuity: the man who created the plastic tomato cutter had not died without heirs. Once we had opened our packets of sugar and spilt most of our sachet of milk on our trousers I opened: 'Young Harding is in America I'm told.'

'I'm so proud of that boy, Yendall. Yes, he is in America and doing very well. America is a generous country, rewards meritocracy. He counsels those who wish to enjoy smoking and so far he has no shortage of customers. Cecelia says he is doing splendidly.'

I thought Mr Sloan looked gaunt. So Halvey had been telling the truth. But I was worried that Mr Sloan welcomed such an occupation in his future son-in-law. It echoed unwholesomely of Lady Bracknell. Retirement did not agree with him. He was no longer intact. Had lost his way. No longer the dependable monolith I had known in the shop. Meritocracy! He smiled so much now that he reminded me of that oaf, Halvey.

I turned the conversation to a happier topic. 'I was talking about the wedding to my wife the other day. She agrees with me, you will have to advise us on the protocol. We have no idea what is appropriate today.' My innocuous inquiry startled him. He began: 'I beg your pardon, Yendall,' and was immediately seized with a coughing fit reminiscent of Todd so many years ago. His eyes watered. I pressed him to drink from his cup. He gasped out: 'Bron,' coughed, 'bronchitis. What – what are you saying, Yendall?'

'A felicitous choice of present, Mr Sloan. We hope you will allow us to be liberal.'

'Oh. Of course. I understand you. I'm as ill-informed as yourself. I'll have to ask Cecelia.'

'When is it to be?'

Mr Sloan began to fiddle with the sugar packet. His uncharacteristic smile had vanished. 'It could be a long engagement, Yendall.'

'That, if I may say so, Mr Sloan, is welcome news. Not that they do not seem fitted to each other but so many today leap into marriage. I'm sure they will do the right thing.'

'The right thing . . . ' Mr Sloan picked up the string and began to duck the tea-bag in his cup. 'The right thing,' he repeated. 'They must do the right thing, Yendall, mustn't they?' I was alarmed in that he showed pain in his face and yet he searched for the smile that nothing could persuade me was his, a borrowed grimace that I had never seen in Montague's. I understood he had not asked me a question. That was all I understood other than that he was not a happy man. He dropped the tea-bag into the cup and put out his hand for his parcel. He pointed to our refreshment.

'Perhaps you'll treat me, Yendall? I think – I think I'll leave you now.'

219

I let him go. I called for the bill. I was told to pay at reception. Neither girl looked at me or thanked me as I paid for the tea.

Seven weeks later Mr Sloan died of lung cancer.

CHAPTER 26

The Plastic Tomato Cutter

I've had six pub fucks out of Nellie Kelly's. It's raining. *The sun is out – The sky is blue – I sit at home – And think of you – And it's raining – it's raining in my heart.* Buddy Holly sounds so soothing coming from the music machine that I guess that makes me an old-timer. My dollars are on the counter. Dave, the barman, helps himself when my glass of Guinness runs down. He's from Tipperary. His hurley and gear bag are beside the coat stand. He doesn't drink. When I say have one yourself he takes the money and puts it in a glass. Every third round he gives me a drink but he doesn't go near the till. Off duty he likes nothing better than to go to Central Park and puck a few balls around. That and the pub fuck. Dave is an authority on the pub fuck. On Sundays he plays hurling for Donegal in Gaelic Park and comes in most Mondays bandaged or stitched. He gets a hundred dollars a game, finds it in his shoe when he comes out of the shower. He used to call me Mr Harding until we became friendly, and now he calls me Mr H. Dave says: 'Sophia's okay, Mr H.' As a pub fuck he means. There is nothing romantic about Dave or Sophia or me anymore.

I knew before Cecelia or even before Mr Sloan himself that Mr Sloan was dying. Donat telephoned me. The Cagneys had never been Mr Sloan's doctor although Donat's father had been a good friend. Because I was once Donat's son and am now Mr Sloan's he decided to give Donat the last bit of business. I am very close to Donat since Mr Sloan became my father. I could cry in Nellie Kelly's. I sent hip letters to Charlie to cheer myself, but I'm not the same man anymore. Bedford Rowe is mad about me. We're on fifty-fifty. Do you worry *all* the time about cancer and heart disease and coughs and spits, we ask them. No, just now and again. Well then, just remember: you don't drown by falling into the water, you climb back out on the bank, change your clothes and enjoy dry land. My work keeps me sane. At night though, in the heat, I hear isn't it divine, isn't it absolutely wonderful? And I see Clancy's face and I go crazy thinking I'm paying for him. I remember him coming to me in my bath the night I played Simpson, the night I was so happy I felt guilty, the night Donat told me she was my sister.

Sophia has big tits but they are a commonplace in New York. Where would you be going without your big tits. Certainly, do not come near Mr H. I love big tits even though Cecelia's were small. Every time I think of Cecelia I try to blot her out with big tits. Sophia Cronin she introduced herself and on her behalf I believe both names. She works in a brokers' around the corner and wears her business suit when she comes for lunch every day. She always sits at the counter but up to now neither of us has made a move. The business suit has its own dignity but it also has its own attraction. Making love to a business suit almost seems taboo – like making love to your own sister. That's why Americans always say 'I'll slip into something comfortable.' No affront to the business suit. If only I could slip into something comfortable. I think like this all the time, one more for my baby, one more for the road thinking. It's the way to get along, to cope.

I waited for Cecelia to write to me and tell me the bad news. I had to promise her that I would come before he died. That's why I'm drinking now at lunch-time before I go to the airport. Donat rang last night and said a week at the most, he's already moved to the hospice. He asked for me. Donat believes he is only hanging on until he sees me. Cecelia is home weeks, has given up her job. I want to go. I want to be with him. But I don't want to see Cecelia. I'm afraid. Afraid of her business suit. Sophia can take an hour and a half for lunch. We can go back to her office which has a shag pad. That's where Dave screwed her. Dave says she has the slinkiest, silkiest, kinkiest underwear.

222

A dose of Sophia might give me immunity against Cecelia. My prick is hard but I'm not thinking of Sophia. I tell her I have to take a raincheck. Pure cornball. But I don't talk anymore, I quote from the slick manual of the fucked up. How do I go on pretending that it's fun going fishing and lounging about in the Catskills with Bedford Rowe? Or that a young Tipperary hurler getting a hundred dollars in his shoe on a Sunday afternoon and burying his face in a pair of out-sized knockers any lunchtime that suits him – how can I pretend that isn't grotty? I've changed. After twenty-eight years being Tim Harding all of a piece I have to acknowledge a scratch in the chrome, walk around myself looking for further evidence of wear and tear. I'm too old for America at twenty-eight, too old for the old Tim Harding, want to trade him in and settle for a fleck of grey at the temples. I want Charlie and Sam and Donat in the tower. I want the Statue of Liberty, true, but without the pub fuck. I don't want to teach maths though. I want to help people enjoy smoking. That's the one pure and clear mission I have in life. So? All that I want is there, spread out in front of me. All I have to do is pull it around me like cushions to an ageing back but I want Cecelia too and without her there is a plate glass window between me and my feast. I can't even pretend to fight against it anymore – I want her. I know I can't have her yet I want her all the more. If a man can't have one sort of life, he's entitled to another. What good is that to me? What did he mean? How do you have another sort of life without it being just that – sort of? When, bombed out of my mind in Nellie Kelly's or in the midst of telling someone to climb out of the water or eating a chicken leg in a boat in the Catskills, I would hear: isn't it wonderful, isn't it absolutely divine?

Charlie and Sam met me at the airport. Charlie took my case and carried it to Sam's car. I sat in the front with Sam.

'How is he?'

'A few days according to Dr Bollix. Why did you fuck off without telling us? Me going around like Sam Spade looking in fucking letter-boxes. What about me winning the handicap?'

'I saw the photograph. You get all the papers in Nellie Kelly's. Charlie, where did you get the outfit? And when I saw Yendall in the photograph with you, I bought a drink for the house.'

'Poor bollix Yendall. I feel sorry for the cunt. He's lost. You won't believe it, we were out to see Mr Sloan, the gang of us, Butsey, Wally, Phil and myself, trying to cheer him up, this is, what, a week ago, and he suddenly says: Charlie, look after Mr Yendall, save him. Can you fucking credit it?'

'Charlie, how's Cecelia?'

'How do I know how she is. Did you have a row, is that why you fucked off?'

'. . . Charlie stop asking him why he went. It's none of your business . . .'

'Shut your face and drive the car Sam Bollix Brown. What's it like when your father's dying. I dunno. My oul fella went when I was nine. Next thing I know I'm collecting slops at a ha'penny a bucket from the lanes. She's miserable.'

Donat and a nun were standing outside the hospice when we arrived.

'Hurry on in there,' Donat ordered me. The nun led me to the room. Yendall and Cecelia were sitting at either side of the bed keeping a vigil while Mr Sloan slept. Cecelia stood up. We put our arms around each other. I held her as a brother might hold his sister in the same circumstances yet even at our father's death-bed the hook-up was still there. What big tits and booze couldn't stunt thirsted for freedom now. I nodded to Yendall. I could not remember him smiling in the Drapers' Club. He wasn't smiling in the photograph with Charlie. But looking at him now, whatever there had been about his features that registered contentment – as when he listened to Mr Sloan singing in the Statue of Liberty – had faded. Cecelia had been crying. But the kick of life was within her without a doubt due to my being there. Yendall looked dead. More lifeless than Mr Sloan who stirred, opened his eyes and appraised us. He smiled at Cecelia and me and then surprised us: 'Leave . . . leave me . . . with Mr Yendall . . . have . . . a . . . cigarette . . . '

In the corridor we both lit up.

'Timothy, you bold boy, why did you stay away so long?'

The intimacy was supercharged. If I had touched her finger we would both have been electrocuted. We would have done it there in the corridor.

'I wanted to come.'

'Then why didn't you?'

'Don't ask. You know.'

We were standing with our backs to a window ledge, a couple of feet apart, not looking at each other, looking straight ahead, smoking, conversation meaningless, unable to talk about our calamity. I knew her now, could say to her: is that a half-slip you're wearing, what colour panties have you on today? We would never be human again until we had fucked each other senseless. I was at a stage with her, sister or lover, when I could say: if that sister coming down the corridor wasn't there which tit would you like me to suck first? The impediment was a magnet, with an insatiable lust for prurience. It was pulling me, and I had nothing to hold on to to keep my feet except to try and stare ahead and not turn to look at her. What little resistance remained was all in my tired legs because I knew her, knew she had gone over to the other side . . . Yendall rushed out and called us in, shouted for a nun. Yendall thought he was dead. He had fallen asleep again. This time when Mr Sloan woke up he indicated to Yendall and the nun to leave, managed to lift his hand an inch above the bedclothes and wave them out. Cecelia and I bent over him. He looked at us both, trying to smile, for a long time before he could speak. He was so frail. He had been frail in the Statue of Liberty but there was so little of him there now. Cecelia was sobbing. I was grief-stricken on her behalf. I did not have what a son must feel when his father is dying. It would have been hollow, false of me to even try and summon love. I didn't know him. Even though I could see he looked at me with what could have been nothing else but love. His lips began to tremble, trying to say something. 'Mm . . . m,' he tried.

I waited for 'my son' or 'my boy', embarrassed at how I would respond. 'Mm . . . m,' he tried again. And, Jesus, when he did get it out it was sweeter than any song. 'Mm . . . m . . . mar . . . marry her . . . ' Then he startled us by saying 'help'. He said 'help' twice and then ' . . . marry . . . ' He would gasp the word through paroxysm and repeat it every time he gathered strength. ' . . . marry . . . ' In between those last words – ' . . . marry . . . marry . . . ' – he interspersed ' . . . help . . . help . . . Yendall.' I thought he was appealing to his old workmate to help relieve the pain, that he hadn't realized Yendall was outside. ' . . . marry . . . get Charlie . . . help Yendall . . . marry . . . '

He lapsed into a coma. We sat watching him in his stillness for ten minutes, neither of us speaking, holding hands. Donat came back and brought us out to the corridor where Yendall was pacing up and down. Sam and Charlie were there too. Yendall, Sam and Charlie all gathered round us, thinking it was the end. Donat was direct: 'You two need rest. There's nothing you can do now. You're staying here, Cecelia?'

'Yes.'

'Then get to bed. Come on, Tim.'

'Can I stay here?' Donat rang for a nun. Charlie, Sam and Yendall left. I could hear Charlie's voice out in the grounds. 'Walk my arse, Mr Yendall, you're coming with us.' The nun led me away from Cecelia to the men's quarters. I slept for ten hours. He died during the night. Cecelia was up at six but she didn't let them rouse me.

CHAPTER 27

The Plastic Tomato Cutter

That Halvey's tentacles were all over the funeral was not that surprising when I reflected that he had laid siege to Mr Sloan's death-bed. Before the transfer to the hospice Mr Sloan had stayed a few weeks at the nursing home in the same grounds. My first knowledge of his illness was a letter I received from him asking me to come and see him. I made haste. This was before his strength ebbed yet it was pitiful to witness the wreck of his conversation. He spoke nonsense. One of the good sisters propped him up in bed and he was comfortable among the pillows as he welcomed me and offered tea. I declined. Too many memories of our elevenses at Montague's.

'I could have gone to St Luke's, Yendall,' he plunged straight in with a smile, enlisting me as a fellow conspirator. Indeed my initial reaction to news of his illness was to wonder why the devil he was not in St Luke's. 'Dr Cagney and I discussed the alternatives. I could have gone to St Luke's but I realized I am not needed anymore.'

'Nonsense,' I protested, 'not needed? How can you say such a thing?'

'Thank you, Yendall. No. I am not needed. As a matter of fact I am in the way.'

'But, Mr Sloan . . . '

'No. I have to think of others. There are those whose happiness would be cramped by my very existence.'

'I don't understand . . . '

'Of course you don't. And I will not burden you with enlightenment. I fear it would cause you sorrow. But please believe me, Yendall, my death cannot come a moment too soon. My illness is providential.'

'I won't have you talk like this, Mr Sloan, you're not yourself.'

'Oh, but I am, Yendall. I most assuredly am myself. If never before, now. When I discovered it was not bronchitis, I exulted.'

'Please, Mr Sloan, please, I beg of you . . . '

It is often more difficult for the visitor than the patient and I have performed my share of the corporal works of mercy often enough to have some tact in comforting the afflicted. But I was at a loss how to minister to my old friend.

'But, Yendall, you must be saved . . . '

He was out of his mind, speaking gibberish. Dr Cagney would have diagnosed as much quicker than I did, perhaps saw no point in curing the body. I was distressed. I looked out the window at the spacious grounds, the greenery – the taxi stopping outside the main door disgorging Halvey and Full Company. I said: 'Halvey.'

'Yendall, you must come again. Promise me.' He had enough sanity to know I would not be at ease with those locusts around the bedside.

'Of course I shall come again, Mr Sloan,' I said but already I could hear the voice of the commander-in-chief: 'This must be it.' We listened to the tap on the door. We saw the face, the happy grin of discovery. I stood up to leave as Halvey led them in.

'We came the minute we heard, Mr Sloan,' Halvey announced, and to me: 'We're not hunting you, Mr Yendall?'

'No,' I said. 'I was just leaving.' Even as I was telling Mr Sloan that I would see him soon Halvey was instructing Thompson and Kirwan to occupy the chairs while he and Rushe planked themselves on the bed. I understood Mr Sloan to have a way with them otherwise I could not have left him alone. As it was he would not be alone again. Cecelia came hurrying over from London and would be with him every day until the end.

While Mr Sloan was in the nursing home I thought it indelicate to visit him daily but I gathered from my twice weekly calls that no such scruples held Halvey and the mob at bay. When I asked Mr Sloan: 'Can I get you anything?' I was told: 'Please don't, Yendall. Look.' He opened his locker. Brandy, whiskey and stout. 'Charlie brings a bottle every day. I tell him not to. He says "give it to the sisters, they can drink it or raffle it."' Mr Sloan smiled telling me this. The poor man's mind was gone. Grapes? Fruit? 'Yendall, Simpson was here yesterday. I have enough fruit to feed a regiment. You should see what Cecelia has taken home.'

Because I restricted my visits to what I deemed acceptable intervals I was acutely aware of Mr Sloan's deterioration. His cough worsened and pained him. His cheeks caved in. He shrank. I was not surprised when he was moved to the hospice. Then I did go every day, fearing that every day might be his last. Cecelia never forgot to say to me: 'You're very good, Mr Yendall.' Sometimes when I called Mr Sloan was asleep. I would not disturb him. Once my bus coincided with the Statue of Liberty taxi. I remained on board and returned to town. Towards the end Mr Sloan was not quite able for visitors. I sat with Cecelia and Simpson one afternoon for an hour and Mr Sloan did not speak at all even though he was conscious. The day before Mr Sloan died, Harding came home from America. I was in the hospice when he called. Mr Sloan was very weak, slipping in and out of sleep in front of our eyes. When he woke up and saw Harding and Cecelia and myself, I was surprised when he expressed a desire to be alone with me. He sent them out to have a cigarette.

Once we were alone he tried to raise his bony hand and point to the bedside table. 'My wallet,' he whispered. I put the wallet in his grasp but he had scarcely the strength to place it on his stomach. His fingers poked about in the wallet. 'Let me, Mr Sloan,' I tried to help him but he shook his head. He managed to pull a fiver out with two fingers and tried to hand me the money. I moved closer to him. He must want something, I thought, puzzled that he had not asked Cecelia. 'For you,' he said. It was my duty to indulge him. I said: 'Thank you, Mr Sloan.' My acquiescence amused him, aroused the deathly smile. He would have shaken with laughter but the effort pained him. He smiled but as quickly turned grave. 'Promise me,' he said.

'Yes, Mr Sloan?'

'Promise me . . . '

'Yes, of course. Anything.'

He was tiring so much from the effort that he had to turn his head on to the pillow for a few moments. Then he tried again. 'Yendall . . . ' I did not speak. I was patient. I wanted him to take his time. 'I want you . . . drink to me . . . after . . . promise me . . . '

Now I understood. 'Mr Sloan, of course. Of course.'

' . . . drink . . . have a drink . . . in Charlie's . . . drink . . . for me . . . '

His head hit the pillow again and I thought he was gone. I rushed out for Cecelia and Harding and the nun. But he was not dead. We all waited until he awoke again. Then his eyes were for Harding and Cecelia. I was standing beside the nun. Mr Sloan switched to us and gulped out: ' . . . alone . . . ' I left with the nun.

I was not at all pleased with Mr Sloan's funeral. The corpse lay in Molyneaux's parlour. Cecelia was seated at the head of the coffin with Harding standing beside her. Distant relatives and female neighbours and of course my wife occupied the other chairs. Having formally paid my own respects I withdrew to an unobtrusive observation stance against the wall where I mourned the lack of a decent turnout. So many of the better people were already departed but so many more whom I would have expected in attendance were absent. Indeed, apart from Dr Donat Cagney, the only dignitary from the professional belt was our own John Moore in his capacity as President of the Drapers' Club. It was not that the turnout was small in number. Alas, far from it. We could not have done better had we rented a crowd. Outside of Moore, Dr Cagney and myself I had to give pride of place to Simpson who was, as one might have expected, suitably attired in black and effected his condolences as would have befitted a gentleman from a higher station. Also, to his credit, Simpson had closed his three shops for two days. His self-abnegation was marked for me when the hearse stopped outside Montague's for a minute's silence to be greeted by jungle music from Deja-Vu's of a pitch intolerable in a ghetto. Not a blind drawn, not a gentleman outside a door with his hat doffed and held to his heart. People went about their business.

Kelly, the politician, was one of the first to arrive. I am not thin-skinned. I accept that a politician sees it as his duty to attend funerals – particularly in his own constituency – given that so many of the emancipated expect such ghoulish ubiquity in exchange for their votes. But I thought even Kelly might have given less value for money. He began with the first seated lady on his left immediately inside the door – my own wife. He shook her hand and expressed sorrow for her trouble. He moved along the line thus, shaking hands with all of Mr Sloan's neighbours until he ran out of them and into one of Molyneaux's sons who must have thought that he was positioned in his professional capacity as anonymously as myself. Kelly condoled with him, almost pulling the young man's hand from behind his back. He shook hands with Cecelia. He shook hands with Harding. He would have taken the paw of a dog, I conjectured, when he was suddenly on top of me shaking mine and telling me he knew how I felt. He had not once looked at the coffin. It may as well have been full of rifles.

Contrast this blunderbuss with the gracious Dr Donat Cagney. Dr Cagney allowed himself a brief nod to the seated ladies, and straightaway stood with head bowed looking at the remains. His hands clasped at the midriff, Dr Cagney posed in the attitude of silent prayer. He then placed the palm of his hand on Mr Sloan's forehead, the appropriate farewell gesture. Now Dr Cagney approached Cecelia. He put his hands on her shoulders and kissed her cheek. Then he held

Harding by the arm for a moment. He did not speak. On his way out, as he noticed me, he paused. Then he came over to me and said: 'A great loss, Mr Yendall.'

Now the hordes came. The Mohican, the jeans brigade, the artists, the criminals, the Wank Mitchell and Johnny Skaw, the down-and-outs, all those who had ever polluted Mr Sloan's pursuit of his constitutional, they were inspired to desecrate his wake. Not a screed of sober dress to be seen. They must never before have attended a corpse. They fell on top of each other in their awkwardness, lining up to paw the lovely Cecelia and young Harding. I deduced the Statue of Liberty must have been closed. I was right. It was. Out of respect. The panjandrum himself now approached followed by his retinue of Thompson, Kirwan and Rushe. Halvey no doubt had done a crash course in etiquette for behold he held his scruffy hat in his hands. His robes of office for the day were muted: a simple red shirt and yellow cravat and white sleeveless jumper, blue jeans and green wellington boots. He shook hands with Cecelia and Harding and then stood waiting like a captain introducing his soccer team to royalty until they had done their duty. And then he ordered: 'Don't forget Mr Yendall, lads.'

I had no choice but to endure the mortification. 'Sorry for your trouble, Mr Yendall,' Halvey said, offering his hand. One by one, Thompson, Kirwan and Rushe repeated the formula. Having now established the precedent that I was one of the bereaved, Halvey and his lieutenants stood nearby as every other camp follower of Halvey's sense of decorum aped him and sympathized with me.

It is the custom that the relatives, nearest and dearest, neighbours, and those who can distinguish between wedding ceremonies and wedding receptions, remain in the mortuary for the prayers. All others usually have the grace to step outside for a quiet cigarette. Not so the Burke and Hares. They stood beside me throughout, muttering the responses to every decade of the rosary. And when finally young Molyneaux approached with arms held wide to clear us all out preparatory to closing the coffin, Halvey ducked under him with the cry: 'I must have one last look at Mr Sloan.' While Harding held the sobbing Cecelia in his arms, the great panegyrist stood peering into the coffin and, after first manufacturing a tear on his cheek, observed: 'He had a lovely voice.' He then kissed Mr Sloan on the lips. 'Sing "Absence" for them in Heaven, Mr Sloan.'

On the morning of the burial the bellringers tolled a muffled peal. I understood the honour must have come through Dr Cagney's agency since Mr Sloan's relationship with the tower amounted to no more than having a prospective son-in-law a member of the Society. My gratification was sullied by the knowledge that Halvey was pulling one of the ropes. During the funeral mass Russell sang 'Moya My Girl', thanks, Simpson informed me outside the church, to Halvey's instigation. Russell did well. Perhaps the most moving tribute was that he did not sing 'Absence'. At the end of the mass as we followed the coffin down the aisle Russell gave us 'Come Home'.

To lament the passing of the horse would probably leave oneself open to ridicule today. Yet I must confess funerals have not been the same for me without having to step adroitly around the fresh green droppings. The motor hearse is here to stay. I accept that. But I deplore the tendency not to walk behind the hearse as frequently happens. Cecelia of course would ride in one of Molyneaux's cars. What, inquired Molyneaux of her, about the rest of us? Who needed a lift? We were outside the church. Cecelia was too distraught to make a decision on such a matter. I was numb at the thought of Mr Sloan being rushed to the graveyard. I worried needlessly.

Cecelia looked to Harding. But the decision was made in a different quarter. Young Molyneaux received a slap in the back. 'Fuck that for a yarn, we're walking. Come on, fall in lads.' The troupe from the Statue of Liberty took their places. Young Harding, being the only near male relative, walked in the front line flanked by Halvey, Thompson, Kirwan and Rushe. I followed on with Dr Cagney, Simpson and Russell.

Behind us, the Bohemians. I noticed Brown in the company of those who must have been there from the tower. Kelly, the politician, did not appear, doubtless having had to attend a different funeral. How tirelessly they work on their own behalf. The bellringers, myself, Dr Cagney, Simpson, Russell, a few more, we were dressed for a funeral. The rest might have been participants in a college rag day. Watching the cut of those encircling the mouth of the grave – apart from Cecelia and Harding – I realized that part of me was being buried.

CHAPTER 28

The Plastic Tomato Cutter

The night Mr Sloan went to the church I was mischievous enough to get Cecelia to invite Donat to Charlie's for a drink. He could not refuse a lady. But he did. 'Thank you, but no thank you. I'll drown my sorrow in the Professional Club.' I asked Simpson and he came though he doesn't drink. Yendall escaped. I saw him outside the church while I was moving through the crowd to get to Sam. Yendall was already linking his wife across the road into one of Jack Molyneaux's cars when I decided to let him go. Charlie's was bursting. He opened the snug especially for us. It's usually closed. 'Those fucking students would close you with their grass.'

Cecelia, Sam, myself and – because it was his first time there and a non-drinker – Simpson all piled in. I bought the round. Charlie served us through the hatch. I handed them their drinks, sat down beside Cecelia. Simpson lifted his orange. 'To Mr Sloan.' Sam echoed him. Then we were rather awkward together. I could not think of how to get a conversation going, did not want to talk snooker. I was distracted by Cecelia's black stockings and black outfit, asking myself was she wearing black underneath. She was. I was purged of my American experience and thought we should wait until our wedding night before making love again. It was my prowess as a debater that first attracted Bedford Rowe. I was part of a team that trounced Harvard. But I was no match for Cecelia. When I brought her home later that night she said: 'Timothy, you're not fair. I don't know what it's like to fuck my brother, I'm entitled to the chance so that I can decide whether I want to marry you or not.' I had no answer to that. I didn't want one.

'I thought Dr Cagney might be here,' Simpson started, 'his father was very popular with Mr Sloan and Mr Yendall.'

'He had a call to make,' I said.

'Dr John Cagney and Sir Thomas Ainsworth, we had to be on our toes. I was given a half crown the night . . . ' Simpson checked himself but he couldn't leave it there. ' . . . it was the night Cecelia was born. Mr Yendall collected me from the Tech to deliver a suit to Sexton Square. As a matter of fact Mr Yendall gave me sixpence on top of it. I was a millionaire.'

'Timothy, where is Mr Yendall? Didn't you ask him?'

'I thought he mightn't like it here.'

'He used to come here on occasions when Arthur Skee had it but you're right. He wouldn't like it here now. Mr Sloan asked me to watch out for him. He said "save Yendall". I'm not sure what he meant.'

'Daddy said the same to Timothy and me.'

I said: 'And he asked Charlie.'

'Charlie would know.'

I took it on myself to call Charlie. He came to the hatch.

'We're talking about Mr Yendall. What do you think? We're all asked to help him?'

'Hang on. I'll be in in a minute.'

Charlie came round and stood with his back to the snug door. He grinned at Simpson. 'What'll we do, Simpson? I've been trying to get him to smile for thirty years.'

'I don't know Mr Yendall,' Sam offered, 'and I didn't know Mr Sloan except to see him. All I know is Mr Yendall in the Drapers' Club. But if you ask me, Charlie, maybe he would have smiled if you didn't roar at him in the street every day.'

'All right, bollix brains, you tell us how to save him.'

'Maybe if you were nice to him.'

I thought Sam was inspired. I said: 'Hold on, maybe Sam's hit on it. Think about it, Charlie. Suppose you were nice to him. Acted the gentleman – wherever you'd learn how to do it. He might smile then.'

'You black English Protestant, you're not listening to me.

I've been trying to be nice to him all my life. Simpson knows. Haven't I Simpson?'

'I don't think being nice to him is the answer,' Simpson spoke so definitely that we all looked at him. 'I think if you really started to be nice to him he would drop dead in the street.'

'What kind of bollix rubbish is that?'

'He liked to be persecuted by you.'

'Perse . . . '

'I know him. If you hadn't always been around he wouldn't have had a target. Even talking to him in the bay window, I don't think we ever spoke about anything else other than Mr Sloan, the changing fashions and Charlie Halvey. You desert him now and he'll have nobody left to look down on.'

'Thanks. Fuck ye and ye're bay window.'

'I agree with Mr Simpson,' Cecelia said, 'Charlie, you don't mind poor Mr Yendall looking down on you. I think if you were even nastier to him then he'd have more to live for. Right, Timothy?'

'No. Not right, Cecelia. I don't know Yendall any more than Sam does but I agree with Sam. But I've seen Yendall's face when Charlie comes into the Drapers' Club. I think Yendall would be happy if Charlie emigrated. That's if Charlie can't learn to be nice.'

'I'm trying to be nice to the cu – I'm trying to be nice to the man. he won't let me.'

'I didn't visit Mr Sloan,' Sam said, 'and he didn't ask me to help Mr Yendall. But Mr Simpson and Cecelia are for Charlie the nasty and Tim, Charlie and if I'm allowed a vote, that's three for Charlie to be nice.'

'That's it. You're allowed a vote, you bollix. I'm going to be nice. Watch me.'

CHAPTER 29

The Plastic Tomato Cutter

I was sitting in the bay window of the Drapers' Club with Simpson for company. Earlier in the afternoon I had been out in the back garden, my head covered with a broad-brimmed white hat against the May sunshine. I have seen my share of mourners having to be restrained from flinging themselves into the grave only to turn up at bingo days later. I do not have such resilience. It was natural that there in the garden my thoughts were of Mr Sloan. I sat down to rest my back. Mr Sloan, Sir Thomas, Dr John, Simpson flitted in and out of my reverie. The gracious days. Arthur Skee's place. But at the periphery of every recollection there was Halvey shouting an indecency. I had not gone near the Statue of Liberty with Mr Sloan's fiver. Restored to his good sense in Heaven he would understand his request to have been melodramatic. And yet, trying to sleep at night or on first waking, I thought of nothing else but his dying plea. I was thinking of it now in the bay window, not paying dutiful attention to Simpson.

'. . . myself a good sign, Mr Yendall.'

'What's that, Simpson?'

'I was just saying, the hall being empty, it's a good sign that youth can still enjoy fine weather.'

'Oh.'

'The Bermuda shorts are walking out of the shop.'

'Yes. I've seen them on half the town, Simpson.'

'You don't approve, Mr Yendall?'

I know how I would have answered a few years earlier. It was the answer I was about to give him now. But I checked myself. I had been in town earlier before retiring to the garden. I had felt the encumbrance of my clothing in the heat. And I

238

had noticed the proliferation of Bermuda shorts on young and old, male and female, lean and fat. But it had all passed me by. It was only when Simpson introduced the topic that I realized I had seen Bermuda shorts that afternoon and on the previous three days of the heatwave. So: did I approve? Or was it possible that I couldn't care less anymore? The violation of modesty and seemliness came from so many quarters now that, perhaps as a man alone, I had given up the stand. That afternoon, had there not been bearded louts dressed in cast-off combat jackets sitting on the pavement outside the former Montague's selling beads and baubles out of suitcases and had they not been there for some months now? And I had let that go. I had not written to the newspaper. There was so much that led me to uncap my pen, too much. My ink was running dry. Part of me was dead: I could accept that. Part of me was dying; I could accept that too. But was that part still in harness mellowing? No. Kill me if to mellow is to tolerate that which is ungracious.

'You find them becoming, do you, Simpson?'

'Charlie bought a pair today. Charlie says . . . '

'I told you he'd be here.' The cry from Halvey as he came in leading Brown and Harding over to us in the bay window. He was wearing the shorts and a matching floral shirt hitherto only seen on those visiting Americans one skirted on the pavements, yielding space to the obesity beloved of a nation where walking is considered dangerous.

'Goodnight, Mr Yendall,' Tim Harding greeted me.

'Goodnight to you,' I said.

'Hey, Mr Yendall, what do you think of the gear? Simpson, what are you doing stuck in stuffy pool halls when you could be out jumping ditches . . . '

Harding sat down beside me while Halvey edged Simpson up the seat, grabbing a fistful of Simpson's thigh and giving it a squeeze.

'Mr Yendall,' Harding in his respectful way asked me: 'Cecelia was wondering if you'd give her away.'

My wife had anticipated that I might be so honoured. 'My dear fellow. Of course, I'd be delighted.'

' . . . I told you there'd be no problem. Mr Yendall and Mr Sloan were butties. God be with the days, Mr Yendall, hah?'

Harding said: 'Thank you, Mr Yendall.'

Halvey was grinning in the good fellowship of the bay window. He positively beamed at me. 'We'll have to dress up, Mr Yendall, top hat, the lot.'

Brown was standing with his back to the number five table. He asked: 'Is it dress for everyone, Tim?'

'It is for you, Sam. You, Donat, Charlie and Mr Yendall. That's what Cecelia says. She's the boss.'

There is nothing like a wedding to bury a funeral. But the idea of Halvey as an usher intruded on my anticipation. I supposed Harding had no way out given that one could possibly understand in the first place why he slummed. Dr Cagney and I would carry the day as best we could.

'It will be a small wedding, Mr Yendall. We're not having a reception. Maybe a few drinks afterwards.'

'I understand. And who is Cecelia's bridesmaid?'

'I don't know. She's digging up one of her old school chums.'

'I'm quite sure Cecelia's choice will be an adornment on Dr Cagney's arm.'

My felicity at first puzzled Harding but then he said: 'Oh. I see what you mean. No, Mr Yendall, Donat's an usher. Charlie's best man.'

On Harding's behalf, Cecelia's, Mr Sloan's, perhaps I should have behaved differently. I will cite nothing in mitigation. All of us beheld the best man. To Simpson and myself the intelligence was fresh. Simpson smiled his benediction. But my urbanity failed me. Halvey was grinning his delight at having been so chosen. I have no excuse. The horror showed in my face. I wiped away his grin, and all of us, myself included, saw me do it. Simpson came to the rescue. 'Come on,' he thumped Halvey, 'talking doesn't pay the electricity bill. What about the two of us taking them on in a four-hand?'

240

I sat on in the bay window, ashamed of having revealed myself.

On the day itself Halvey succeeded in invoking a solemnity appropriate to the nuptials. In fact, releasing Cecelia from my arm at the top of the aisle, I admitted that Halvey cut a solid figure in tails. Father Brock, the chaplain attached to the Society of Bellringers, performed the ceremony. Brown, also from the tower, gave the first reading. And Simpson, I was very pleased to see, read the responsorial psalm. There was a symmetry about the balance of representation from Montague's and the tower that was untouched by the choice of Butsey Rushe in his capacity as standard bearer of God knows what to give the second reading. At that stage of the ceremony I had the sensation that I had been kidnapped and I succumbed to the fatalism that prompts those in captivity to strike a rapport with their abductors. Russell sang 'Ave Maria'. There were so many contradictions that it was difficult to see the hand behind the wedding. That Montague's and the tower were there in what strength remained to those institutions was understandable and a credit to the guiding spirit. But scattered about the church and indeed lounging against the portals, the gaudily caparisoned denizens of the Statue of Liberty were also there in force: Thompson, Kirwan, the lot.

I could imagine Cecelia and Harding planning their wedding as all young couples do – although with the cloud of Mr Sloan's death hanging over them. Cecelia sent me an invitation card but not as an invitation. It was formality in case I disapproved of the wording.

Mr Henry Yendall requests the pleasure of your company at the wedding of his friend Cecelia Sloan to Timothy Harding at 7.30 p.m. at the Redemptorist church and afterwards in the Statue of Liberty.

There wasn't an RSVP. They were given out as complimentaries to all walks of society from the labour exchange to the jails. I made a decision the moment I saw the invitation card. I would sail through Cecelia's big day on her behalf. So, we were going to the Statue of Liberty. So. I would sail through if we were going to a sewer.

We were photographed in the registry and in the grounds. I was braced to hear 'All together now lads, say cheese; Mr Yendall, say cheese, you'll ruin the photograph.' But no, Halvey managed to contain himself. Outside in the church-yard my wife and I talked to Simpson, my wife congratulating him on my perfect fit. Indeed I was pleased that in a grey three-piece with buttonhole Simpson had not stinted on himself. Halvey, as best man and Master of Ceremonies, was going from group to group in the yard and when I saw him come towards us I was prepared to suffer the worst. But he swept off his top hat and greeted my wife: 'Nice to see you, Mrs Yendall.' My wife accepted his hand. 'Simpson, you're look-ing well but I wish I had Mr Yendall's elegance. It went off well so far anyway. A pity Mr Sloan isn't with us. God be with the old days, Mr Yendall. I'll see ye later.' My wife had been listening to me for over thirty years on the subject of Halvey. She said to me now: 'That hasn't been so bad, Henry, has it?'

But the Statue of Liberty was to come. Again, I was surprised. Unless I was mistaken the place had been cleaned. All the bar stools had been taken out and a long buffet table, laden tastefully, ran parallel to the counter. There was a notice on the pub door that read PRIVATE FUNCTION but it seemed to me that the place was as full of the regulars as I had observed on my previous visit. But then the clientele to a man had been invited to the wedding. Halvey's sister had charge of the catering and I had no fault with my plate. The long bench was reserved for the principals, the rest made do by standing or sitting on the floor. Halvey and a few conscripts staffed the bar and soon there was a contented buzz of conversation and supping and dining. The drink was free. I turned to Cecelia and said: 'You're too liberal.'

'Me, Mr Yendall? It's all on Charlie, that's his wedding gift.'

Now the reception was neither fish nor fowl in so far as with

242

Mr Sloan scarcely cold in the grave one could not revel, yet the melting pot of exuberance yearned to bubble over. Arthur Skee's old piano was in its place, but had long since been superseded by the guitar as the instrument of accompaniment. Halvey took a break from behind the counter and came out to mingle with the guests. Dr Cagney was standing talking to Father Brock. The priest was drinking a glass of whiskey. Did I approve? I most certainly did. If the Redemptorists had a fault – and they had many – it was their tendency to promote hysterical abstention in their undernourished subjects rather than the measured contemplation advocated by the Jesuits. Beside me my wife cleaned her plate. I tried to ignore the mob wolfing away while I took in Russell talking to Simpson. Of course they reminded me of Mr Sloan and prompted me to imagine what gentle animation would have pervaded the gathering had he been still with us. And I was conscious of his fiver in my wallet. I went to the counter to get a drink for my wife and myself and offered the money to none other than Johnny Skaw who was quite happy to take it. But then I heard: 'Skaw, what in Christ's name are you doing?' He grabbed the fiver. 'I'm sorry about that, Mr Yendall.'

'The fellow is doing right,' I said. 'You may as well know, Mr Sloan's dying wish was that I should have a drink here in his memory. That is Mr Sloan's money.'

'Did he say that, Mr Yendall?'

'Yes.'

'The light of Heaven to his soul. But please, not tonight, Mr Yendall. Spend it another night. And listen, any chance you'd do me a great favour?'

He held me by the arm and pulled me gently towards him so that we were out of earshot. 'Look around you, Mr Yendall, this is a very delicate matter. We can't send them off without a song. If I let one of my crowd loose, you wouldn't know what they'd come up with. But we have to have some song. There's a few here I can trust but I want the right man to lead the way. Will you give us one?'

I was flattered but suspicious of him. He could not have

243

heard me sing. 'Where did you get the notion that I have a voice?'

'Come on now, Mr Yendall. I used to have my ear to the door when Arthur Skee had it. 'When Other Lips', right? The very first time I heard it I asked Mr Sloan and he told me you sang it. And he agreed with me. Nobody can do it justice like yourself.'

'Thank you for the compliment.' I was confused. I had not suspected such a type of having an ear.

'Will you let me call on you so? I think it has to be done for Cecelia, in honour of Mr Sloan.'

'I must ask my wife. Is your piano in tune?'

'Sure, what about it if it's not, someone can bang away on it.'

My wife was amused but willing. 'If you'll put up with me, Henry.'

'*Order*. Everybody shut up . . . close yer gobs for Mr Yendall . . . '

My diffidence in the surroundings was dispelled by the reassuring smiles of Simpson, Dr Cagney, Father Brock, Russell, Cecelia and Harding, the people from the tower, as my wife led the way to the piano. It was out of tune but I had known my wife to master more recalcitrant instruments. Her delicate introduction sufficed to quell the last cough. I began: 'When other lips and other hearts . . . ' One knows when one does well. A rendition that invites a raucous chorus is deficient. When I came to the final 'will you remember, will you remember . . . ' Dr Cagney, Father Brock, Russell, et cetera, joined in softly and we were allowed fidelity to the last note and a second's silence before the applause. We might have been back in Arthur Skee's. I moved quickly through the congratulating crowd back to my seat before Halvey could orchestrate the cries of 'more', 'more'. We did not have encores in Arthur Skee's. I shook my head and waved away their insistence.

'We won't be greedy,' Halvey declared. 'Someone from the tower now please. I call on Dr Cagney.'

I had not had the pleasure before, but I had heard of his

'Burlington Bertie'. It was a joy. And of course my wife well knew how to complement the saunter. We had Father Brock with a stirring 'Road to Mandalay', and Russell gave us 'Take a Pair of Sparkling Eyes'.

Somebody shouted a name, calling on the Mohican to show us the way to Amarillo. Halvey shouted back: 'I can bring ye no place. Amarillo my arse.' I cringed for my wife, but she was enjoying herself so much at the piano that she did not seem to notice. The entertainment did degenerate from there on. Not Halvey's fault, I hasten to say. He could not be responsible for the thin talent at his disposal. I drifted away with my own thoughts when someone from the tower sang that gruesome rugby anthem, 'Beautiful, Beautiful Munsters'. That did invite a chorus. Cecelia left the bar and went upstairs to change and my wife left the piano to go with her. Soon we could take our leave. I could not pretend to have had a day to remember; neither was it an occasion I wanted to forget. It was tolerable and that was more than I had hoped for. Yet to have had fears at all was an indictment of the age. Cecelia and Harding were young and youth is lost in the democratic embrace, the mad ideology that would have us all equal. We all went to the street to see them off in the taxi that was taking them to Kilkee for the honeymoon. I could overlook the extravagance of the taxi in the light of the romantic choice of resort. It took an effort to remain deaf to some of the coarse instructions offered to the happy couple by the regulars, and I thought it singularly self-restrained of Halvey not to have dipped into his own bag of morsels. As the taxi moved away, so too did such as Dr Cagney and Father Brock, and I decided my wife and I had also done our duty. Unfortunately, we also had our obligation to the host of the evening. He was standing at the door shouting 'Riff-raff back inside, don't give me a bad name.' I offered him my hand. I said: 'I must commend your hospitality. I think we can safely leave the rest of the night to the younger brigade.'

My wife stood beside me. 'Yes, it was a lovely evening, thank you.'

'Don't mention it, Mrs Yendall.' He smiled at us both. 'Ye've a good act, ever free on Wednesdays I could fix ye up with a gig here.' My wife was amused and so might I have been, could I be sure he wasn't joking.

CHAPTER 30

The Plastic Tomato Cutter

An appropriate eight and a half months elapsed by the time Donat and Brock finagled the adoption. The baby, George, is almost a year old now. Our stay in New York covered the myth of Cecelia's pregnancy. It was such a pity, Mrs Yendall said, that we were that close to home – Dublin – when Cecelia delivered. But also, Mrs Yendall observed, the birth did not knock a feather out of Cecelia. And as the baby grew Mrs Yendall was decisive – George was taking after Cecelia.

I put the 'Fagstart' ad in the weekend newspaper and my first client was one I had helped to quit, Mrs Lillis. Of course she was a cheat. She had been falling into the water but it wasn't that. My fee was based on a month's smoking, how many she would like to smoke comfortably. She claimed to aspire to five a day. I let her get away with it. In New York when someone tried that our answer was that we did not school the nursery slopes. Twenty a day minimum. The fanatics are working day and night with their letters to the papers, and the government is under pressure from the European Community. Already, in London, one toe in the Underground and you can't light up anymore. Here, the cinemas will be next for the chop. Those who wouldn't know a dog biscuit from *haute cuisine* are clamoring for smoke-free restaurants. The beleaguered are queueing up outside my door.

Donat wrote to us in New York and so did Charlie with the same news and yet neither Cecelia nor I could believe it. But it was true. Charlie says he meant it as a joke but he would have meant it seriously if he thought he would be taken seriously. He met Mrs Yendall one morning in town and by way of one of his salutations greeted her with: 'Morning, Mrs Yendall, lovely day. When are you coming to play for us?' Mrs Yendall conceded that it was lamentable, the demise of decent singing, that so much that was graceful could be choked by the squawk of pap.

Charlie pounced. He says Yendall hasn't a bob, that those people would be out on the streets if the rates on private dwellings had not been abolished. He calls Yendall the last apostle of genteel poverty. He worked on Mrs Yendall that morning in the street. She tittered and pooh-poohed the very idea that he would pay her, but Charlie's darting eyes can see through people and he says women are the ones with the balls anyway; they're tough, they have to be, married to such fucking apes as Yendall. Charlie promised that he could deliver at his end, get Russell to round up a few, and through the bells Charlie would get the choir mob and everybody knew somebody else who was languishing with a voice and a song and nobody to listen and no place to sing any more. Yendall came in with her the first night with a face that made Charlie almost shit himself with fright, but when Yendall saw the crowd – the quality of the crowd – he softened and spent Mr Sloan's fiver. Yendall was so taken with the charm of people he had forgotten existed that he relented and accepted the role of Master of Ceremonies.

They are there every Wednesday night, keeping something alive, Charlie spruce in a dress suit and dickey-bow. We get a baby-sitter that night. Sam is always there and Simpson is a regular sipping his orange and glued to Yendall's performance as MC. Donat comes and does his turn and so does Brock. Everybody has a song and sings the same song every Wednesday night but there are so many of them there that you don't notice that. And Charlie and the singing have tamed Charlie's regulars, and also, younger people, my age and younger, they come, because they have heard of the novelty or because they are getting pissed off with their own culture. And when it's closing time, and I linger on with Cecelia and Sam our hearts throb to see how happy Charlie is. Though he always manages to scowl:

'That bollix Yendall won't let me pay him.'

All Fourth Estate books are available at your local bookshop or newsagent, or can be ordered direct from the publisher.

Indicate the number of copies required and quote the author and title.

Send cheque/eurocheque/postal order (Sterling only), made payable to Book Service by Post, to:

> Fourth Estate Books
> Book Service By Post
> PO Box 29, Douglas
> I-O-M, IM99 1BQ.

Or phone: 01624 675137

Or fax: 01624 670923

Alternatively pay by Access, Visa or Mastercard

Card number:

Expiry date ....

Signature ....

Please allow 75 pence per book for post and packing in the UK. Overseas customers please allow £1.00 per book for post and packing.

Name ....

Address ....

....

....

Please allow 28 days for delivery. Please tick the box if you do not wish to receive any additional information. ☐

Prices and availability subject to change without notice.